Tor Maddox:

UNLEASHED

by Liz Coley

Liz Coley

Tor Maddox:

UNLEASHED

by Liz Coley

FOR KATE

Who wanted a heroine for herself.

ACKNOWLEDGEMENTS

Thanks to my husband Brian, who was listening to NPR news in the car with me when inspiration struck and who encouraged me to write this story. Thanks to NaNoWriMo for giving me permission to do nothing but write in November. Thanks to my kids Ian, Connor, and Kate for their honest reactions along the road to creating a manuscript. Thanks to everyone at the SFF Online Writing Workshop who ever responded to a posted chapter. Thanks to my agent Nancy Coffey, who saw the promise in this story and family of characters and continued to believe in them through thick and thin. Thanks for unflinching support and friendship from my writing communities: Northern Ohio SCBWI, Cincy YA, Ohio YA Writers, and Binders Full of YA Writers. Finally, thanks to the readers who will spend the next few hours with me and Tor Maddox. You can make the world a better place.

CHAPTER ONE

UNDER THE RADAR

Are you paying attention? Are you aware that Man's Best Friend just became Public Enemy Number One?

~ www.governmentsecrets.us
First posting: September 6

I couldn't get those words out of my head as Cocoa yanked his leash with all the strength of his twenty-five pounds and tugged me toward the dog park. Sure, I know it was just another one of those weird conspiracy blogs, like the ridiculous ones I like to read about Apollo missions being faked with special effects, or 9/11 being planned by the CIA. I follow enough *real* news that I know there's no way our government could pull off a stunt that big and keep it quiet for long. As Shakespeare, my absolute favorite wordsmith said, "The truth will out."

I'm not the kind of girl who believes everything she reads on the internet, but this entry had an unusual ring of authenticity. Okay, so Cocoa didn't look like the next scourge of the ages with his dark brown tail wagging frantically in anticipation of social time. Still, this new blogger's message resonated (echoed and hummed) in my mind while Cocoa pulled me out of our typical So Cal suburban cul-de-sac and over the bridge across the dry creek bed. I've never seen a drop of water in the creek, but, in theory, if we ever got enough rain, it would run down from the nearby mountains. Well, not exactly mountains—more like parched, rocky, scrubby hills.

What exactly had that blogger said? I pulled up the webpage on my phone.

> *Are you paying attention? Are you aware that Man's Best Friend just became Public Enemy Number One? It's easy to be distracted by all the other potential disasters looming on the horizon. You count on the media and your government for clues.*

I don't know about the government, but I do count on the media. I admit, I'm glued to CNN from the moment Cocoa and I get done with our daily walk and romp. I have after-school dog duty, and my brother Rody does the six a.m. walk because he's one of those annoying people who wakes up ready to roll when the alarm goes off. Plus, except for his crazy long bangs, his short clipped brown hair takes about two seconds to wash and dry, whereas my long dark tresses demand lather-rinse-repeat as well as conditioner. This arrangement works out great for me because Cocoa is a morning pooper and Rody has to deal with it. Totally fair.

Cocoa's legs were full of stored up energy, prancing

along as fast as I could walk, even with the stride of a giant—well, not exactly a giant, but five ten on a girl is pushing the limit. Before letting him inside the fence to mingle with the other dogs, I planned to take our usual lap around the park so he wouldn't be quite so overwhelming. He came to a dead halt, yanking me backward, and pushed his nose through the chain link of the Small Dogs Only pen, where he traded sniffs with a white Westie.

"Come on, Cocoa. I'm the human here," I insisted, giving a slight snap to the leash. "I'm supposed to be your pack leader. So follow me."

He heard my exasperation and came willingly to heel. Six years ago, Cocoa had adopted me at the humane society when he was just a motley-looking puppy. All we could figure was that somewhere in his family tree was a beagle who gave him shape and stature, a chocolate lab who gave him color and sweetness, and a terrier who gave him spirit and a mustache. He's a fine example of the American canine melting pot.

I set a good pace around the chain link, waving at familiar folks on the benches. Still, that crazy blog was tickling my brain, demanding attention. Much of what it said was true:

> *You count on the media and your government for clues. And what are they doing? Watching for hurricanes on the Gulf Coast; monitoring the northern border of Pakistan for terrorists; measuring seismic tremors along the San Andreas Fault. They are scanning the night sky*

for inbound comets and asteroids; tapping your phones and reading your emails and profiling charge card bills across America looking for terrorist sleeper cells. They are sweeping the skies for migratory birds carrying avian flu; scrutinizing North Korea and Iran for evidence of intercontinental atomic missiles.

I couldn't argue with that, although some threats were more realistic than others. Bird flu was old, old news. We'd been getting ready for that since 1998, for eighteen years. (Our quarantine emergency supplies would have expired long ago except for Dad's compulsive restocking.) And by the way, the blogger had left out mudslides and wildfires, a couple potential disasters that are especially worrisome to us here in San Diego.

That's where we've all been looking for the next major disaster—he/she/it went on—*looking up, out, and in. But it flew in under the radar. We should have been looking down, down at that cold, wet nose pressed lovingly into the palm of our hand.*

We came around to the gate of the pen reserved for medium and large dogs, and Cocoa pressed his cold, wet nose lovingly into the palm of my hand. I dried it on the silky fur between his ears. "You're not a modern day flea-infested plague carrier, are you, fuzzy face?" I asked him.

He looked at me blankly, as usual, with an innocent dog smile. See, I only asked because the blogger had gone on to spout some weird theory about a coming pandemic that was going to be caused by dogs. But he never got any more specific. Undoubtedly a total nut.

When Cocoa tipped his head on one side and stared at his friends running free, I opened the gate for him and unclipped his leash. He bounded onto the grass with a happy woof.

The white Westie in the next door area raced up again, yipping a greeting that sounded like a fistful of gravel in his bark box. I knew I hadn't seen either him or his owner before, because I would have remembered the human specimen, for sure. He was about six feet of lean surfing muscle, sun-bleached hair, and clear blue eyes. The tight tank top he was wearing showed off his well-spent hours in a weight room and proclaimed his allegiance to UCSD—he was a college guy.

What was he doing here in Poway, fifteen miles inland, instead of cutting class and hanging out on a Del Mar beach where he so clearly belonged? His loss, my gain.

I smiled openly at him. He lifted one eyebrow in my direction. Very charmingly, I thought.

Our pets exchanged polite butt sniffs through the fence. Then something about Cocoa's scent launched the Westie into sneezing spasms, and a glob of yellow mucus sprayed out and stuck to the dark brown fur on Cocoa's toes. He twisted and licked himself.

"Oh, no. I'm sorry," the owner said. "That's gross. Must be allergies. Westies are prone, you know?"

"No, I didn't." I froze a smile onto my face. "Learn

something new every day! Cocoa, come." I turned away ASAP, my stomach flipping over.

"Hey, are we okay?" the guy called after me. "Are you mad? I just got Wessex back from the kennel, but he's perfectly healthy. I promise he's had his kennel cough vaccine."

He said *We*? I peeked back over my shoulder. His sweet blue eyes were worried. He was extremely cute again, and I could be very forgiving.

"Don't worry about it," I said. "Cocoa's had his Bordetella vaccine, too." I wasn't showing off, just making myself sound a little more mature. No, really.

Cocoa barked and raced off to mingle with the big dogs. Before I could follow, the guy's hand shot out and landed on my shoulder. Zap. A fizzing current ran straight through me to my feet. I spun my head to look over my shoulder (we ballerinas can do that, you know, for spotting) and found myself pupil-to-pupil with him. His eyes were so ocean blue I heard the surf crashing in my ears. The Earth stopped spinning. Time itself refused to move on. Excuse my hyperbole, but this was a new experience for me, the mutual "whoa!" of the eye-lock.

He blinked first. "You want to go get ice cream? With the dogs, I mean?"

I was stunned for another microsecond. Was this a date? Mom had said I wasn't allowed to date till I'm sixteen—forty-eight long, long days away. So no, this wasn't a date. Because then I wouldn't be allowed to say, as I did, "Yeah. That would be great!" Because really, it would just be walking Cocoa...to the ice cream shop...with another dog...who happened to have an owner.

"My treat, this time," he said.

This time? My brain sang wild, crazy melodies that even Mozart never thought of.

"Thanks. I didn't bring my purse," I said, and that covered the reason he was paying, because God knows, it wasn't a date and I'd swear to that if Mom caught me. Cocoa was confused when I called him back and snapped on his leash before he had finished socializing. "Trust me, fuzzy face, you're going to like this," I promised.

We walked the dogs up to the main road toward the Super Scoop. I have to admit, I noticed that we turned a few heads as we went along, him with his tall blondness and me with my tall brownness. I bet they even thought we were a couple. I checked out our reflection together in a store window and approved.

It was easiest to talk about the dogs (I guess that's why grownups always talk about their kids), so I learned that his little guy, Wessex, was allergic to grass, loved the car, and preferred banana ice cream. I found myself accidentally spilling the tale of my most embarrassing moment, right after we got Cocoa when my Mom caught me trying to bleach him with L'Oreal hair coloring because I wanted a golden retriever. It was logical. Mom's own Doris Day blonde look came out of the same bottle.

At Super Scoop, he ordered two kid scoop dishes of banana for the dogs and two double fudge chocolate waffle cones for us. I couldn't decide whether it was very manly of him to order for me or slightly obnoxious, so I decided to go for manly. I double-blinked as he peeled a twenty off a roll. I was right.

Definitely manly.

"Wait a second," I said with the realization that we'd been chatting like old friends. "I don't even know your name. I can't take ice cream from a stranger."

"Sorry, I've forgotten my social graces," he said with a very old fashioned, unexpected, and adorable bow. He stuck out his hand. "Erich. With an H."

"Herik?" I teased. I slipped my hand into his. Strong. Warm. Wow. I almost forgot to reply, "Tor."

"Tor? That short for Victoria?" he asked.

"Uh, no. Torrance," I admitted.

"Torrance. Like the beach?"

I nodded.

"Gnarly waves," he said with a hint of a suggestive smile and a raised eyebrow.

That trick with the eyebrow gave me happy shivers. I pretended the goosebumps on my arms were due to ice cream. I can't remember much of the banter after that, just that the ice cream disappeared too fast, and we wandered back.

"This isn't my regular park," Erich said as we came in sight of it again. "When are you usually here?"

"I get over here most afternoons about this time," I said. "How come you're so far from campus?"

He sighed. "Long story, but basically my folks are making me live at home to save money. How about you?"

"Oh, I live at home, too." Well, it was true.

"No kidding. Small world. What year are you?"

"Sophomore," I answered briefly.

"Hey, me too," he said with a disarming grin. "I'm assigned to Warren. I don't think I've seen you before, but it's a huge place. Which school are you in?"

I chose this crucial moment to answer without thinking. "Poway High."

Hello, Tor. Anyone home in there?

His eyes went from soft and friendly to wide and shocked in an instant. He took two steps backward. "Well, yes. No wonder," he stammered. "Oh, God. Look at the time." He checked his arm, which, to his obvious chagrin, had no watch. His eyes darted around, slightly panicked. "Nice to meet you, Tor."

"Nice to meet…oh, spit," I whispered at his retreating back. So much for my first, secret not-a-date.

In spite of my dimwittitude, I couldn't wait to tell Sioux about Erich.

Sioux's my UBF, ultimate best friend, knows me better than anyone in the world. She's not one of those *fashionable* girls who look with envy at my body and say, "God, Tor. You should be a model. You could even be a supermodel if you got a boob job." It mystifies them that my fashion choice is men's slim jeans (28-32's, which are not easy to find), a faded brown Padres T-shirt, and a baseball cap slammed down over my long straight brown hair. When we hang out at the mall, they play dress up with me, beg me to put on the micro styles that make them hate their own thighs.

Even Sioux sometimes teases me for my lack of feminine taste, but she knows my darkest secrets. She has seen me dressed from my perfect, tight hair bun to the tips of my pointe shoes in glittery pink and floaty white. She has seen me twirl and leap and sauté arabesque. She has seen me in mascara and eyeliner and red blush and lipstick. For creeps sake, she has seen me in a gauze tutu. My secrets are safe with her, a girl with her own multiple personalities, so to speak.

So I finally got her alone the next day as we were fixing up our black bean burgers at the Fixin's Bar in the cafeteria at lunch. Swiss cheese, fried onions, and ketchup. A small slice of heaven on earth.

"How old do you think he was?" Sioux asked after I had laid bare the whole un-sordid story.

"I don't know. Twenty? Twenty-one?"

"You vixen, you!" Sioux said enviously. "Can I come with you next time?"

"Sioux-san! What would your mother say? Besides..." I grinned. "The way he ran off with a big 'jailbait' sign flashing in his dilated pupils, I'll never see him again. Not at my dog park."

So I was half right, as things turned out.

During last period study hall, I added *governmentsecrets.us* to my bookmarked blogs and indulged in my usual "nuts and news" scan. The teachers don't care whether you're really doing homework as long as you're quiet and not trying to break through the site-blocks. Today's cryptic, paranoid message was annoyingly brief: *Watch the news carefully.*

When Cocoa and I got back from our walk (alas, as predicted, no Erich today), Rody was already home from fall baseball practice, thumping around in the kitchen and fixing himself a snack. The TV was playing extremely loud music videos. Mom and Dad weren't home from work yet.

"If you don't mind," I said and switched straight to CNN.

He stood at the kitchen counter, smoothing huge amounts of peanut butter onto six stalks of celery. "Does it matter if I do?" He glared at me through the strands of his long, dark bangs, still wet from the shower.

"Nope." At least I'm honest. "Hey, how was the chem lab write-up? You done?" I reached over his shoulder and snatched a piece of plain celery. I tower over him by four inches, much to his dismay. Judging by the way he was eating and his unusually thick look, he was getting ready for the growth spurt that would elevate him to Dad's respectable six foot two.

"Yes, I'm done, and no, you can't copy," he said. He crunched violently for emphasis.

"Duh. Just wondering," I shot back, trying to sound hurt. I'd been hoping to…not copy…just compare… data and analysis. That's all. That's fair. I help him with Language Arts, after all.

See, we're both in tenth grade, and for three hideous months of the year we're the same age, even though my birthday is October 24th and his is the next August 14th. People who don't know us very well assume we're twins. When I explain that I am actually nine and three-quarters months older, they smirk and say, "Oh, I see. Irish twins," which if you didn't know is an ethnic slur and inappropriate way of pointing out that our parents had sex and got re-pregnant mere days after I was born when Mom was supposed to be resting and recovering.

There are just some things you don't want to know

about your parents. That's one of them. And now I can't un-know it.

I sat down at the table with my vocabulary worksheet, one ear on the TV.

"How can you concentrate with all that talking?" he asked.

"It's relaxing," I said. "I need to know what happened today."

Call me a news junkie. I won't argue. At school, they think I'm just a smidge odd for caring about what goes on in the world. I've had this reputation ever since sixth grade when the other kids found out that I'd helped my parents hand out lawn signs to elect our current president. (Okay, so maybe passing out campaign buttons in the cafeteria wasn't such a great idea.) Well, they're welcome to their high school oblivious ignorance. I, on the other hand, know that one day, I'm going to have to live in the real world. I'd like it to be a decent one.

Rody doesn't share my enthusiasm for news. "Fine. Whatever." He grabbed his plate in one hand and shouldered his backpack, yielding the TV to me, his elder.

"Hey, take that with you." I pointed to the bag of reeking practice uniform.

In the background, the newscaster was talking about our war casualties in Africa. I glanced up from trying to write a sentence using the word "mitigate" (which, as I had just discovered, means to lessen the effects of something), and I caught the very tail end of the words crawling across the bottom of the screen, the part they call the ticker:

...0 CONFIRMED CASES OF MYSTERY FLU IN
NORTHERN CALIFORNIA TOWN...

That caught my attention, and my natural curiosity kicked in. What had I just missed? Was it actually zero confirmed cases? That wouldn't be news. Twenty confirmed cases? More interesting. Two hundred confirmed cases? A disaster in the making! And if they were calling it a mystery flu, they must have already run some tests on the victims and decided it wasn't the deadly Avian flu breaking into fortress America.

I watched for another hour, but strangely enough, no one reported anything about it, and the tag never recycled. That should have told me something.

CHAPTER TWO

OUTBREAK

How come no one else is talking about this? Something weird is going on up in Northern California. Cluster deaths. A new disease. Better get those flu shots before they run out.

- www.governmentsecrets.us
Posted: September 12

The blogger kept posting alarming notes, notes that bore a strange sense of truthiness, and I kept reading it daily because (A) it was entertaining, (B) truth can be stranger than fiction, and (C) even a nut can find a squirrel every once in a while. Hang on. I don't think that last one is exactly right. But the actual news, which normally panics at the first hint of a measle, reported nothing on this mystery flu for the rest of the week, so I figured it had run its course and vanished. The bark was worse than the bite, so to speak.

Then, suddenly, it was back with sharpened teeth. I was working on a vocab worksheet in front of the news, learning great words like *antipathy, virulence,* and *vacuous,* when out of the corner of my ear I heard the familiar voice of anchorman Alex Fletcher saying,

"...mystery flu and are in critical condition. We now are reporting one fatality from complications of pneumonia. The first victim has been claimed." Dramatic pause. "Is this just the tip of the iceberg? Dr. Narlee Wave of the Centers for Disease Control is with us in our Atlanta studio. Dr. Wave, should we be worried? What more can you tell us about the so-called mystery flu?"

I suppose there's hope for someone like me, named after a beach, if someone with a name like Narlee Wave made it into med school and ended up as an epidemiologist at the CDC, the Mecca of infectious disease tracking and research. But what were her parents thinking?

Side bar. Actually, a lot of us ask this question regularly. *What were our parents thinking?*

Take Sioux-san. Her parents wanted a good, old fashioned name that sounded like Mary or Frances or (hey!) Susan but carried all the faux Native American panache of a trendy tribal name like Dakota, Cheyenne, Sequoia or Wyoming.

Take us, me and Rody. Oh yeah, Mom and Dad were embarrassingly creative about our names. They called us after the places we were—ahem, excuse me?!—*conceived* back when they lived in L.A.: Torrance County Beach and Rodeo Drive. That is *way* TMI more than I expected when I asked where my name came from. *Way*. All I can say is I'm glad my parents weren't interlocking on a beach towel a little farther north toward Redondo on the famous RAT beach the night I was invented. Just as glad Rody hadn't been saddled with Ford Taurus Maddox, the other possibility they considered.

Anyhow, in spite of this horrendous handicap of a name, Dr. Narlee Wave had risen to the rank of CNN's expert du jour. She gave a concise yet extremely unsatisfying answer.

"Well, Alex," she said with way too much familiarity in her body language. "At this point, there's not much we do know. With a cluster of current cases, we're able to do some genetic testing on the disease itself. The curious thing we're finding so far, apart from the unexpected virulence of this strain, is its novel composition. All fifteen cases are of the type H3N1."

Alex the news anchor acted impressed. "Is that so? H3N1. Serious indeed." As if he had a clue. I wanted him to ask the obvious follow-up question for those of us without a medical degree, like "What's an H3N1?" But instead he asked, "What does the CDC plan to do now?"

"We're emphasizing contact tracing," she replied. "That is, finding anyone who had contact with the affected people during the time we believe they were contagious. The more cases we find, the more we'll know about this outbreak. I'd caution anyone who experiences flu-like symptoms to maintain vigilance and call their family doctor."

"So is that the official term for what we have here? An outbreak?" Alex asked.

Dr. Wave shook her head slightly. "Officially we call this a Phase Three Pandemic Alert. But it's not—"

"Pandemic?" Alex interrupted. "Are you saying a pandemic has started?" He turned a shade paler, and tiny beads of sweat broke out on his upper lip, as if he were beginning to experience flu-like symptoms.

Dr. Wave wrinkled her brow in amusement. "No, no, Alex. *Phase Three* means that we have a new, self-limiting influenza subtype. *Self-limiting* means it should run its course as we take the appropriate measures. *Appropriate* measures means the steps I just outlined. We have as yet no firm evidence of human to human transmission. That's where contact tracing comes in."

Alex wiped his brow theatrically and smiled. "I'm sure we're all relieved to hear that. So would you recommend that everyone go out and get their flu shots early?"

Hey, that's what the blogger suggested, come to think of it.

Dr. Wave shook her head. "Alex, unfortunately, the flu shots prepared for this season weren't based on this novel combination, H3N1. The CDC's *official* position is that they'd be practically useless against this new strain. However, it's never a bad idea to protect yourself against the endemic, familiar varieties. But truly, there's no need at all to worry the public. You can trust that when we get to the bottom of this, vaccine work will be initiated."

"Ah, good. When can the public expect a vaccine for the new flu?"

"Generally, vaccine development takes twelve to fifteen months. We may be able to fast track this one, if we're lucky."

"How long will that take, if we're lucky?" the newscaster pressed her.

"At least six months."

By the time Mom called me and Rody to help her fix dinner, CNN had a really dazzle logo for the NEW FLU in code orange colored letters and an ominous (totally foreboding, like in a minor key) theme song and no new information. They kept replaying the part of the interview where Dr. Wave said, "We'd call this a Phase Three Pandemic Alert," and, "Generally, vaccine development takes twelve to fifteen months." I read between the lines. *Ladies and Gentlemen, start your panic.*

Mom and Dad believe faithfully in the old-fashioned family dinner. Dad's job as a hospital pharmacist gives him predictable hours, so he's always home on time. And even though Mom spends her days teaching Culinary Arts over at the J.C. (junior college), she still has the energy to make us a healthy, delicious, well-balanced dinner. Rody and I are often called into service as her sous-chefs at home. She does try earnestly to train us, bless her optimism.

When we presented ourselves for kitchen duty, Mom handed Rody a hunk of Parmigiano-Reggiano and a heart of organic romaine. "Rodeo, grate and chop, please," she commanded. "Torrance, you can mince two cloves of garlic. Thanks, sweethearts."

She whacked three homegrown tomatoes into dice-sized cubes, while I was still peeling the first clove of garlic. The entire piece skittered off the cutting board when I took a knife to it, and Cocoa hoovered it up from the floor by my feet. I'm sure it could only improve his breath. He sat back with his hopeful, begging face on. His little teeth smiled at me.

"Go on, git, you silly old beast." I nudged him with my knee.

By the time my garlic was reduced to smithereens, Mom had demolished a crown of broccoli and had started boiling rigatoni. I stirred for her while she magically transformed a bunch of chopped vegetables into a fresh pasta primavera with creamy parmesan sauce. And somehow, while I wasn't looking, she had put garlic bread under the broiler and tossed a salad. Sigh. She makes everything look easy.

Dad slid in the door right on time, and I ran up to give him a hug. "Hey Dad, I've got dinner news," I said, all excited to tell him about H3N1, the New Flu.

He pulled me tight with my feet off the floor. "Hey, punkin," he said, which I admit, I cherish, because who else would call their giant daughter a cute little name like that. "Save it for the table so we can all enjoy it." He loves table talk.

We gathered around Mom's beautiful creation and held hands. "Will you say grace tonight, Torrance?" Mom requested.

"Grace," I said. Family joke. Then I said a real one, a shorty. Well, I was hungry.

"So what's your news?" Dad asked me.

I was bursting to tell. "Dad, do you know anything about this quote unquote mystery flu on the news? Does anyone at Palomar Hospital have it?"

"Mystery flu?" he echoed. "As a matter of fact, we do have a new patient with an unresponsive flu strain. Outrageous fever. On oxygen support. Pathology hasn't typed it yet. They called me from the ICU today to see if I could develop a more potent antiviral cocktail."

I knew what that was. That's like a mixture of two or three different medicines, but without the cute little umbrella they put in tropical juice cocktails.

"I'd say it's probably H3N1," I offered in a matter-of-fact way. "It's a novel combination."

You could practically see his ears perk up, like Cocoa's when he hears the clink of his leash. "H3N1?" he repeated. "Why? What do you know about it?"

Dad has always had this suburban survivalist streak. Not only do we have a portable generator, a three month supply of food, and an entire wall of water gallons in the garage, but he has studied up on how to live off the land when civilization as we know it falls. Thanks to the pharmacy, he even has a few doses of Eradiflu for all of us stashed away in cold storage.

Mom has hinted that he wasn't quite so extreme when she first met him. But then 9/11 happened when Rody was less than two weeks old, and all his protective dadly feelings kicked in. On top of that, when Rody and I were preschoolers, Dad got called up for Army Reserve duty and got his foot blown off in Iraq even though he only went to help set up some medical clinics. So unfair. Having seen the plunging chaos in the Middle East first hand, he realized that everything could go to hell in a handbasket in no time flat, and, as the leader of our little tribe of four, he'd better be alert and ready for it.

So that, in a nutshell, a really big nutshell, is why he was as interested in news about a mysterious new disease as I was. It was more than just professional curiosity; it was intelligence gathering.

I had run out of brilliant news, however. "That's all

the CDC knows so far," I confessed. "They just announced it a couple hours ago."

Dad squeezed his lips thoughtfully. "A new strain, huh? Could be serious."

Rody shrugged, cynical and unimpressed as usual. "What's the big deal," he said. "I had the flu last year. I got over it."

"Not this kind of flu," I said. "Somebody already DIED from it."

"Hey, survival of the fittest," he said, striking a stupid bodybuilder pose.

"Oh, shut down, you muscle-bound moron," I snapped.

"Torrance, please," Mom said. "Be civil at the table."

"Yes, Mother," I said dutifully. I glared across the table at Rody. "But just wait till I'm excused, you vacuous peon." Score double points for two vocab words in one insult.

"Torrance!"

"Sorry, Mom."

Since it was a ballet night, I ate lightly then ran upstairs to do the caterpillar into butterfly thing. My jeans and t-shirt slithered to the floor like a discarded chrysalis, joining the rest of the *detritus*, a lovely word for the debris I leave by the side of my bed. I pulled on long pink tights and a black leotard. Poof, a butterfly. A long gray sweatshirt jacket and my old rubber clogs completed the ensemble. Okay, maybe a moth. I leaned over and stretched, palms flat on the carpet, then grabbed all the brown hair puddling on the floor and twisted it into a bun. Four hairpins later, I was set to go.

◆——————◆

21

"Come on, Mom," I yelled as if I'd been ready for hours. I jingled the car keys at her.

She transferred to Dad the pile of dirty plates in her hands, and secretly winked at me as she grabbed her purse. She didn't flinch even once while I was driving, and after I parked, we both signed my driving log. Another twenty minutes toward my license requirements. Yay.

From her cavernous purse, she pulled out a paperback book with a patient sigh, but I knew better. We did this routine three nights a week. She savored her peaceful time, reading by visor light in the parking lot.

I slid my dance ID card through the mag-reader and waited for the green light.

"Hey, Tory," came at me as I opened the door.

"Hey yourself, Felix," I answered. If Felicity was going to screw up my name on purpose day after day, I could do the same. She smiled, catlike, at me, but she retracted her claws.

I chucked my shoes and sweatshirt into a cubby and folded myself in half to slide on my ballet slippers. A familiar hand patted me on the high point, that being my butt.

"Ooh, what a target. Couldn't resist."

I turned to face Sasha with a grin. "Yes, you could, and you know it."

Sasha was almost everything a girl could want. He was eighteen and over six feet tall. He was built like a racehorse, with chest and arm muscles out the wazoo. He had long, sinewy thighs, as they say in those awful romance novels Mom devours. He had the face of an angel—long-lashed hazel eyes, high cheekbones, and wavy black hair. He was graceful, charming, and witty. He was an excellent dancer. He was gay. Duh. I said *almost*, didn't I?

Sasha was like a brother to us, all the pink little ballerinas who'd grown up together in the studio. He stood up to jock-teasing at school with a simple question—"Would you rather be in a locker room with a bunch of sweaty guys or with a bunch of half-dressed ballerinas?" Hah! That always shut them down.

"Hey, Alexander," Felicity crooned. "Ready for auditions next week?"

Okay, we all know he isn't really Russian, and yes, he's really Alexander Bromwell, but Sasha always uses his stage name to go with his stage personality. And Felicity knows it.

Sasha grinned at the name-abuse. "Gorgeous sweater," he said, eyeing the burnt-orange cashmere cardigan she was wearing backward. She has a perfect, petite dancer's body, and the men's V-neck sweater hung down to mid-thigh on her, the V opening showing off her black straps and shoulder blades. It was quite effective, in all honesty.

"May I?" Sasha stroked her cashmere-covered arm with a teasing gleam in his eye. Felicity's shiny, glossed lips parted. She looked up through her long Latina lashes with her huge, dark Bambi eyes. It was a look that melted the boys at school when she pulled it out of her weapons cache, but it only made Sasha laugh. Everyone knew she'd had a warm spot in her heart for him since fifth grade. It had moved farther south into her panties since then. (Did I really say that? Meow.)

Got to give her points for senseless persistent optimism, though.

Auditions. The holiday show always included a beautiful *pas de deux*—partner dance—and, finally, Felicity and I were old enough to try out for it. Sasha's place was, of course, guaranteed, as the only male dancer in the studio who was old and strong enough to lift.

My traitorous brain painted a beautiful picture of tiny, dainty Felicity floating above the stage, balancing her gently curved torso on Sasha's upraised arms. I splashed some mental turpentine on the image and repainted it with myself, more gravitationally challenged, yet still a mere cloud in his gentle hands. Then Sasha's knees and elbows buckled and the imaginary me rolled thuddingly to the floor. Ack. Maybe I'd skip a few meals before tryouts.

I watched the news daily for breaking information, but it was always more of the same, until three more Northern California flu victims died on Friday, only four days after the first one. This cranked up the official anxiety level—four dead out of fifteen sick was lousy odds.

"How's the patient at Palomar doing?" I asked Dad.

He frowned. "Not so well, I'm afraid. You'd think a young, healthy man would be able to bounce back once we got the antivirals into him, but his lungs are in horrible shape. It's terribly sad, and quite honestly, I'm frustrated. He's stuck in a vicious cycle."

"What do you mean?" I asked.

"It's like he's drowning himself. They call it a

cytokine storm. His body is trying too hard to fight the infection and swamping his lungs with fluid. They put him on a vent tonight."

"Does he have it for sure? The New Flu?" A cold feeling filled my stomach.

"Mmm. It's confirmed now. The sequence is identical to the ones up north."

"Dad…" I started. Then my words choked off.

"What is it, punkin?" His arms were around me, and I talked to his top button.

"Please be careful around him, Dad. Don't breathe or anything."

He squeezed me tight. "Hey, don't worry, hun. Gloves, masks, the works. I promise."

Four nights later Dad dragged in looking pale and beaten. "Hiya, little one," he said in an exhausted voice. "How's my girl?" He tossed the mail onto the kitchen table and plopped down with a thud. Cocoa put his head on Dad's knee. Dad scratched Cocoa's ears. "Yeah, you too, boy. How's my dog?" He sighed and rubbed his right leg, where his prosthetic foot attaches. This upgraded version is practically bionic, with pressure and balance sensors and toes that he can move, but just like always, he still gets sore by the end of the day.

I rubbed his tight neck for a second. It was as hard as rock. "How's my Dad?" I asked.

He kept his eyes down, sorting through the evening paper.

"Dad, you look awful. You're not…you're not getting sick, are you?" I was careful not to let my voice shake like the rest of me.

"No. I'm okay," he said. "Mostly." He had the paper open to the obits. I don't know why he reads them. It's a habit of his any time a patient at the hospital dies. Completely depressing, but it's his way of paying his respects or something.

I peered past his ear with my chin resting on his shoulder. "Who was it?" I asked. But then my eyes locked onto a familiar face. "Oh dear God," I whispered. "Oh spit." It was a high school photo. It was Erich with an H.

Dad pointed to the picture. "We lost him yesterday morning. I asked to attend the post today. It was really rough."

"The post?" My stomach rolled.

"Post mortem. The autopsy."

"Yeah, I know, Dad. I meant, why would you go?" My eyes filled up with tears. A couple dropped onto the newspaper in big, fat plops.

Why put yourself through that? Why watch them dissect and cut and measure and analyze someone who was alive and well and buying me ice cream less than two weeks ago?

Dad pulled me down onto his lap. He brushed the tears off my cheeks with his fingertips. "I'm sorry, punkin. I shouldn't have brought it up. I know you're the sensitive type."

"I, uh, I sort of knew him," I confessed. I rubbed a runaway tear. "I saw him around the dog park."

"Really? When?" Dad's ears went on high alert. Code yellow.

"Like two weeks ago. But it was his dog that was sick, not him. His dog had allergies."

Dad's eyes drilled me. "You spoke to him?" Escalate to code orange.

"Well, yeah, a little," I said. "I mean, people are friendly with each other at the park."

"How close was he standing?" Dad demanded.

"I don't know," I said. "Like people stand. He didn't kiss me or anything."

"Kiss you?" Dad's voice rose to a squeaky high note. "Why would he kiss you?"

"No reason!" I said, a little too loudly. "It was only ice cream, I swear!"

Dad looked at me with a perplexed, baffled, protective, kind of angry jumble on his face. "Torrance Olivia Maddox, what are you talking about?" All three names. Code red. Now I was really in trouble.

But Dad surprised me. He put his lips to my forehead. "Normal, I think," he announced. "You feeling okay? Physically?"

Of course not. My heart was bruised and bleeding. "Yeah. I'm okay," I reassured him.

"You know, just the same, I'd like to start you on a regimen of Eradiflu antiviral. And a regular flu shot."

"Why?"

He put an arm around my shoulders. "Just in case. If that poor kid was walking around two weeks ago as healthy as you say....You wouldn't believe how torn up he was inside. Lungs like dishrags." He squeezed my hand. "We don't want to take any chances, do we?"

"Nope," I said. "We don't."

"After dinner, I'll take you over to Wal-Mart for the flu shot."

"Dazzle." Somehow my shocked grief over Erich

had been smothered by my own sense of self-preservation.

I knew I was in for a long night on the internet. H3N1. Just what might this beautiful, friendly, now dead guy have breathed on me, anyhow?

CHAPTER THREE

PATIENT ZERO

They know more than they are saying. They have known for weeks—the source, the vector. Why aren't they doing anything? The trickle has to be stopped before the levee breaks.

- www.governmentsecrets.us
Posted: September 20

Here's what I learned the night Erich died. First of all, flu, real influenza, is a virus. That's why it's stupid to take antibiotics for it—those only work on bacteria. Got that? So a virus is basically made of a protein package full of a bunch of genes that hijack your cells to do the heavy lifting for them. The virus lands on the cell surface (and believe me, it looks just like those old moon lander photos; you should check it out) and pops its genes into your cells, which go crazy making copies of the virus, and then explode and send out the new baby viruses to invade the next bunch of cells. It's like a microscopic alien landing fleet. In you.

Meanwhile, your body notices the invasion and creates a bunch of puzzle-piece-shaped antibodies to try to figure out which fits the virus. The right one will snap in, lock on, and yell, "Yo, guys, come haul off this virus." Then you go into mass production of the right puzzle pieces to find and disable all the virus particles. That's how it's supposed to go. If you've ever had that virus before, your body is really quick and efficient, which is why you don't get so many colds when you get older—lucky you, you've already had them all.

But while the invasion is just getting started, before the racking cough and copious (that is, grossly plentiful) snot tip you off, you are still going to school and the mall, breathing virus particles all over your friends. It isn't till the battle is raging that you find yourself lying in bed with a feverish pounding head, aches in every joint, and shivery crawling skin, wishing death would hurry up and take you. *Usually* you get better. And the virus marches on to new territory—your friends.

It sounds like your body is smart at dealing with viruses, right? Well, they've been around a lot longer than people, by billions of years, so they have more experience and expertise. They've worked their way up. All animals get viruses. Even amoebas (amoebae?) get viruses. Spit, even plants get viruses! And influenza viruses are really smart. They morph. And then the puzzle pieces don't fit, and they can get a good, strong invasion going before they get shut down.

Back to H3N1. (I know you were wondering when I was going to get there. Hey, it took me an hour of Googling to get this far!) Influenza has two hugely important proteins on its shell, H and N. They're a tongue twister: hemagglutinin and neuraminidase.

Don't panic. There will not be a quiz.

Because of the morphing, H comes in 15 flavors, just slightly different from each other; N comes in 9. That makes a lot of potential combinations (quiz: nine times fifteen equals what....?)(So I lied. There was a quiz. Did you get 135 combos?).

H has to do with how easy it is for the virus to grab onto your cells; N has to do with busting out the baby viruses. That's why they're so important. And according to Dr. Narlee Wave, the New Flu was H version 3, N version 1.

Which meant...what, exactly?

I found this great webpage that had information on old flu epidemics. Take a look at this:

H2N2: Russian Flu killed 1 million 1889-90
H1N1: Spanish Flu killed 50-100 million 1918-20
H2N2: Asian Flu killed 1-4 million 1956-58
H3N2: Hong Kong Flu killed 2-4 million 1968-69
H1N1: Swine Flu killed 300-600,000 2009-12

Killed?! Millions?!

Until these numbers slapped me upside the head, I thought we humans were pretty good at fighting off germs, almost kill-proof. I was wrong. Influenza isn't just a bad cold—it's ruthless. Every year hundreds of thousands of people die of regular, familiar influenza if they are very little, very old, or otherwise kind of feeble. But *millions* died in those epidemics when a new, unfamiliar, and especially harsh combination of flu invented itself. The Avian Flu is H5N1. That was a new combination. So is H3N1.

At this point, Dad came over to the computer. He looked at my screen and asked, "What are you working so hard on?"

"I'm learning Virology," I said. "There's all this information on flu in general, but nothing on where H3N1 came from. I'm trying to find out."

He gave me one of those aren't-you-clever smiles that makes me glad to be alive. Then he patted me and said, "Strong work. But it's bedtime. You can crack the case tomorrow."

I started up the stairs, but as I looked back, I saw him sitting down at the computer to do some of his own sleuthing—a dark silhouette against the eerie blue glow of the screen.

Right after that first fatality, Alex and Dr. Wave became a daily news snippet, a part of Alex's regular afternoon segment, *Fletch in Focus*. While the death toll gradually rose, Narlee offered no new information on where this flu had come from or how it had spread to Southern California. On September 20th, Day Nine of CNN's New Flu watch, Alex asked, "Dr. Wave, I know it's early days yet, but can you tell us how the New Flu compares with prior flu outbreaks?"

Dr. Wave was becoming addicted to the limelight. She rocked a new bobbed hairstyle. Dark blondish highlights replaced her old gray streaks. How did she have time for the hair salon? Wasn't she supposed to be working madly in a laboratory or crunching data to figure out what was going on?

"Alex, so far we're seeing some similarities and some differences." She rested a hand on the sleeve of his jacket, and I noticed she'd also had time for a French manicure. "In terms of similarities," she said, "New Flu has appeared as a recombination of existing subtypes. We call that an antigenic shift. However, there are also a number of point mutations in the virus, which may account for its virulence." She patted his arm. "In layman's terms, its strength. And that, we call antigenic drift. Whenever we get shift, there's the possibility for a major outbreak, perhaps a local epidemic."

Rody, snacking with me at the kitchen table, shook his head. "How can you stand listening to her?" he asked me. "Ninety-nine percent of the watchers have no idea what she's talking about."

"Do you?" I asked pointedly. "I do. All it takes is a *modicum* of effort to learn about it."

"What's a freaping *modicum*?"

I rolled my eyes. "A smidgen. A tad. An itsy bit. Look it up. It's on this week's vocab list." I stabbed at the page in front of me with my eraser.

With the *modicum* of research I had done, I knew all about the shift/drift thing. Drift is small scale, just a copying error when the baby viruses are being mass produced inside your cells. Sometimes it has no effect; sometimes it makes the new virus harder to recognize; sometimes it can make things much worse, depending on which genes get the error, the mutation. Shift is huge. It's like exchanging arms or legs with someone. It's new, it's weird, and there's no telling what the new combination might do. Of course, you can only exchange arms or legs with someone if they're in the same room as you are, so to speak. Shift happens only rarely, when two kinds of influenza viruses are in the same place at the same time, and they get all tangled and switchy in the dark. Then the combo has to be strong enough to survive and multiply.

Shift is what creates super-viruses. And then, millions die.

Alex followed up with, "And what about those differences you mentioned?"

Dr. Wave answered. "There are two main differences so far, Alex. First the good news. Fortunately, this virus seems to be transferring slowly. We still haven't *formally* identified a *vector*, that is, in layman's terms, a carrier, or determined whether it's moving directly from human to human. We're working with an extremely small number of cases. In addition to the fifteen recent cases in Northern California and single case in San Diego, we've traced hospital records back to last year and found only 18 more tentative cases."

"If that's the good news, what's the bad news?" Alex asked.

"Of those 16 confirmed and 18 possible cases, 28 are no longer alive. That's an 80% mortality rate if it holds up. Compare that to 20-40% for smallpox, 50% for avian flu, and up to 70-90% for Ebola."

"Are you serious?" Alex's eyebrows formed a tight line across his forehead. "Are you telling us New Flu is as fatal as Ebola? What—what—" Cool as a cucumber Alex Fletcher actually spluttered. "What are we dealing with here?"

Dr. Wave tightened her lips, like a coach preparing a stern pep talk. "Alex, Alex, Alex. There's no need for panic. At this very moment, in this very town, almost a dozen scientists are working hard to crack this nut. And when they do…we'll have our answer."

"Almost a whole dozen," Rody commented. "Boy do I feel safer now. Do you, Tor? Do you feel safer knowing that *almost* a dozen scientists are trying to figure out what causes an 80% fatal flu?"

"Oh shut down, Rody," I said automatically. "I'm sure they're doing the best they can."

"No spit," he said with a smirk. "My point exactly."

It's really weird how you can multitask your life. The school counselor calls it compartmentalizing— meaning you can be different people in different places at different times and each of them feels natural. Think about it. Are you the same person on the soccer field that you are at your religious service of choice? I don't think so.

Like back when I was taking Taekwondo and ballet at the same time, I was the rough, tough, screaming, kicking chick on Tuesday and Thursday, and the graceful, pink, twirling music box doll on Monday, Wednesday, and Friday. Then my ballet studio insisted that I had to pick one after I broke my big toe in a clumsy wheel kick right before the end of year dance recital. I folded my do-bok into a box with tissue paper and hung my hard-earned red belt in the closet. Another year and I might have made black belt, but the choice was clear. I put the rough, tough, screaming, kicking chick somewhere away in my psyche for safekeeping until I needed her.

Multitasking. Part of me was doing the school thing.

Part of me was maintaining vigilance for any more info about New Flu and monitoring my own vital signs. (So far, so good.) Part of me was stretching, dancing, and thinking lofty thoughts in preparation for auditions. I was keeping lots of balls up in the air with this mental juggling act.

Audition day came, a sunny, breezy Saturday afternoon, and I waited nervously outside Room Three. I could hear the music—I could hear it in my sleep these days—and my toes and fingers twitched. The music stopped, and Felicity came out looking like the cat that swallowed the canary. Yellow feathers poofed out of her mouth as she spoke. Just kidding. But seriously, she purred as she said, "I got it in the bag, Tory. Go home. Save yourself the effort."

"We'll see," I said. Calm, calm, calm. I couldn't let the fact that I wanted to let fly with a roundhouse kick to her left ear ruin my compartmentalization. Center. Focus. I am ballerina.

Sasha and two teachers were waiting in the room. He gave me a big thumbs up sign, and I swept a graceful bow to him with a little smile. Then the music started, I put on my game face, and all my focus became technical. I became a precise machine with complete control of the position of every part of my body, from the curve of my fingertips to the tilt of my chin. I flowed like a current of air.

Sasha moved me around like a crane handling a china tea cup, incredible power and at the same time gentle control. I floated above the ground, I spun in dizzy circles, I puddled at his feet, and somewhere in the distance, there was music playing.

Sasha helped me up from my puddle and leaned close. "I hope you get it," he whispered into my ear. His cheek brushed mine as he pulled back, and I gazed up into his hazel eyes. He gave my hand a squeeze. Then the evil teachers broke the spell.

"Please send in the next girl, Ms. Maddox."

In all, six girls auditioned for the number. Felicity and I were the noobs. Still, two of the others had danced the role in past years, and two weren't as good, to be honest. There was hope.

Sasha came out of the room, shining with a fine layer of sweat, and I followed him to the drinking fountain. "How'd it go?" I asked, all casual.

"Can't say anything," he said coyly. But then he draped an arm around my shoulder and led me off to a quiet corner away from the other girls. Felicity was throwing eye daggers at me. Smiling, I caught them in my teeth.

"What, what?" I asked.

His face turned serious. "No really, they told me not to say anything. But there's something I wanted to ask you." Long pause.

"Well, what?" But he still hesitated. What couldn't he ask me? We were like sisters.

"I was wondering," he said. "Wondering whether you might consider coming with me as my date to the Homecoming dance next Saturday."

"I don't get it," I answered. Well, I didn't.

He coughed. "This is awkward. I, um. There's this…Things are weird for me at school right now. I just thought that maybe. Well, you're a great partner. We look good together. I thought they'd cut me some slack if you..." He was clearly having trouble completing a coherent. Sentence.

"You thought I could come with you for cover? Be your...what do they call it...your beard? You know, you can't exactly go back into the closet, Sasha."

"God, I'm sorry. You're insulted, aren't you?"

My mind did a calculation at the speed of light. Faster, even. "Nope. Not a smidgen. I'll come with you. I'd be happy to."

See, what I figured out was that even though Mom and Dad won't let me date (for another thirty days), going out with a gay male friend isn't a date. No one could reasonably call that a date. Mom and Dad are reasonable. They couldn't call it a date. Plus it would get me into Homecoming with a senior. Sioux would absolutely scream.

While my brain replayed every glorious moment of the audition, I scooted up to my room with the best of intentions—to change and contact Sioux and dazzle her with my news. However, the computer screen jumped to life right where I had left it, on the "government secrets are us" page, and I was hooked. That blogger was driving me crazy with all these hints that the government knew something it wasn't telling, that what I was hearing on CNN from Narlee Wave wasn't the whole story. So where did Narlee fit in? Was she ignorant or incompetent or evil? I stared and stared at the blogger's page, trying to read between the lines. What was he trying to tell me?

I jumped about a mile when this furry snout suddenly appeared in my lap. Cocoa had his leash in his mouth and was gazing at me with those melting brown eyes.

"What is he trying to tell me?" I asked Cocoa. Cocoa just tipped his head to one side and dropped the leash. "I'm in the middle of something here," I said to him.

Cocoa batted his eyelashes. I swear he did.

"Yeah, yeah. I get it," I said. "Resistance is futile." I ruffled his ears. He slurped his love and appreciation all over my hands as I clipped the leash onto his collar.

At the park, tail vibrating with joy, Cocoa dashed into the melee (that is, the confused throng of his species), and I sat down on a shady bench with mine and whipped out my phone. Something had just occurred to me. In the very first posting, the blogger had mentioned dogs. I'd assumed he was talking about fleas and black plagues, that sort of thing. But maybe not. Could dogs get the flu? I tapped the question into Google, and the answer on the teeny screen blew my mind. There it was—canine flu—a new disease.

Where had it come from? Back in January 2004, a bunch of racing greyhounds in Florida came down with a strange respiratory disease that turned out to be horse flu, a fifty-year-old new disease, and that came from a bird flu—not *the* bird flu, the H5N1 version, but a different combo. Apparently birds carry a lot of different flu viruses. They call them "animal reservoirs," like they're this huge lake of disease about to break over the dam.

I glared at the sparrows scavenging for crumbs on the sidewalk.

Horse flu isn't contagious to people, thank gladness, so it stayed in horses until someone had the disgusting idea of feeding raw horsemeat to greyhounds, and the virus passed into them. The virus didn't get digested; it mutated (drifted) in eight spots and suddenly it was canine influenza, passed from dog to dog to dog, like 100% contagious.

Really. Look it up.

It's so contagious that by December 2005, only two years later, it had spread to twenty-three states. So contagious that even dogs without symptoms can still spread the virus around in kennels and vet offices and parks.

Parks. An itchy feeling ran down my spine. Cocoa was nose to nose with another dog. Holy spit.

"Cocoa, come," I called him. "Co...come here, boy."

A tremor of nerves shook my voice. I don't know why. The canine flu is H3N8, and people can't catch that. And besides, there's a dog vaccine for it now. That's what I read, right there.

So why was the blogger blaming dogs?

"Cocoa, come," I yelled more urgently. He slunk to my feet and whined. "I don't like it here." I explained. I had to get Cocoa out of the park, away from all these drooling, barking, sniffing creatures carrying God-only-knows what germs on them.

Sometimes things just come together as if by fate. I think they call it synchronicity—that's *syn* "same" and *chronos* "time" from the Greek, according to my OED app. Or it might have been a coincidence—that's *con* "together" *incidere* "to fall into or upon" from Latin. Either way, fated synchronicity or lucky coincidence, that evening, in front of the TV news, things did fall together at the same time. And that was the beginning of things falling apart.

Dr. Narlee Wave had added a bright blond streak to her hair, part of her new signature look. "I've got breaking news tonight, Alex," she said. She'd lost her long-winded pedantic style—pedantic, I love that word—and learned how to do the cadences of newscasterese. I wonder who coached her. And I love the way she took credit for what was accomplished by *almost* a dozen CDC scientists.

"I've located Patient Zero, Alex. I've pinpointed the original outbreak of the New Flu. It seems to have arrived in Northern California last October, almost a year ago."

"So have you spoken with this so-called patient zero?" Alex inquired.

"That would be impossible, I'm afraid, Alex. He died in November."

"I see," he said, and without missing a beat: "CNN would like to express deepest condolences to the family. Dr. Wave, what about family? Friends? Have they been able to shed any light on the mystery?"

"His wife died of New Flu a week after he did. The children are now living with relatives who've denied us access. They're too young to make accurate witnesses, in any case."

"How can you be sure then that it was New Flu?" he asked.

"Forensic pathology confirmed it from both medical records and exhumation."

"Exhum…" Alex turned a shade paler.

Exhumation is pulling you out of the humus, in

◆━━━━◆

41

other words, digging up your decomposing body for study. Ick, right?

"What about his friends?" Alex continued. "Do they have any information on where he might have caught this flu?"

"No, Alex. That's the whole point of a *patient zero*. That would be the first person who contracts a disease. The First. That's why he's called *patient zero*."

"Seems like *patient one* would make more sense," Alex quipped.

Dr. Wave was not amused. She continued. "His primary friends were his hunter comrades. Two of them fell ill and died. The fourth man in the group had a mild case and recovered."

"Is that what you epidemiologists call a cluster, Dr. Wave?"

"I'd call it a local outbreak. It's logical that the first few cases of a contagious disease would be people who associate with each other."

"Did these hunters pass it on to another group of people?"

"As far as we have found, only to their immediate families. That implies that the disease is very difficult to spread. It seems to require more than casual contact."

"Well, that's great, isn't it?" Alex asked.

"On the other hand," Narlee carried on, "there are other interpretations. We see a long gap until the next micro-outbreak, longer than a normal incubation period. So either we are missing the cases that link the first and second group of patients, or the disease has an extremely long latency, or the disease is maintained in a non-human population—an animal vector."

Hunter buddies. Animal vector. My brain went click....click....click....why would a bunch of hunters get sick? And what would they be hunting? An image of Elmer Fudd popped into my head. Was it duck season or wabbit season? Duck season...Wabbit season...Duck season...DUCK SEASON! And then like puzzle pieces popping together or maybe Tetris pieces falling down the screen and fitting perfectly, I had a theory.

Suppose a duck carrying avian flu gets shot by a hunter. And suppose that hunter's dog is trotting around with a slight case of dog flu. And suppose the dog gets a good dose of avian flu germs when he retrieves the dead duck. Then you've got two flus in the same place at the same time, waltzing around in the dark, and...tahdah...the stage is set for a major shift. An exchange of pieces. An entirely new flu.

Would it work? I grabbed a napkin and the pencil in front of me and scribbled down a pair of equations:

$$H5N1 \times H3N8 = H3N1$$
$$\text{avian flu} \times \text{canine flu} = \text{new flu}$$

I was so proud of myself I could hardly stand it. I waved the napkin at the TV. "I got it. I got it," I yelled.

"What did you get?" Rody called as he walked in from the garage.

"C'mere. They're going to announce the source of the New Flu, and I figured it out. All by myself. I'm so smart. Look." I shoved the napkin in his face. He started to say something, and I clamped a hand over his mouth. "Shut down. Listen."

I waited for Dr. Narlee Wave to tell Alex the punch

line. I waited. But she kept on with her coy, "We're still working on it" "Don't know the origin" et cetera party line. And then the segment ended.

"So…what?" Rody moved toward the fridge. "They didn't say anything. Same old, same old."

I grabbed his arm. "Wait. Look at this. You're the science guy." I explained my theory to him.

"Well, yeah. Makes sense," he said. "But if it was that obvious to you, they have to already know."

"I know," I said, not at all insulted by his implication. I was thinking the same thing, quite honestly. "I know. So why aren't they saying?"

He shrugged. "Some secret left-wing liberal media conspiracy?"

"She's not media. She's government," I corrected him.

"Okay, then. Some secret right-wing government conspiracy."

I punched him.

Which still left me with the question. Why wasn't she saying?

If a New Flu was running around in the dog population and people were catching it and dying, surely it would be wise to get the word out. Right?

CHAPTER FOUR

SASHA

When the AIDS epidemic first started, no one connected the dots. There was a book published about it, a must-read called "And the Band Played On." You know what happened when the Titanic sank? The band played on. That's what's going on here. You're going to hear the same old merry tunes, while all around, disaster looms. You've only seen the tip of the iceberg.

- www.governmentsecrets.us
Posted October 1

I brooded and brooded (which means sitting like a hen, worrying over her eggs). I brooded over my flu equation. The H5N1 avian flu started when wild birds in Asia infected domestic birds. Families in remote villages then caught the disease from their backyard chickens or ducks or geese. But the numbers stayed small and far away.

So the flu news migrated from the front page to the middle section to the last international page like geese flying south for the winter, until, finally vanishing from sight, it wasn't even news any more. Of course, the

World Health Organization kept track, but the bird flu never shifted or drifted in a way that let it jump from person to person. Only 160 people died before the first human vaccine for bird flu was approved in 2007.

So are we done with bird flu? Not exactly. Our edible poultry is vaccinated for about nine horrendous sounding diseases, but Avian flu is not among them. So yeah, it's still out there, in our wild and domestic feathered friends: *flying vectors.*

The other part of my equation, the canine flu, had me stumped. There's a dog vaccine for that, so there shouldn't have been dogs running around with flu unless their owners were negligent. Right? But then I thought, get real Tor. How many people adopt a cheap dog from the pound and go out and spend $200 on a flu vaccine right away? I don't even know if we did that for Cocoa (mental note: ask Mom). After I woke up dreaming about this stuff on Saturday morning, I Googled the recommendations for new puppy vaccines. Prepare yourself:

6 weeks: distemper, measles
9 weeks: distemper, parvo, corona
12 weeks: distemper, parvo, corona
16 weeks: distemper, parvo, corona, rabies

And then every year we're encouraged to do distemper, parvo, corona, rabies, heartworm, Lyme, and Bordetella?! Is that like a thousand dollar vet bill? And canine flu isn't even required.

I bet there were a LOT of dogs running around without their flu vaccination. A new puppy, fresh from the Super Duck Hunting kennel, wouldn't have finished his basic vaccine series, never mind the optionals, like flu and Lyme and Bordetella. A final depressing thought—maybe the canine flu vaccine we have doesn't even work on New Flu because of the different genes. And if that's the case, then all the dogs everywhere are vulnerable. All of them.

My brain flashed to Wessex the Westie, yellow snot and a coughy bark. I was absolutely, deeply, depressingly positive that Erich had caught New Flu from Wessex.

That's when I acted in haste. Fine, I'll admit it. Impulsively.

I fired off an angry email to Alex Fletcher through the CNN comments link. I asked him to pass along my message to his good pal Narlee because I didn't know how to get in touch with her. I told him that the government had to know that dogs were the carriers, the vectors, the "animal reservoirs" for this New Flu, and it was incredibly irresponsible of them not to warn people. I included my equation and my wild duck theory. And then I forgot about it.

How could I forget about it? I had other things on my mind. Very important things. Like what to wear to the Homecoming dance. Tonight.

Somehow, I'd left it till the last minute. Spit, I hadn't even told Sioux yet. She'd kill me, for sure. I called her and pleaded for forgiveness and help.

"Minx! Vixen!" she squealed. "I hate you! Let's go shopping! I'll pick you up in ten." It was actually twenty by the time she screeched into my driveway. I slid into the car. Picking up Sophe and Valaree must have slowed her down.

Sioux grinned. "I brought consultants."

"Reinforcements, you mean," I said. Sophe and Valaree were always fashionably turned out. I'm sure I was a sad, sad case for them.

Sophe tapped me on the shoulder. "C'mon. This is going to be a blast."

Valaree held up three fingers and ticked them off. "Priorities: dress, hair, nails."

"Not hair," I said, straightening my baseball cap. I had to draw the line somewhere. "Or nails."

"Oh please, can't we do your hair?" Sioux tossed her silky blond curls with a manicured hand. Pretty pink nails and all. She was Sophe and Valaree's project last year. To look at her, you'd never have known she was taking Physics and AP Chem this year. As a sophomore! She looked like a pompom chick. But that girl was going to win a Westinghouse National Science Award before she was through. She'd sneak up on everyone. She was well-camouflaged.

As they pulled hanger after hanger for me, tossing things at me to try on and offering a running fashion show commentary, I decided they were living a little too vicariously. I declared a timeout and sent them off to find themselves new shoes. I had an idea.

Shamelessly stealing inspiration from Felicity, I headed over to the men's department, where I found what I was looking for—a size 44 Long black merino wool cardigan. Over in the lingerie department, I picked up a black lace camisole—the kind my Mom would kill me over if she ever saw it. But my date was gay. So it was safe.

I found a pair of black sliders, these new strappy sandals with three-inch heels on sale. Heels! Oh joy. I could wear heels and still be able to look Sasha straight in the eyes.

I texted the girls when I was done, told them to meet me in the dressing rooms. Their giggles preceded them into the area, and Valaree was whispering, "It better not be brown."

"Or orange." Sophe replied. "I can't believe we let her pick something out herself."

"Hey, I heard that," I said.

"Now," Sioux demanded. "Show us your stuff."

When I stepped out of the changing room, their mouths fell open. The soft knit fabric slinked down my body, clinging to what little I had up there, and ended abruptly at a dangerously high level on my thighs. Long lotioned legs stretched down to my high black sandals.

"Wait, here's the best part," I said. I twisted my hair up into a bun and spun around. The deep V of the sweater went down to the curve of my back, showing the black stretch lace camisole with flashes of white skin peeking through.

Sioux fell over backward in a fake faint. Valaree and Sophe had their hands on their cheeks. "Oh my God, Tor. Oh my God," they said in perfect unison.

"Dazzle," Sioux whispered from the floor. "I hate you. You look absolutely perfect."

"I'm *still* doing her nails," Valaree said to Sophe.

That night I showed Mom the totally wrong outfit, a demure little dress with a high neck, cap sleeves, and flowers (shudder). Then I dressed for real and put on a long raincoat. I'm not stupid.

Mom and Dad and I watched through the kitchen window till Sasha's headlights turned into the driveway. Mom tucked a stray hair into place around my bun and kissed my cheek. "Have a lovely time with your friend, sweetie. And don't slow dance with any of those other high school boys, you hear me?" She twinkled a knowing, maternal smile at me.

Dad's eyebrows wrinkled, no doubt at the image that had just jumped into his head of me slow dancing with a grinding groper. He shot me a nervous look as he handed me off to Sasha, who was unfairly stunning in a silky maroon shirt and tight black pants. Dad's look said, "Are you sure this is right? Are you sure he's safe?" I shot him back a confident nod.

Dad dictated Sasha's orders about getting me home on time, no drinking, et cetera, and went back into the house. I paused by the passenger door as Sasha opened it for me. What a gentleman. Then I slid off the raincoat and tossed it into the back seat. Sasha appraised my outfit under the street light. "Spin," he ordered. I twirled around in the sodium orange glow.

"Oh yeah. Nice, very nice."

I gave him a winning smile. "Thanks."

"No wonder you didn't want Daddy to see that." He winked and laughed quietly. I sank into the soft leather seats and Sasha drove off, a bit too fast. But that was okay. I felt like going fast. I felt like flying, in fact.

Of course, we danced beautifully together, fast and slow, after all the years we've spent with each other in studio. If Sasha's goal was to be noticed, well, we got noticed. He hovered over me protectively, and when other guys came up and asked me to dance, he had a smooth way of sending them off. I did my best to glow and shine and gaze adoringly at him, which, somehow, was no effort at all.

All too soon, the ball was over, the pumpkin was waiting, and the footmen were getting squeaky. We abandoned the clean-up crew in the bright, noisy gym and slipped away to the comfortable stillness of his car. Sasha was much slower on the drive home. But that was okay. I felt like going slow. I felt like savoring the night. We pulled up into my darkened driveway. I turned to him to say goodnight, and he put a hand on my shoulder.

"Thanks, Tor. I really mean it. Thanks for coming with me tonight."

Somehow, I melted along his arm and ended up snuggled under his armpit. I looked into his beautiful hazel eyes, and the next thing I knew, my mouth moved five inches forward and I was kissing him, dissolving in his Sasha-ness. A thousand hours of togetherness compressed into this delicious, lingering touch of lips.

The warmth of his breath scattered across my cheek twice as I sank completely into his perfect embrace. The kiss was slow, sweet, silent.

We came apart. I blinked in surprise. "I felt the earth move," I said shakily.

Sasha gave me a rueful smile. "Sorry Tor. I didn't."

I looked at him for a moment; then I burst out laughing. Otherwise, I would have cried.

When I woke up on a soggy pillow next morning, I had to check in the mirror to make sure I wasn't morphing into Felicity. Look at the evidence. (A) I actually bought and wore in public a deliberately sexy, provocative outfit. (B) I was stupidly, hopelessly in love with my friend Sasha. How couldn't I be? He was almost perfect.

My own face stared back at me, somewhat the worse for a long tearful night. What had I done?

At least my instincts had worked. At least I had laughed. At least I had saved Sasha from a horribly embarrassing scene. So when I met him Monday night at ballet, I could still pass it off as a spur of the moment joke, a quick peck on the cheek between friends that accidentally missed. Maybe.

To keep going, to avoid driving myself crazy, I had to compartmentalize. I had to stuff all my turmoil about Sasha into a lockbox and turn the key. I had to cram my feelings in a car trunk and drive them off a cliff. I had to stick my heart in a carton and mail it to Peru.

I had to distract myself. I skipped breakfast and leashed up Cocoa. He rubbed round my legs like an excited cat and licked my hand with doggy gratitude. He bounced toward the door and through it. Off we went for a long walk, a walk where I tried to blank my mind, even though I could hear it hammering on the lid of the lockbox. I concentrated on appreciating the blueness of the sky, the smell of eucalyptus trees, the song of a mockingbird on the telephone wire. I don't know why they even have telephone wires when everyone has a cell. Maybe the Audubon Society makes them keep them up for the birds.

There. It was working. I was distracted. I wasn't thinking about Sasha. Oh, spit.

Dad was reading the L.A. Times comics when I got back from walking.

"Up early, punkin. How was the dance?"

"Okay," I said.

"More details?" he requested.

Sigh. Fine. "Mostly okay," I added.

"You look like you've got something weighty on your mind, punkin," he said. He opened his eyes wide in a friendly, gosh-I'm here-for-you way.

As I searched for a response, it occurred to me that there was room for one more weighty thing on my mind, besides Sasha—my ongoing search for the truth (cue dramatic music) about the New Flu. "Daddily," I said. "Is there any way to get in touch with the family of Erich with an H?"

"With an H?" he asked.

"Sorry, that's how I always think of him. That's how he introduced himself."

"Why do you want to get in touch with them?" he asked.

"How can I find out what happened to his dog, Wessex?"

"You're on a first name basis with his dog?" Dad frowned. "How well did you know this guy?"

"Not. Not well at all. Mere acquaintances, passing in the park," I said.

He raised one eyebrow dubiously (meaning it didn't look like he totally believed me). "I can't get a phone number, you know, with patient privacy. But maybe the chaplain's office at the hospital could contact them. So tell me, why Wessex?"

"I have a theory," I said.

Dad had tons of medical training from pharmacy school. I pulled the tattered napkin out of my pocket and showed him my equation.

"Punkin, that's very intriguing, very clever." I basked in his praise until he said, "Don't you think the CDC has that line of inquiry under control, though?"

"Not you, too." I sighed.

"What'd I say?"

"Rody said that if I thought of it, it must be obvious."

"Sorry, hun. That's not what I meant to say."

"Sure, sure. I forgive you. I'll admit, I thought so too, but I've been following the CDC reports on the web and TV and I haven't seen anything like this yet."

"Tell you what," he offered. "I'll see what I can dig up."

"Thanks, daddy-o. You're the best." I punched him gently on the arm. Well, I was getting kind of big to smooch him on the cheek. On second thought, I did that, too.

Monday night, heading into ballet, I gave myself a pep talk. Act natural. Be yourself. For God's sake don't let Sasha guess that you weren't kidding. Of course, this *would* be the night we were going to practice some of the *pas de deux* techniques with the whole class.

After warm up at the barre, we smashed our feet into pointe shoes to practice our promenades and pirouettes. Promenades basically involve holding a lovely position, while your partner walks you around and spins you slowly. In pirouettes, you spin quickly, with your partner supporting your waist. The two teachers and Sasha took up positions, and we all had to go down the line.

A week ago—no problem. Tonight, though?

It was easy getting through the teachers. They had experienced hands, supportive and impersonal. But then I got to Sasha's line. He gave me a look that turned my knee joints to putty, and I slipped off pointe. His hands snapped out to grab and balance me. As his long fingers wrapped around my waist, they burned through my skin-tight leotard. I could feel every finger tip individually, as if all the nerves in my skin had migrated to my middle region. When I leaned forward slightly and raised my right leg into an arabesque, his hand slid into position high on my thigh, and I nearly swooned. Just a couple days ago, this was all business, all technique. Now, all of a sudden, it was pulse racing, shallow breathing, skin prickling madness. It was all I could do to keep from turning myself just slightly into his arms and wrapping myself around him. Sanity prevailed, but barely. Crazed and distracted, my timing was off for the entire night.

Next day, Sasha texted my phone during history: *Call me asap after.*

You can imagine what that did to my concentration. Had I totally betrayed myself? Did I ruin our friendship? Or had he unexpectedly realized he danced both ways? Did he want me to be his for always and ever? I drove myself nuts. I didn't hear a word for the whole afternoon.

With trembling fingers, I called him.

"Hey yo, Tor." He sounded normal. What did it mean?

55

"Hey Sash. What's up?"

"Are you free now? Can you meet me somewhere?"

"Like where?" I asked. My heart was thumping, caught between scared and excited.

"Are you on the bus yet? How about if I get the car and pick you up in front of school?"

"Yeah, okay," I said. As long as I was home by dinner, Mom wouldn't know I went out in a car without her permission. I couldn't bother her at work for something so trivial anyway. And they knew Sasha. It wasn't like I was driving off with a stranger. So I paced back and forth in front of the school until his dark green car pulled up.

I hopped into the passenger seat and did everything I could to not remember the last time I sat here. I sang loudly in my head. I dug my nails into my palms in the heavy silence. Sasha called this meeting. It was his job to start.

He pulled into a strip mall parking lot on Poway Road. "C'mon. I'm buying."

Great. We were at the Super Scoop. "You know, the last person who bought me an ice cream here died," I said, by way of a conversation killer.

"You're kidding, aren't you?"

"Nope. Dead serious."

Sasha laughed. He thought I was kidding.

We sat down at a little café table in the sun in front of the shop with our cones. "How's your ice cream?" Sasha asked.

"Um, cold. Chocolate. The usual. But thanks."

He studied his cone carefully and caught an escaping drip. He worked away quietly on his ice cream. We'd never had this awkwardness between us before. Ack. What had I done?

Fine. Fine. I'd have to start the meeting. "Why are you buying me ice cream?" I asked in a tiny voice, crossing my toes so hard they cracked.

"I, uh. Sorry. I have something hard to tell you. I'm softening the blow with ice cream."

My heart squeezed into a painful, small rock inside my chest. My lungs froze up and refused to inhale. Here it comes, I thought. The dump. I balanced on the brink of emotional chaos and peered over the edge at the long fall.

But then he held my hand. And he wouldn't have done that if he wanted to end our friendship. I breathed. I listened.

"Tor, I'm sorry," he said. "I wanted you to know before you heard it tomorrow night. They gave the part to Felicity. I know how much you wanted it. It was really close, but..."

I guessed the rest. "But after the way I screwed up yesterday..."

He shrugged sadly. Truly, this devastating news was cushioned by the fear that it could have been much, much worse. I'd have plenty of time to beat myself up over losing to Felicity, but at least I still had my friend, my Sasha. "Thanks for the warning," I said softly.

He squeezed my hand in a friendly, encouraging, nonromantic way. His eyes flicked toward the parking lot, and his face lit up like I'd never seen it before. A tough-looking guy with spiked hair, gauges, and a nose piercing walked toward our table.

"C'mon over, Blade," Sasha called. "Meet my best

buddy, Tor. Tor, this is Blade."

Blade rested a hand on Sasha's shoulder. Comfortably rested his hand on Sasha's shoulder. Rested his hand on Sasha's shoulder like it was a habit.

"Hi Tor," Blade said in an unexpectedly soft voice. "It's super dazzle to meet you. Sasha's always like Tor this, Tor that. I feel like you're family."

Which made him, what?

My brain said: *Blade. I've never heard about you. Why does Sasha look at you like that? And not at me?* But what came out of my mouth was, "It's really nice to meet you, too." And I stuck out my hand and shook his, like a mature grown-up person, not like someone who wanted to run away and hide under her bed for a month.

"Sash, can you take me home before my parents know I went out without permission?" I asked in a steady voice.

Sasha looked to Blade for the okay, and it broke my heart all over again. But Blade nodded and smiled. A nice guy. Maybe I'd eventually like him. "Hey, I'll be seeing you later anyway," he said to Sasha. Sasha handed him his unfinished ice cream cone, a level of intimacy I'd never even imagined.

On the short car ride back home, I put my mouth on autopilot and put my brain to sleep. It was too much to process all at once. And that was before I got home. I had no idea what was just around the corner.

CHAPTER FIVE

QUARANTINE

Don't they understand that the longer they wait, the farther it spreads? It's like the smoldering undergrowth that blooms into a raging inferno. Water won't put out this fire. But they know what can; they know what to do. They make plans and more plans and contingency plans. And still they sit on their hands watching the days tick by, watching the clock countdown to November.

- www.governmentsecrets.us
Posted October 4

It was four o'clock when Sasha dropped me off. "So you liked him? Really?" he asked.

"Yeah, Sasha. He seems nice," I said for the fifth time. "See you tomorrow."

I watched his car drive away till I couldn't see it any more. I told myself, "Out of sight, out of mind." Yeah. Sure.

As soon as I opened the door, a brown bundle of excitement skittered into the entryway, nails grappling for purchase on the tile floor until he crashed into my legs. Cocoa rubbed his head on my knee, his leash between his teeth. His eyes pleaded with me. Walk? Walk?

Out the door moments later, I noticed an unfamiliar black car ominously parked by the curb. We have a park-in-your-garage rule, so a car on the street stuck out. Ominously, as I said.

Cocoa pulled me toward the car to investigate, and, as we walked past, he slowed and sniffed the doors. The windows were so darkly tinted I couldn't see inside, even when I shaded my eyes and pressed my forehead to the glass. No obvious clues.

We were about a hundred feet away when I sensed a change—the background noise altered by the subtle sound of tires moving on asphalt. The car had pulled away from the curb, rolling steadily in our direction. So stealthy, it had to be electric. Oh, spit. Had someone been looking out at me when I was looking in at them?

A hugely creepy feeling made my feet fizz inside my running shoes, and it wasn't just me being paranoid. The hair on Cocoa's spine rose, and a rumble sounded deep in his throat. I gave the leash a quick jolt and hurried Cocoa along until we could turn left into a neighborhood side street. The car made the same corner and continued cruising along behind me. I could feel it breathing down my neck. Don't look, I warned myself. Something bad always happens if you look.

Cocoa sensed my growing alarm. He turned, barking aggressively, but I urged him forward as fast as I could walk. I knew if I broke into a run, it would end up like a bad movie, with someone leaping out of the car and shooting me down in the street. Then the headlines would say something about a fifteen-year-old gunned down in an accidental drive-by shooting; assailants unknown and at large; drug dealers suspected in a deal gone wrong. News at eleven.

Next corner, as soon as I whipped out of the car's line of sight, I ducked between two houses. Flipping a mental coin in my head, I opened the gate to the backyard on the right and pulled Cocoa in behind me. I peered back through the cracks between slats. Moments later, the black car glided past, paused at the next intersection for a long while, then headed off to the left.

My heart pounded in my ears. My hand on Cocoa's muzzle kept him from barking. I think I aged ten years while we hid there. The gate creaked as I opened it. The latch clicked loudly behind us. My eyes scanned up and down the street. Empty. For now.

I slinked like a spy or a secret agent or perhaps a fugitive, ducking from bush to bush. Dizziness reminded me I'd forgotten to breathe. With a final dash to my front steps, I locked and bolted the front door. Were we safe? My heart hammered with unrelieved tension. Cocoa stood rigid behind me, barking and barking. I peeked at the street through the kitchen window. Spit. The black car lurked at the curb again, right in front of my house. Surveilling.

Two Men in Black got out. No, I'm not kidding— they were really men in black. Black suits. Impenetrable black glasses. Big black bulges under their black jackets. They walked to the front door and rang the bell. Surprising. I had expected them to kick it down. I froze behind the door, peering through the peephole. They rang again. One of them dragged his hands through his thinning hair. The other one gave a visible sigh. He leaned his face right up to the peephole so that it became huge and distorted. He backed off and pointed at the hole. Spit. He knew I was watching. He reached into his coat, and I closed my eyes tight. I braced myself. I took a final breath. This was the perfect end to a miserable day. I prepared myself to die.

Yet I still had so many unanswered questions. Was there an afterlife? Would I meet God? What would my parents think? How would bullets feel drilling into me after they used up their energy penetrating a door. Would it be over quickly? What was taking so long?

What was taking so damned long?

I exhaled, opened my eyes, and peered out again. One of the men was holding up an embossed gold badge to the peephole, too distorted to read. The other one knocked twice.

Fine. I opened the door. "You can't come in," I said firmly. "My parents aren't home."

The guy with the badge folded it away into his coat and extended his hand. "Ms. Maddox? I'm Agent Turner. This is my partner."

"I'm Solly," his partner said.

"Seriously? You're sorry? I'm sorry I ever got up this morning. What do you want?"

The agent muttered back "I didn't say I was sorry."

"Well, you ought to be," I said. "Scaring the spit out of a teenage girl. Harassing and following me. Breaking into my house."

"We're not in your house," Agent Turner pointed out.

"Right," I said. "And stay out." I slammed the door,

barely missing the hand he was still holding out to me. I put my eye to the peephole.

Solly ran his hands through his hair again. If he did that all the time, no wonder it was thinning. Turner rang the bell.

I opened the door four inches. "What?"

A well-shined shoe slid into the opening. "Ms. Maddox," Turner said through the gap. "We really don't mean to alarm you. You're not in trouble. We just need to ask you a couple of questions."

Great. I'd given him a literal foot in the door. If I slammed it now, I'd be assaulting a Federal Agent. Most likely.

I opened to slightly more than a B-width shoe to size them up. "Are you guys Federal Agents?" I asked, just to be clear on my risk here.

"Yes, ma'am," Solly said.

"What's the penalty for assaulting you?"

A slow smile spread across Turner's face.

That made me mad. Totally mad. So mad I flung open the door, reached down deep, and found my dormant rough, tough, screaming, kicking chick and woke her up. "Heeeeey yaaaah!" I yelled as I dropped into a back stance, ready to let loose with a powerful side kick.

Solly stepped forward, in front of Turner. "Now sweetheart, don't be..."

"Sweetheart? I'm not your sweetheart, you balding male chauvinist swine!" My foot flew up as if it had a mind of its own, planted one dirty sneaker in the middle of Solly's chest, and sent him sprawling across the sidewalk. He rolled and came up in a crouch, a menacing black gun pointed straight at me. I lunged forward, ready to deliver a breaking kick to his gun hand and felt myself pulled back abruptly. Turner had my arms twisted behind me in a full Nelson, and I couldn't get a leg into position to break his knees.

"Calm down, Ms. Maddox," he said with a soft, silky voice in my right ear while I struggled helplessly. His breath smelled like peppermint. "In answer to your prior question, right now, you're looking at under a year. But if you do serious harm to my partner there, we're talking ten to thirty."

I glared at Solly. He stood and holstered his gun. He smoothed down his coat and raised his hands to his head. I just couldn't help myself. "Stop it," I yelled. "You're pulling all your hair out with that stupid habit."

Turner shrugged. "She's right, you know. Now, young lady. Let's take this off the street and inside where we can have a quiet, civilized chat." He relaxed his grip and set me loose.

"I know how you guys do this. I have your number. I watch TV. Are you supposed to be the good cop? You know the good cop doesn't wrench the victim's shoulders out of their sockets." I rubbed my shoulders for good measure.

"I'm sorry," Turner said.

"I thought he was Solly," I said, recovering my wittitude. "Okay. You can come in and wait. But I'm not saying anything till my parents get home. I'm a minor."

"You may be a minor, but you're a major pain," Solly grumped.

"Ha, ha. Wait till your boss finds out you pulled a gun on a fifteen-year-old girl."

"Aw, crap. Fifteen? Really?" Solly rubbed the sore spot on his chest.

Turner chuckled quietly, a nice laugh. He let me go and patted me on the shoulder. "Hey. Sorry about your shoulders. I didn't want you leaping down the barrel of Solly's gun. It might have gone off, and then where would we be?"

Where indeed? I'd be lying in a pool of my own blood and Turner would be trying to revive me and then my parents would come home. Dad would see this stranger with his face all over me and then he'd go all Rambo on him. Awful. Time to step it down a notch.

"Fine. Apology sort of accepted," I said. "But the door stays open."

So these two Federal Agents followed me into the kitchen and sat down at our table. Where I eat breakfast. Where I do my homework. Where I watch CNN. It was a bit surreal.

We stared at each other. I broke first. "You guys want coffee?"

The silence, except for the gurgling coffee, was deafening. I couldn't stand it. Solly watched me suspiciously as I opened the snack cupboard and reached in. "There's no gun in the cookie jar," I babbled nervously. "I'm just going to make a snack. You guys don't stop breathing if you smell peanut butter, do you?"

Turner shook his head, smiling.

Drat. So much for my secret weapon.

I grabbed a handful of gingersnaps and began

smearing each with a glob of peanut butter, conscious of Solly's narrowed eyes. I dealt four mini-marshmallows onto each snap and set them in the middle of the table. Turner helped himself while Solly crossed his arms.

"These are very good," Turner said. "Thank you. Cute dog, by the way." Cocoa was begging at his feet. "May I?" He held a cookie just out of Cocoa's reach.

"Just one." If he thought I'd weaken just because he was nice to my dog...

Turner balanced the cookie on Cocoa's broad nose and scratched him behind the ears. Cocoa held perfectly still, holding Turner's gaze, his eyes wide. Turner lifted a finger, and Cocoa flipped the cookie into his mouth and crunched. Then that traitor lay down, his nose resting on Turner's gleaming black wingtips, a devoted hound.

I poured three cups of coffee, even though I hate it. I figured it made me seem more mature. I added three teaspoons of sugar. Turner raised one eyebrow. Was that too much?

We sipped and crunched in silence. Solly stared out the window above the kitchen sink. Turner patted Cocoa. They were calm, contained, content to wait forever.

I glanced at Mom's old-fashioned kitchen clock. It was getting on toward the Alex and Narlee show. "You guys mind if I turn on CNN?"

"Be my guest," Turner said, as if it were his house. "Do you watch a lot of news?"

"Sure. I always watch in the afternoon. While I'm doing my homework. Which I should be doing now. It's important to know what's going on, right?" I realized I was babbling again.

"What is going on, Ms. Maddox?" Turner asked in a gentle voice.

I pretended not to hear him. The New Flu logo and theme song were rolling. Dr. Wave looked quite businesslike in a red silk blouse and blue blazer. The lab coat look was out, I guess.

"Nice suit, Narlee," I said under my breath.

"Do you know her?" Turner asked, demonstrating the hearing of an owl.

"What? No, of course not. How could I?" I asked. "Shhhh. It's starting."

Alex Fletcher began with his usual welcome, New Flu Day 23. "Narlee, I understand that tonight the Director of the CDC will be making an unprecedented prime time appearance on all stations. Can you give us a hint about what she's going to say?"

Progress? Were they finally going to tell America what was going on?

"Oh yes, Alex," Narlee said with a tight smile. "Tonight we have a critically important announcement for the country. We've narrowed down the source of the influenza virus, and we'll be announcing some important public health guidelines for dealing with the risk of human infection until we isolate the vector."

"Can you be more specific?" Alex urged.

Dr. Wave lifted her eyebrows at him. "Are you honestly asking me to preempt my boss?" She turned to look straight into the camera. "I advise everyone to tune in for the press conference at 9:00 p.m. Eastern Standard on any news channel."

Alex recognized the stonewall and made the best of it. "Let's make that 9:00 p.m. Eastern Standard Time on CNN, where we'll give you the most accurate and up to date information on the New Flu. You'll rejoin us for that coverage, won't you, Dr. Wave?"

"Of course." Her bright red lips formed a smug little smile.

"Can you verify the rumor that your scientists were helped out by an anonymous tip?"

I sensed four eyes boring into the back of my head. I glanced around to see Turner watching for my reaction. I flushed and focused back to the screen.

"Alex, our scientists have been working this problem day and night. We've consulted many expert sources. And we broke the back of the problem long before any so-called tip."

Turner was still studying me intently.

I sensed it. I spun again in my seat. "What? Why are you staring at me?"

Turner's eyebrows pressed together. Like he was working very hard to understand something. "Ms. Maddox," he finally asked, "who fed you the information that you sent to CNN?"

"What? Are you guys reading my email?"

Solly let out an exasperated sigh. "Honey, we read everyone's email."

"No way. That's impossible."

"Yes way," he said, flaring his nostrils.

I frowned back. "Don't call me honey. That's sexual harassment. I'm pretty sure."

Turner put a hand on Solly's arm. "Solly, please don't call Ms. Maddox honey. She doesn't like it."

Solly's hand rubbed his chest unconsciously.

Then Turner spoke to me again. "The CDC director contacted the Agency when your so-called tip came through. We're following up to see who passed that information to you."

"Why?"

"They need to determine whether an insider is leaking information out or if an outsider is attempting to send information in."

"But why? What are the...the implications of those options?" Surely my sophisticated wording would impress them.

"It's complicated. What can I tell you?" He paused for a thoughtful sip of coffee. "If there's a leak, the CDC wants to know whether it's one of their own, or someone from the West Wing. Ms. Maddox, if there is a potential whistle blower inside the CDC, that person is going to need some protection."

"From what?"

"From the government, for one," Solly replied.

"But you are the government," I said.

Solly snorted. "Not the whole government, honey. It's like tribal warlords over in D.C., each with his own—"

Turner cut him off with a quick hand gesture. "Excuse me. If I may continue. On the other hand, if an outsider has independent information about the origin of the virus, we have a whole different scenario. We'll have to investigate the possibility that the outbreak was planned."

As he spoke, Turner watched my eyes carefully. I wondered what they were telling him. "And if it was planned, we have to determine whether the infectious agent is naturally occurring or bioengineered."

"Bioengineered? You mean, like bioterrorism?" My voice squeaked. In all my research, I'd never even thought of that. "But...but it's 'E, none of the above.' I didn't get the information from anyone. I just guessed."

Solly snort-laughed again and his lips sounded a raspberry of disbelief. "Oh, yeah. A fifteen-year-old girl just happens to be an expert in virology?"

"No, seriously," I said, forgetting that I had sworn not to talk without my parents present. "It's not that complicated. I've just been reading what's available on the internet."

"Which web sites?" Solly asked, whipping out a notebook.

I looked him straight in the eye. Of course, all I saw was myself reflected in his stupid dark glasses. "CDC dot gov. Flu dot gov. Wikipedia. Nothing nefarious. That means wicked and criminal."

"I know what nefarious means," Solly said. "What else."

"Nothing," I insisted. "Nothing. Oh yeah."

"Oh yeah...?" Solly's hand remained poised over the page.

"There's a new blog called government secrets dot us."

Solly shook his head. "You're kidding, right?"

"No, seriously. That's what put me on to the idea that it had to do with dogs. But I have no idea who posts it."

Solly's eyebrows rose above the rims of his glasses. "And Bingo was his name-o," he sang softly. He and

Turner exchanged a meaningful glance.

Turner reached into his pocket and handed me a business card. All it said was Agent Steven Turner and a phone number. "You think of anything else, you call me, Ms. Maddox."

"I'd rather call you Steve," I said. "And you can call me Tor. You're not going to wait for my parents?"

"Nope. We're done. For now." There he went, being ominous again. As he gave his and Solly's coffee cups a quick rinse, he added, "Please don't speak with any other agents before contacting me. And do let us know if someone other than us does try to contact you."

"I thought you guys in the black uniform all play for the same team."

Solly laughed. "Good one, Ms. Maddox."

Why was that funny? I wasn't even making a joke.

They were just rising to leave when Mom came in through the front. "Why is this door open? We'll get flies," she called before she looked. "Oh, goodness." Her eyes darted from Solly to Turner. "Tor? What's going on? Are you in trouble? Is she in trouble?"

"Mom, meet Agent Turner and Agent Solly. They were just leaving. Weren't you guys?"

"Evening, Mrs. Maddox," Turner said smoothly. He slipped her a business card and shook her hand. "A pleasure to meet you." He flashed her a gleaming smile.

Mom's hand went to her hair, and I suddenly noticed how handsome he was, in an old kind of way. "What—?"

"No trouble at all, ma'am. We just had a cup of coffee. Sorry to bother you. Have a pleasant evening."

Mom's eyes flew from the business card in her hand

to the sink to the coffee cups in the draining rack and back to me. She was trying to slot this peculiar scene into her world view. Turner and Solly took advantage of her momentary confusion to glide out of the house faster than she could put polite words together to request an explanation.

"Torrance Olivia." She fixed me with the gaze that makes me want to confess everything I've ever thought of, never mind done. "If you're not in trouble, what in the world is going on?"

Why did people keep asking me that? "I...uh. I don't exactly know. It's all..."

Words failed me. I needed time to figure out (A) how this fit into *my* world view, and (B) what I was going to tell my parents. Cocoa, bless his little doggy heart, came to my rescue. He appeared from under the kitchen table and pawed at my leg, leash still on.

"Hey, I was just about to take Cocoa out," I lied. "Come on, Coke! See ya, Mom."

Leaving her sputtering and yelling after me, I beat a hasty retreat with the dog, and I didn't look back. I'd had enough of probing, suspicious people. The street was empty, the men in black definitely gone. I figured that was the last I'd see of them. (Of course, I figured wrong.)

My escape was a very temporary solution, because I did have to come home for dinner. I waited until the last possible moment and slipped into my seat just as Rody was putting the bread on the table. Mom had prepared her thoughts even if mine were still in a tangle. The grace she said went something like this: "Our Father, we thank you for this food and for a close and trusting family. Watch over all of us, and especially those of our children who might be getting into something over their heads. Amen."

Dad and Rody both raised their eyes and looked straight at me.

Why? Why did they automatically suspect me? I tried a clever ruse (in other words, a distracting trick). "So Rody, just what have you been up to lately?" I asked.

"Keeping my head low and my hands clean," he said. "So who are your new friends?" He smirked. "I'm so Solly I took a wrong Turner and got home late and missed them."

"Oh spit," I said. I threw a guilty look at Mom, who was wearing that face, the face that makes me three years old all over again.

Dad, who had just made it home, was completely out of the loop. Mom hadn't briefed him yet. "New friends, Tor?"

"Oh. Yeah. Two guys stopped by. No big deal."

Mom glared at me. "Two Federal Agents stopped by to interrogate our daughter while we were out. And she let them in."

"Hey, wait a minute," I said, trying to defend myself. "That was only after Solly pulled his gun on me."

"Pulled his gun?" Dad's face flared a frightening shade of purple and his eyes grew two sizes. "On my daughter?!" His weight shifted to rise from the table, though where he thought he was going, I have no idea.

"Well, to be fair, that was after I side-kicked him in the solar plexus."

Dad thumped back into his chair and gasped.

Rody's chin went up, and he looked at me with a curiously respectful gleam in his eye. "You side-kicked a Federal Agent? That's brilliantly stupid, in a cool kind of way."

I smiled.

Dad was not amused. "You side-kicked a Federal Agent?"

"He was harassing me. He called me sweetheart," I explained. "And honey."

"But sweetie," Mom said gently, "you can't attack people for trying to be kind to you."

"It wasn't kind. It was condescending. And grossly inappropriate, don't you think?"

"Get. To. The. Point. Please, Tor," Dad demanded, his complexion warning that a paralytic stroke was imminent—mere seconds away. At this point I wasn't entirely sure whether he was mad at me or the agents. So I spilled. Everything. Even how Cocoa abandoned his post and became a lap dog for Steve. Agent Turner.

Rody looked proud of the way I took down Solly. Mom looked proud of the way I served coffee and biscuits to the guests. Dad continued to look explosive.

"I don't like it. I don't like it at all. Feds can't come bursting into a man's house when he isn't home without a warrant."

"Actually, they can, Dad." I reminded him.

"Okay. Technically yes," he conceded. "But it isn't right. It isn't American. It isn't what I went over there to represent." Over there always meant the Middle East.

"Well, no harm done," Mom said cheerfully, if a bit forced. Amazing. She could be madder than anything, but if Dad joined in and his blood pressure started to rise or his mood started to fall, she turned into the reasonable, soothing one.

Mom took his hand in hers. "Torrance hasn't been hauled off on assault charges. There are no bullet holes in our house or in our daughter. They left without a fuss, and that nice Agent Turner was very polite. He even washed out his own coffee cup."

"I think it's all over, Dad," I said. "They're off to investigate some poor blogger now."

Dad breathed heavily, but Mom touched his cheek, exuding calm. He shook his head slowly and looked at me as if I weren't quite real. "I still can't believe you stirred all of this up with an email. I mean, they had to have already known."

"Thanks a lot," I said. "For your vote of confidence."

"Welcome." His smile was a little twisted as if he were trying too hard, but I could tell he was winding down. "By the way," he said, "I heard back from the Chaplain's office today. They did contact Erich's family to inquire about the dog. He died on the same day as Erich."

"Oh wow," I said. "And was it H3N1? Like Erich?"

"We'll never know. In all the turmoil over losing Erich, they had the dog's remains cremated immediately."

At nine o'clock, Dad and I sat in front of the TV, waiting for the promised CDC announcement. Here it is, verbatim (word for word):

"I'm Dr. Marta Ruiz, Director of the Centers for Disease Control. Tonight, we can confidently announce that the New Flu is a cross hybridization between the antigenic versions H5N1 and H3N8, the Avian Flu and Canine Flu. In layman's terms, the Bird Flu and Dog Flu have exchanged genes to create a new strain deadly to both humans and dogs.

"This is the kind of thing that can occur completely naturally under very rare conditions. Fortunately, the new combination is not backward transmissible to birds, so for the time being, it is confined to the North American continent. It is highly contagious among canines who have not been vaccinated for H3N8. It is also highly transmissible between canines and their human caretakers both in saliva and moist breath. The disease is estimated to be 25% fatal in canines and up to 80% fatal in humans.

"For this reason, we are making the following quarantine recommendations for all dog owning households in the continental United States. First, keep all dogs inside except for minimal trips outside as needed for sanitation. Second, keep dogs and all members of the household at a distance. Wear a face mask when interacting with a dog, and wash hands after any physical contact. Thoroughly wash any materials that have been in contact with a dog's saliva. Report the appearance of any dogs in public areas to your County Health Department.

"Although we have no confirmed cases of human to human transmission, we still recommend avoiding travel and large indoor gatherings. If you experience flu-like symptoms yourself, seek immediate medical assistance. Doctors' and veterinarians' offices will be tracking the disease as we work toward complete containment. We anticipate that a full three months of diligent quarantine will break the cycle of infection. Thank you for your attention and cooperation."

Dad and I turned to each other. I spoke first. "Three months? They've got to be nuts. People will never do all that. It's going to be a disaster."

Which is pretty much what the blogger said a month ago.

CHAPTER SIX

PROTECTIVE ISOLATION

So now the secret is out and the finger is pointed at our dogs. Have you any idea how many flocks were preventively destroyed in the early days of the Avian Flu? How do you think they're going to deal with our sixty million best friends?

- www.governmentsecrets.us
Posted October 5

Dad's cautious, survivalist mind was a step ahead as usual. The morning after quarantine was announced, he caught me on my way to the school bus stop. "Punkin," he said, "Mom and I were talking last night. We thought it might be a good idea to take Cocoa in for a booster on his flu vaccine. It's been at least five years since he was immunized."

Ah, so Cocoa did get it back when. Good to know we're responsible pet owners. "Sounds smart to me," I said. "Even if they're not sure it'll do anything."

"Can I ask you to take care of that after school? By the time Mom and I get home from work, the vet will probably be closed."

So that afternoon, I leashed up Cocoa and walked over to our local vet, about two miles up the road. The autumn air refreshed my troubled soul. My steps were lighter than in days. But my bubble burst as soon as I left the comfort of my street. The few people we passed on foot stared at us with hostility, and one car honked long and loud. The driver waved an angry fist at me and Cocoa. What was up with that? Okay, I was technically breaking quarantine, but it's not like I had any choice. No way was I going to drive illegally with an unsecured dog as my copilot.

The waiting room was packed, and it took over an hour before the vet tech called me back to an examining room. His name badge advertised that his name was Ryan—"a member of our caring team." Well, he seemed nice enough when he asked, "Do you need to see the vet today or are you just here for the booster?"

"Oh, just the shot," I said. "This is a *just-in-case* kind of thing, you know."

He smiled in an understanding way. "I hear you. There's a lot of that going around."

"Is that what everyone's here for?" The waiting room was just as full when I was called up as when I had arrived, a steady stream of dog owners.

"You bet," Ryan said. "You're lucky you came in today. We're going to be all out by noon tomorrow if this keeps up." He prepped the syringe, flicking it to settle an air bubble.

"Holy spit. Then what?"

He shrugged. "We've called our supplier, but they're cleaned out. I guess when we're out, we're out."

He slid the needle into Cocoa's flank without a flinch by either of them.

"Wow, you're good," I said. "He didn't even feel it."

"Thanks. That's about my fiftieth of the day." He patted Cocoa on the shot spot. "All set, boy. Let's hope that keeps you healthy."

"Thanks a ton." Relief flooded my brain. Then another thought dribbled in. "Did you try getting more doses from Arizona or Nevada?"

"Yeah, about an hour ago. As soon as we realized there was going to be a run on it."

"And?"

"They're not sharing. Said something about building an immunity blockade along the border towns."

"I guess that makes sense from their perspective," I conceded.

"Sure," Ryan agreed. "But it doesn't help us. I bet this is over-exaggerated. It'll calm down in a few days."

I prayed he was right. After reading that quarter of a billion birds were killed in the early 2000's, I was thrilled that people were stepping up and vaccinating their dogs and that our government was finally showing sense by ordering quarantine before things could get out of hand. When I had predicted that people would never cooperate with quarantine, I had never been more wrong. The news reported that the announcement was being taken seriously all over the country. The great American big red panic button had been pushed.

On Friday, there were a noticeable number of empty desks at school.

With the newspapers running front page articles on the quarantine every day, and the TV running reminders as a public service announcement at the bottom of every screen on every channel, I guess I couldn't blame people for turning paranoid about it. They even considered closing the mall over the weekend.

On Monday, the desks were over a third empty. On Tuesday, half the kids were out, and several classes were cancelled for lack of subs. The teachers were calling in scared as well. Our pets had been under quarantine for exactly one week out of the expected three months, and everyone was behaving like the end of the world was near.

Poor Cocoa had resigned himself to being locked indoors. He lay on the kitchen floor with his head on his paws, looking sad. It was stupid that we couldn't keep him outdoors in our own fenced backyard, but Dad said we needed to follow the quarantine rules precisely. I explained the situation to Cocoa, but he just sighed at me and twitched one ear.

Feeling pretty low myself, I walked alone over to the dog park. Totally eerie is the only way to describe it. No one was out on the streets or sidewalks, even though it was a beautiful evening. Over at the park, the romping areas were deserted. The gates swung open. The graffiti scrawl that usually said, "Clean up your own shit" was covered over with an official poster that read:

CLOSED UNTIL FURTHER NOTICE.
ALL DOGS TO REMAIN UNDER QUARANTINE.

Another hastily printed cardboard sign, posted on each fenced section, read (errors and all):

ALL DOG OWNER'S USING THE PARK ON OR AFTER OCTOBER 1 MUST REPORT TO THE COUNTY HELTH DEPARTMENT FOR EXPOSURE SCREENING.

The phone number was printed at the bottom. That struck me as sort of futile. I mean, no one was supposed to be here, right? So who would see the sign?

I debated with myself. Wessex was here long before that. Should I call County Health and say the flu was already here in September? Should I tell them to change the date? Did I want to be screened? I looked all around and couldn't spot any security cams. They'd never know that I was here. They'd never know I saw the sign. There really wasn't any point in reprinting a sign no one would see. And besides, I hadn't come here at all in October.

I cast one last look around the park. How soon would we get back to normal? When would we hear the click-click of little toenails on the sidewalk? I imagined the pens full of frolicking dogs so vividly that for a moment I wasn't surprised when I heard a bark. Then, of course, I was. They were all supposed to be under lockdown. I whipped my head around. A kid, must have been about eight, was being pulled along by a large black Labrador. His transparent school backpack was stuffed to bursting with brown kibbles.

"What are you doing out here, kid?" I asked as he got nearer.

His eyes were red, and he kept glancing back over

his shoulder. "Nothing," he whispered.

"Can't be nothing," I argued. "You've got a pack full of dog food on your back. I'd say that's kind of unusual."

"We're leaving," he said morosely.

"We're leaving?" I echoed. "What are you? Eight?"

"And a half," he replied. "Midnight and me are taking off."

"Why?"

"Dad says we gotta get rid of him before he makes us sick." A single tear ran down the dirty little face.

I studied Midnight. Cold, wet, black nose. Clear bright eyes. He looked perfectly healthy. "Who says he's sick?" I asked. "He looks okay to me."

"Dad says 'looks can be deceiving.'" The kid was a perfect mimic of a paranoid adult. "Mom says he could still have the flu germs in him."

I couldn't argue with that. Mom was right. But, still.

"So where are you planning on going?" I asked.

"North. Gramma lives in Santa Barbara. I think that's in the North. But I'm kind of lost. Could you maybe draw me a map?" He was so cute, I wanted to take him home and keep him.

What a dilemma. I was a perfect stranger, and he trusted me. His dog, sniffing my pants with interest, trusted me, too. My skin crawled at the idea of what an easy target he was for some villainous perv. And I couldn't believe his parents would just get rid of their dog. Maybe he'd misunderstood the whole discussion. "What's your name, kid?" I said all friendly.

"Gary Francis," he replied.

"Okay, Gary Francis. If you tell me your phone

number, I can give you directions to Santa Barbara, okay?" He gave me his phone number, which I thumbed into the phone in my pocket. I pointed him way down the street, a straight run where I could see him for a few blocks, and told him where to turn right.

"Thanks, lady," he said. He trudged off in the direction I had sent him. As soon as he was out of earshot, I called his house.

"Is this Mrs. Francis?" I asked the woman who answered. "Are you missing a little Gary?"

"Who is this?" the frantic voice asked. "Oh my God, yes, yes. Please don't hurt him. I'll do anything. Who are you? Where are you?"

"Calm down ma'am. Before I say anything, I've got one condition for my information."

"God, anything. How much?"

Holy spit! What kind of person did she think I was? "You have to keep the dog. Forever," I said. "Gary's running away to Santa Barbara because he thinks you want to get rid of Midnight, who looks perfectly healthy to me, by the way."

"It was all my husband," she protested. "He said we had to get Midnight put down in a hurry. We got into a blowup over it, and Gary heard us."

"Mrs. Francis, that's a healthy dog and a miserable boy. So do you want them both back? It's a package deal."

There was no hesitation. "Absolutely."

"I'll be walking along Oak Knoll with him for the next five minutes. Then we'll be turning up Carriage. You know where that is?"

"Yes, I do. I'll be right there. I'm just in the mobiles

behind the park."

"Okay then. See you soon." I hung up the phone and hurried to catch up with Gary. "Hey kid, I decided to walk along with you a ways," I said. "It's a pretty night for a long walk."

That encounter by the park was only the tip of the iceberg as the blogger suggested. The local news reported that dozens of dogs with running noses or coughs had been abandoned at the humane society. With their "no kill" policy, they were overwhelmed.

In spite of quarantine, after one week there were eighty new cases of sick dogs and forty human cases in the Northern California cluster. Down in Southern California, the numbers were still small, only thirty sick animals and ten sick humans. But as soon as a couple of cases popped up on the Pala Indian reservation and three across the state line in Nevada, Congress passed an immediate ban on the interstate transportation of dogs. I'd watched footage on CNN of a big, burly truck driver being held at the state border sobbing man-tears as he handed over his best friend to the highway patrol for temporary storage while he completed his haul.

I thought about Wessex, our local "dog zero," and wondered how he had gotten the flu from Northern California and how many other dogs he had infected in the park before he died. I envisioned rings spreading out from the rock that had been dropped in our placid pond.

Gloom hung over everyone's spirits. It wasn't just school and the mall, either. People carefully avoided each other even casually. They hoarded garden dust masks and wore them if they had to go out. If someone coughed or sneezed in the grocery store, everyone else adjusted their masks and moved away. The eyes above them wore a tight, nervous look.

Dr. Wave displayed the daily tally, like a body count. The more people who caught it, the CDC said, the more the risk that the virus would drift to a form people could give to each other directly. But for now, contagion depended on the dogs. They were the only vector, the animal reservoir.

The good news? With more cases being counted, the human fatality rate had been downgraded to 65%. The bad news? According to the CDC, we had no idea how many animals might already be infected and contagious.

I noticed the one crucial point they hadn't emphasized—quarantine did nothing to stop dogs who were already infected and still in the incubation period from getting sick. Then, all breathing the same indoor air, their families would be exposed to the deadly virus. The germs were already out there. For a few weeks the infection rate and death toll were going to rise until they turned around and dropped off. Quarantine wasn't a cure—just a way of cutting the losses, human and canine, until the disease finished running its course. That may be kind of cold, but it's true.

By the end of the second week of quarantine, Narlee Wave reported ninety human cases on record—twenty newly admitted to hospitals, forty-five dead, and twenty-five recovered or recovering. She insisted that this was totally expected, that quarantine was working the way it was supposed to. The President gave several prime time mini-speeches basically saying the same thing. His calm, smiling face assured us that we were following pandemic prevention procedures that had been laid down over years of careful planning. In his deep, warm voice he asked us not to succumb to fear and worry.

But either people didn't understand the message, or they didn't like it. They bombarded the government with emails and phone calls and tweets demanding DO SOMETHING. Reporters incessantly asked (as in on and on till they were blue in the face), "Quarantine—is it enough?" What exactly did they think the alternatives were?

But Narlee's official line, every afternoon at 4:15, was, "Be patient. You've got to give it the full three months."

Those three months stretched out ahead of us all the way through the holiday shopping season. What would Christmas would be like this year? In-store pre-holiday sales were way off. On-line shopping wasn't going to fill the gap. UPS drivers were refusing to approach houses where they heard barking. That piece of news ran on the nightly business report. The finance guys blamed the flu scare, and the commentators worried that quarantine might affect voter turnout in November. The President and his challenger agreed on one thing—they both started running political ads for absentee ballots and early voting.

It was Tuesday, October the eighteenth, exactly two weeks after quarantine began, when the CDC or Congress or someone in Washington or maybe just someone in Sacramento panicked and took us to

DEFCON 1, figuratively speaking. (That's when all of our missile-holding planes are flying around madly on highest alert.) Marta Ruiz, CDC Director, told us in another prime time broadcast on every channel, there were too many unknown infected dogs out there still spreading the disease to other dogs in their households and to their owners. The *animal reservoir* needed to be assessed and contained. Affected states would soon receive guidelines for a new *protective isolation* policy.

A special order came down from the California Governor's office:

> *All citizens owning dogs in the State of California are required to bring them for a free health screening at their nearest veterinary care center. Infected dogs will be held in isolation and cared for until their recovery. Healthy dogs will return home to stay in indoor quarantine until the cycle of transmission is completely broken.*

He also ordered everyone to stop panicking and return to work and school.

Good ol' Narlee took center stage for the television news commentary after the official announcement. She was fluent in the government's official talking points. "Alex, I hope all the citizens of California feel a great sense of relief at this time. Infected animals will be placed in protective isolation with far better care than their owners can provide at home. Animals with a clean bill of health will be protected at home, and the weight of uncertainty will be lifted from their owners. We'll all be able to go about our usual lives without any fear. The CDC commends the Governor of California for providing the kind of leadership and foresight needed to intervene and control the situation before it becomes a crisis. We expect similar measures soon will be enacted in Arizona and Nevada."

In the morning, school buses were running again, and I watched the crowds lined up at all the nearby vet offices as we rattled past. Those poor vets were going to have their hands full today with hundreds of dogs to test. I wondered if little Gary Francis's mom would be first in line so she could prove to her husband that Midnight was safe. I hoped so, for his sake. I talked Mom into waiting until the crowds thinned down, promising to take Cocoa over to our vet with Sioux-san and her Irish Wolfhound, Talisker, after school.

I clearly underestimated the number of dogs in our suburb. It was *still* packed when Sioux and I got to our clinic. Cocoa was so happy to be out and on a leash again that he danced along the road. Sioux had a little trouble holding back Talisker, who had to outweigh her by at least twenty pounds. It was like a party, a big dog party. The line buzzed with excited chatter as the line snaked forward. We were outdoors; we were taking action; we were all taking responsibility for protecting ourselves and our community instead of hiding inside houses with fingers crossed. I admit, it did make me a little nervous, having all these dogs standing in line together, but I didn't see any yellowish-green snot or hear any coughing. And anyway, what was the alternative?

The line inched ahead. Two police at the door kept calm and order. On second thought, they weren't regular police. Their uniforms were more armyish, a dull gray suit with a weird backward flag on one shoulder. Maybe we really were at DEFCON 1.

"Who are they, Sioux?" I asked. "Soldiers?"

"Looks like National Guard," she replied. "They always help out in emergencies."

"A bit over the top, isn't it?" I said. "This crowd is pretty tame. Even the owners."

They let only a couple of people in at a time to be processed. It reminded me of waiting to pick up a spiral ham on Christmas Eve. I watched the door, trying to guestimate how long it would take us to get through. I had homework waiting.

They'd set up a one way system. People were exiting through a side door near the back of the building. The person going in at the moment was very recognizable, a heavyset woman in purple with a plump bulldog. I glanced at the time on my phone.

In just over nine minutes, the woman came out alone, dabbing her face with a Kleenex. Nine minutes seemed super efficient. Too efficient. Paperwork? Test and results? They must have this down to a science in there. Then I had a thought, a dark disturbing one. I hadn't seen any pets come out the whole time we'd been standing here.

"Sioux, have you seen any dogs come out?" I asked casually.

"Sure," she said. "I think so. They can't all be sick, right?"

Right. Of course not.

After about five more minutes, the guards beckoned the two of us. As we stepped inside, the two people before us were just being led off to the examining rooms with their pets. Sioux and I stepped up to the check-in station. "Fill this out," the vet-nurse said curtly. "Name, address, phone, pet name." She shoved a clipboard at each of us. At the bottom of the page was a tear off sheet with a ten digit number. As soon as we were done, two techs came and split us off in two directions.

"See you in a minute," I said to Sioux. She gave me a jittery thumbs up sign.

My tech was wearing a mask and medical gloves, but a glance at his badge showed it was Ryan again, the nice tech who had given Cocoa his booster shot.

"How's it going? Another crazy day?" I asked him.

He shot me a strange look over his mask. "Yeah," he said. "It totally sucks."

He didn't even bother weighing Cocoa or checking out his eyes, nose, throat, heart, or lungs. He just grabbed a long swab out of a jar on the counter, stuffed it up Cocoa's nose and dropped it in a plastic bag. "Stay here while I run the test," he ordered in a weirdly sarcastic voice. He slammed out the back door to the lab area.

That swab must have tickled Cocoa's nostrils. He huffed a couple of times and sneezed. A spray of greenish mucus splattered on my jeans. Holy spit. My blood ran cold. Not Cocoa. Please God, not Cocoa.

I stared at the back door in shock. Right now, the tech was running whatever kind of instant test they had for New Flu on a glob out of Cocoa's nose. He would test positive. They would take him away from me, and I'd have to walk home alone and tell the rest of the family.

From the back area came a scuffling sound and a single bark. A single deep bark. At my side, Cocoa gave an answering yip, but it wasn't returned. Not another sound. That was weird. There should have been a chorus. You know how dogs always set each other off. How many dogs were back there? How many isolation cages did they have, anyway?

"Oh crap," someone yelled. "This one bites." Then a moaning howl rose and trailed off into silence.

Cocoa yipped again once and looked at me adoringly. How could I turn him in? Spit.

My brain spun, trying to get into gear, trying to decide what to do. In a flash the sputtering engine in my cortex caught and raced. Logic outpaced trust and headed down a scary road. Since I'd been here, I'd seen at least thirty dogs go in. Not one came out. And they had tested dogs all day. How could you isolate a few hundred dogs in a building this size? And what kind of medical test for a new disease could be invented in a week and only take five minutes? What exactly was going on in here? I was afraid even to think of the possibilities.

I opened the exam room door as quietly as I could and slipped out with Cocoa. I hurried down the white corridor to the red emergency exit sign at the back of the building, praying hard that there wasn't an alarm hooked up to the door. I pushed through into the fresh air and listened. Silence. Thank gladness.

A large truck was parked out back, the kind with a

rollup door to the cargo area. No one saw me come out, and I dashed out of sight around the side of the building to where I was supposed to exit, casting one last look over my shoulder. I stopped dead in my tracks. One of the gray guards was back there rolling up the cargo door. Two more came through the rear exit and heaved something into the truck. Something limp and gray and furry. Huge and familiar.

My chest tightened. I gasped. What had I just seen?

The guards went back into the clinic, and I took three careful steps toward the truck. Just enough to catch a glimpse that burned itself into my memory forever—bodies large and small, brown and white, long-haired and short, carelessly piled on top of each other. The exit began to swing open again, and I darted around the edge of the building.

I jumped with panic as the side exit door opened, almost smashing me. It was Sioux. Just Sioux. And then the look on her face hit me. She was wiping tears off her cheeks and clutching a torn piece of paper.

"Oh good," she said, seeing Cocoa. "I'm glad he's okay." I didn't say anything. "Talisker...Talisker tested positive," she said between hiccupping sobs. She waved the receipt at me. "They'll take care of him and call me when he's better. They said that 95% get better." She tried bravely to smile. "See, I've got my claim check for him. They told me keep it in a safe place."

I didn't say anything.

It was too late, anyway.

CHAPTER SEVEN

REFUGEES

The time to act is now. Terrible things are happening before our eyes. I am reminded of the warning that if I don't speak for others, no one will be left to speak for me. Why do I feel so helpless?

- www.governmentsecrets.us
Posted October 19

I felt just awful as I left Sioux to tell her parents that Talisker had been taken into "protective isolation." Awful because I still had Cocoa. Awful because I hadn't trusted my suspicions soon enough, when we were waiting in line. Awful because, to be brutally honest, I hadn't even thought of going back to find her in the building—all I could think of was escape, for Cocoa. Awful because I couldn't bring myself to tell her what I had seen.

I was pale and shaky and sweaty by the time I got back home. Mom was already prepping vegetables for dinner. She froze, mid-chop. "Oh. You're back." She looked at me over her shoulder and went back to chopping fast and hard. "Torrance, the vet's office called a minute ago." I stopped breathing. "You forgot your purse. They're sending someone over here with it. Isn't that thoughtful?"

"Mom," I said. "They're lying."

She turned. "Oh? Where's your purse?"

I glanced down at my empty shoulder. "I mean that's not why they're coming. They're going to take Cocoa."

She sighed and laid down the cleaver. She rested her hands on my forearms. "I know, sweetie. I'm sorry. They told me the test results over the phone. If Cocoa's sick, you know the best place for him is the animal hospital. They'll know what to do."

Mom is basically a trusting person, a what-you-see-is-what-you-get person. Rody's totally cynical, and I'm somewhere in between. Realistic enough to know that the supposedly friendly voice on the phone was lying through its teeth.

"Mom, they're taking all the dogs. All of them!" My voice cracked, and I started to sob. Fear, tension, fear, anger, fear. "They're putting them all down. Get it? All. Down."

"Don't be ridiculous, Torrance. They don't do that to healthy animals. Now, calm yourself and be reasonable. Don't go all teenage hysterical on me."

"Mom, I saw it. I saw it!"

"Sweetie. You saw a vet put down a healthy animal?"

"No, no. Not exactly. But there was a truck, the truck where the soldiers just dis...dis...dispose of them!"

"Soldiers? Sweetie, calm yourself. I'm sure you're

misinterpreting what you saw. These are good people. They've been our vets for years."

"I know, I know. I don't get it. How could they turn evil overnight?" I stomped around the kitchen floor. I was screaming. What an awful time for Mom's intuition to fail on me. I couldn't break through her reasonableness. The truth was just too unreasonable. But I was sure. I was positive. I was right.

Cocoa ran to the front door and growled. The doorbell rang. Before Mom could stop me, I grabbed Cocoa's leash and hauled him toward the back door. I didn't wait to see who it was. If there were soldiers with them, Mom would cave. And Cocoa would be gone. Before the front door opened, we flew out the back. No time to say a word. No time for second thoughts. Escape was the only option.

We ran across the narrow gap behind the backyard fences and down into the dry creek bed along the edge of the park. The trees were thick and sheltering. Cocoa and I hunkered down in their deep shadow, waiting.

Cocoa's tongue lolled as he panted softly. I scuffed at the parched clay under our feet. Bone dry. No help there. I knew there was a water fountain by the playground attached to the Community Center, just beyond the dog park. For that matter, each of the pens in the park had a faucet. Didn't help. I hadn't brought a bowl or any other sort of container. I was completely unprepared.

Cocoa made an odd snuffling noise, and some more disgusting green mucus dangled in the opening of his nostrils. Oh spit. I knew that wasn't normal. Worse, I had read that "green or yellow nasal discharge is a symptom of canine flu." Undoubtedly a symptom of the New Flu version, too. I wiped it off with a large leaf and carefully avoided touching any. I couldn't let Mom and Dad see Cocoa in this condition. No way would they keep him in the house now and risk infecting all of us. They'd knock me unconscious (or, to be fair, wait for me to fall asleep) and then take him to the animal hospital.

After what I'd seen, I didn't trust any vet. Not if our own was involved. Plus they couldn't have come up with this idea on their own. Somebody had called in the National Guard. Somebody had a big truck ready and waiting. Somebody had ordered a silent massacre. Lambs to the slaughter. The silence of the pups. Somebody had pulled the plug to drain the animal reservoir. Who had that kind of power?

I had a suspicion this wasn't just happening in my neighborhood. It had to be playing out all over California, but silently. The governor had called for *protective isolation* as ordered by the CDC. Who controlled the CDC? I pulled out my phone and checked Wikipedia. Okay, so the CDC was a section of Health and Human Services. And the head of that was the Secretary of Health and Human Services. And his boss was POTUS, the President himself. A terrible idea forced itself into my head. My fingers flew across the screen. It took a *presidential* order to call out the National Guard.

I thought of his friendly, crinkled eyes and kind smile. I thought of the campaign button stashed in my top dresser drawer. Spit. My President had to know about this, must have okayed it, maybe even planned it.

That's what I figured, hunched under a bush in the cool of the evening. I shivered, but not from the cold.

Evening birds hopped about, looking for food, beeping at each other. Other than that, my nervous, angry breathing was the only sound. Then my cell phone blared, sending me reeling back into a tree in surprise. Ouch. It was home. I refused the call and silenced the phone. We waited till the sun set a bit after six. By that time my phone had logged fifteen missed calls, all the same number. In twenty more minutes, it was pitch dark all around me and pretty darned dark in my heart.

I decided to go home and try one more time to get through to the parents. If that didn't work, well, maybe I'd follow Gary Francis's example, load up a backpack full of dog food, and head north. All the way to Canada if I needed to. Except, I reminded myself, the border was closed to refugee dogs. "Come on, Cocoa. Ready for dinner?" Cocoa had to be feeling pretty hungry by now. I was.

I sent Cocoa straight into his doghouse and ordered him to stay. Peering around the edge of the house, I didn't see any strange cars in the driveway or on the street. I quietly entered through the back door. Not quietly enough, obviously.

Rody came thudding downstairs. "Where the heck were you? What happened? Mom is totally nutso frantic."

"Where is she?" The house felt empty of parents.

"She's with Dad, going door to door, looking for you. We didn't even eat dinner," he said accusingly.

"Oh. Sorry," I said, even though I wasn't.

"Are you going to tell me?"

"Are you going to believe me?"

"Why wouldn't I?"

"Mom didn't." That stunned him. "She hardly even listened to me," I complained.

He sat down on the bottom stair. "I'm listening."

Wow. Sometimes you can still be surprised by someone you've known for fifteen years.

I sat on the floor across from him and told him what I'd seen, what I thought. My voice was kind of shaky, and a couple of times I had trouble going on, but he didn't interrupt.

When I finished, he asked a perfectly reasonable question, darn him. "Have you had a chance to check out for sure whether any of the other vets around are involved?"

"Of course not. I had to get Cocoa to safety. That's about all I could deal with for the past few hours." My voice whined with tension.

"Okay. It's okay." He squeezed my arm in a rare and painful gesture of support. "I'm glad you got Cocoa out of there, no matter what. Where is he now?"

Could I trust him? I sure needed an ally. A strong one. "He's in his doghouse out back. I need to get him some food and water."

As my hands were still trembling and unreliable, Rody carried out the full water bowl and kibbles. A grateful Cocoa licked his face, and Rody scratched him behind the ears. "What are you going to do now?" he asked.

I'd thought about nothing else while I was crouched in the undergrowth. "Tonight? Call Mom and Dad. Tell them I'm home. Try one more time."

"What if they don't believe you?"

"Then I play along. Act penitent. Buy time."

"What about tomorrow?"

I had that worked out, too. But I wasn't about to trust him that far. "Tomorrow is another day," I said mysteriously.

Mom answered her cell phone before the ring finished. Through the hiccups, I sensed she was torn between screaming at me for running off and crying with relief at finding me alive and safe. She and Dad arrived home in no time flat, and Dad gave me a tight hug. Mom handled it in the best way she knew how— she started making dinner.

"Where's Cocoa?" Dad asked, looking between me and Rody.

Rody watched my face, let me take the lead, and kept his thoughts to himself.

"He's safe in his house," I said. "He's—"

"I'll be right back." Dad headed out to the yard. Eventually he returned with a heavy step and dark expression. He wouldn't meet my eyes, but he shook his head slightly from side to side when he looked at Mom.

"Oh dear," she said on a sigh. She stepped up and put an arm around him. "Help me carry these in, will you, hon?" She handed him two plates of steaming omelets. She balanced the other two. Rody grabbed the basket of rolls. I carried in the pitcher and filled the water glasses. All in strained silence.

After grace, Dad looked at me expectantly. "What's going on, punkin? It's not like you to run off. Not like you to avoid the obvious. Not like you at all."

"I had a terrible shock," I said matter-of-factly. I had to keep my bubbling "hysteria" under control. "I don't know what Mom told you…" I trailed off.

"I'd like to hear your version. From you." How I loved him when he said that. He's always so reasonable, so fair.

I swallowed the lump that wasn't eggs in my throat. Just sheer exhausted, relieved, terrified emotion. "While we were in line for the vet clinic, mind you, the one with soldiers guarding the doors, I didn't notice any people coming out *with* their dogs. That struck me as very strange. Ominous, even. Now, I would have thought that at least some of them would be healthy."

"Perhaps," he said, considering. "But remember three things: first, this bug is probably a hundred percent contagious between dogs since their immune systems have never seen it; second, dogs live a particularly active social life in our part of the world so they're exposed to a lot of other dogs; and third, our very own suburb is the center of the southern California epidemic. If you went up to L.A., for example, I wouldn't expect such a high percentage of sick dogs. But down here, only two miles from the outbreak point, I can well believe it. They might *all* have been exposed. And the authorities have to err on the side of caution."

Ack. Dad was too logical. Too reasonable. I hated that.

"But Dad. Even if they were taking them all in for quote unquote protective isolation, how much room would they need? The clinic's not big enough to store all the dogs that didn't come out."

"Honey, that's probably why they had a truck waiting, to take them to a bigger facility," Mom chimed in.

I tried Dad again. "Dad, I heard a bark and a shout and a howl that faded away, like they were killing the dog. Then a minute later, these guys threw a body into the truck."

"Punkin, they probably just anesthetize them for transport. Can you imagine a huge truck full of panicked, barking dogs? They anesthetize them, just like on airplanes. I'm sure that's all you saw. You don't really think our vet would be involved in something so macabre as tricking people into giving up their dogs and...and destroying them. Do you?"

Of course I did.

One last, hopeless try. I had to. "What about the instant lab test? That has to be fake. There's no way they could have invented it so fast."

Dad pondered my point. "I can see why you'd think that, but they're probably using the regular canine flu test. It would work if it's based on the common segments of the two viruses."

It sounded so reasonable when he said it, but I knew in my heart that he was wrong, wrong, wrong. I stared at my hands in my lap, trying not to cry.

Mom broke the weighty silence. "Sweetie, I know this is terribly difficult for you. The men who came by with your purse showed me the printout with Cocoa's lab results. Your father saw them too. You know we have to take Cocoa in for professional treatment." She looked to Dad for backup.

Dad took her hand in his, a united front. "Tor, you

can't deny that Cocoa's showing signs of congestion. I've seen him. He *does* need professional treatment."

"But Dad, why can't we treat him here?" I pleaded. "You've got all that antiviral junk in the emergency medical kit. Why can't you treat him?"

"Punkin, I'm not a vet. If he needs respiratory support, I don't have any of that equipment. And if we wait too long, and he gets a complication like pneumonia, all the facilities may be full and we'll lose him. Furthermore..." He patted me on the head. "Furthermore, I don't want to risk exposing the two of you any more than you've already foolishly exposed yourselves. This is a very dangerous disease in humans, far more risky to us than it is to the dogs."

Then he played his best card last. "You wouldn't want me or Mom to come down with New Flu, would you? Keeping a sick dog in the same environment with us is too dangerous."

Spit. He and Gary Francis's dad would get along great.

Horribly disappointed, I put plan B into effect. "I guess you're right Dad. All your points make sense. But can we please wait till tomorrow to take Cocoa in? If we do it tonight, I'll be up awfully late. Then I won't get a wink of sleep worrying, and I have a math test tomorrow."

So by the time we got done with dinner, I had them convinced that I was embarrassed to have made such a stupid mistake. (My performance deserved an Academy Award.) Tomorrow, I agreed, we'd take Cocoa in together for proper supervised treatment. Dad gave himself, Mom, and Rody a dose from his stock of

Eradiflu. We all went off to bed happy and reconciled. Yeah, right.

I lay awake making lists in my head until three in the morning. Then I slipped out of bed silently and started phase two of plan B. My backpack accommodated two water bottles, two plastic bowls, two sweatshirts, one of Dad's emergency mylar blankets, and a small flashlight. I filled up a gallon Ziploc bag with dog food. I grabbed an unopened box of chocolate chip granola bars and a bag of craisins for me. I wouldn't need that much food just for an overnight, but if something stopped me from sneaking into the empty house tomorrow, I'd be prepared. For a change.

Last task before heading out, I woke up my computer and sent off another email to Alex at CNN. I figured since he paid attention the first time, it was worth a shot.

Dear Alex,

Ask Dr. Wave if she knows that mass murder is going on in Southern California. Healthy dogs are being put down without the owners' knowledge and consent. They're slaughtering the innocent. How wide has this atrocity spread? How high up does the order come from? Find out. Please.

Then I slipped out to the yard. Cocoa shot from his dog house to greet me, dark as it was, with an encouraging burst of energy. "Come on, Coke," I whispered. "Gotta be super quiet now."

Under the wheeling stars, the gibbous moon sat fat and lopsided on the western horizon. It would be even darker soon. I coaxed Cocoa along toward the creek bed, toward our uncomfortable but proven hiding place. Sense-blind to my urgency, he tried to stop and sniff everything. My heavy hand on the leash tugged the fur under his collar.

"I'm doing this for you, you oaf," I hissed. "Come on."

It was spooky climbing down the slope under the dark trees. I bent low under the overhanging branches and walked east along the lowest part. Twigs tugged at my hair. Wisps of spider web caught my cheeks. Under cover of the slope, I dared to turn on the flashlight to scan the rocks underfoot. If I broke an ankle out here, I was nailed. Cocoa panted along beside me. I say panted, but there was a definite wheezy quality to it that made my own chest ache. We'd hardly gone any distance. He shouldn't be tired yet.

When we were safely out of sight of houses and humanity, I found a less gravelly spot to collapse into at the base of a tree. Cocoa curled up against me, a nice warm body. Still, I put on a double layer of sweatshirts and opened up the mylar blanket to spread over both of us. I flipped the flashlight around in my hand, covering the clear plastic with my palm. The red glow was all the nightlight I thought safe.

Even with three layers of clothes and an insulating blanket, I shivered and shivered in the night. I was terrified that heat-seeking rattlesnakes would slither under the blanket with us. Terrified that spiders would drop out of the bushes. Terrified that Cocoa would take off after a wild rabbit. I was afraid of men in black suits. Afraid of men in white coats. And especially afraid of falling asleep. My eyes ached. Exhaustion battled with adrenaline.

At 5:15 a.m. all the batteries ran out, both mine and the flashlight's. I slept, pursued in restless dreams by the vengeful spirits of barking dogs.

At 6:51 a warm, pink light penetrated the underbrush. A rising swell of birdsong served as alarm clock. At my stirring, Cocoa yawned and stretched. He lifted a leg against the tree I was leaning on and streamed against it.

"Hey, watch it," I scolded. "I mean, good boy. Come, Cocoa. Lie down."

Down? His puzzled eyes asked me. He knew it was time to stretch, time to play, time to go for his quick morning walk with Rody.

"Sorry, fuzzy face. We can't. Have some breakfast." I poured dog food into one bowl and water into the other, but Cocoa turned his head away, uninterested. "I guess you need a walk first. I'm sorry." He whimpered softly.

"I hear you, bud. Me too." I rolled my shoulders, stretched my legs out in front of me. Every square inch of my body hurt. The granola bars tempted me not.

What was going on at home this morning? By now, Rody would have discovered Cocoa was gone. Would he say anything?

Mom was probably wondering why she hadn't heard the shower go on and off in my bathroom. Maybe she was knocking on my door right now, calling me to wake up. Maybe she was cracking open the door and walking over to the tousled lump of covers to run her hands softly through my hair and kiss me on the cheek. Maybe she was turning in horror from the empty bed, running through the house, calling to my Dad, crying, "She's gone...she's gone."

My throat ached. I did that to her. A tear slipped out of the corner of my eye.

I pulled out my phone and sent her a text message: *Mom I'm safe I'm fine don't worry don't search.*

I hoped she could live with that. I doubted it.

I huddled with my dark thoughts as the sky brightened. In the distance, on the playground, toddlers laughed with their own mothers, enjoying their morning playtime before naps. A knife twisted in my heart. Life went on for the innocent as well as for the ignorant. But knowing what I knew, I could never be that carefree again.

I checked the time. With Rody gone and parents off to work, I could sneak home, shower, and resupply.

Leashing Cocoa to the tree, I ordered him to be quiet as a mouse. "I'll be back in a flash," I promised. I could easier pass unnoticed on my own.

Two steps away, he started whining. Another step and he let out a bark. This was not going to work. Spit. I set him loose and, with a firm grip on his collar, told him "Hush." Escaping with a dog in hand required perfect timing.

We tiptoed out of the brush and over the rise to the bridge. I imagined fifty-three pairs of eyes following me from all directions as we bolted for home.

Thank gladness Mom and Dad had left the secret key under the plastic rock in the yard. We entered the house and closed all the blinds—the way lots of people do to keep the furniture from fading. It wouldn't look out of place.

Once inside, I experienced a huge sense of relief, which didn't make any sense. Think about it. I was actually *less* safe here where people knew I lived than huddled in the creek bed. But it was warm. It was home. Cocoa felt the same way. He went straight to his dish and cleaned out the leftover kibbles in a flash. I helped myself to a bowl of Wheat Chex, human kibbles, and stowed the bowl in the dishwasher.

Cocoa wasn't used to going upstairs and followed me reluctantly, but I had to keep him nearby. I shut him into my room while I showered. The hot water jets shot into my skin, pulsing on my aching muscles. I stayed under way too long (we're supposed to keep showers very, very short in drought years, like this one), but it felt like heaven. I tossed my filthy overnight clothes into my hamper and dressed for another day. Four hours of safety here was a luxury I could indulge before I had to retreat to my hideout for the evening.

I was about to put my phone into my pocket when I noticed the message notification. Mom had texted me: *Come home, sweetie. We love you!* with all the correct punctuation. How cute. How compulsive.

Sioux had texted: *Where ru I'm in cafeteria.*

I texted back: *Invisible long story ask rody.*

Rody had texted: *You cudv freapin told me.*

What do you do when you're a refugee? I watched CNN Pipeline on my laptop at my desk. I finished the homework I could do online. I ate enough calories to equal lunch and dinner. I did my ballet stretches and barre warm up. I replaced my flashlight batteries. I lay on my bed and read with Cocoa curled up snoring at my feet. This wasn't half bad.

I cried when it was time to go back to the hideout. But I had to. We had to.

CHAPTER EIGHT

BACK IN BLACK

Something has people stirred up around here, people asking questions, reporters showing up and trying to get interviews. Maybe it'll break soon. Thanks to someone on the outside. Are you reading this? Thank you.

- www.governmentsecrets.us
Posted October 21

After another horrible, uncomfortable night, which ended with mourning doves sobbing at me, I lurked near the house to make sure Mom and Dad both left for work and didn't lie in wait. For the first time in my life, I couldn't rely on them. They didn't believe me, and therefore, I couldn't trust their instincts. Acid corroded my stomach. But I swallowed a small TUMS® of hope. As mad and worried as they must be, I believed we could work it all out somehow when Cocoa was better. They'd see that I was just being sensible. And I could make up the school work. One bad quarter wouldn't ruin my transcripts for college applications. I hoped.

Just one thing concerned me. The regular old canine flu could last up to a month. I wasn't sure I could last that long living under a bush. So I prayed New Flu was quicker.

As soon as I verified the coast was clear, Cocoa and I dashed inside for a hot shower, food, and batteries. I was going to run out of batteries too fast at the rate of two per night. Maybe I could leave Rody a note to buy some more. Then I remembered Dad's battery-free crank flashlight in the emergency box in the garage. Duh. That would be perfect.

Cocoa followed me into the garage. I was rummaging around in the emergency box when Cocoa let out a low throaty growl. "What?" I asked. Cocoa rumbled again, winding up for a bark. I clamped my hand on his muzzle. "Shhh. Shut down."

I strained my ears. And then I heard them. Voices inside the house. Familiar voices, but not the ones I wanted to hear.

"Maybe she's got a computer upstairs."

"Good thought. I'll check it."

No doubt about it. The men in black were back.

I smashed my ear against the inside of the garage door. Voices retreated along with footsteps. Had I left myself logged in? Would they be able to read my outbox? I slapped myself on the head, but it didn't jar the memory loose. I couldn't remember how I'd left the laptop.

Then the voices were right on top of me. "I'm checking out the rest of the house. Looks like she's still here, no matter what the parents say. I found warm dirty clothes in the girl's hamper."

Oh gross. That was Solly, fresh from pawing through my clothes. "I thought the mother must be lying," he said. "She just didn't seem upset enough for the mother of a runaway."

How dare he call Mom a liar! I'm sure she was upset, on the inside. Polite and coffee-making on the outside.

"At least she hasn't been picked up by our friends," Turner said. The way he said *friends* suggested that they were anything but. "Be thankful for that."

"Cocoa, over here," I whispered. I eased open the door to the spare car, the family weekend car. Mom and Dad's mini-electrics had taken them to work. Cocoa hopped in without any encouragement, and I slid in behind. We crunched down in the foot space, which is amazingly hard if you're five ten, but where there's a gun nearby, there's a way. Someone opened the garage door to the house, hovered for only a moment, and left. Click.

Tears of relief sprang to my eyes. I made Cocoa sit in that cramped car for another hour, just to be sure. Then I snuck out alone. The house was empty and the curbside clear. Solly and Turner had left no sign they'd ever been there. My clothes were still in the hamper. My computer looked undisturbed. Even my crumpled paper towel was still on the counter. Creepy. More than creepy.

I started to pack my backpack, thinking: breakfast, lunch, dinner, breakfast, lunch, dinner. I sure was going to get tired of granola bars and peanut butter and jelly sandwiches. I filled up two gallon Ziplocs with dog food. The forty-pound bag in the garage was starting to run low. We had six meals to get through before we could sneak back in on Monday. Plus I had no idea how

I was going to live with myself through Saturday and Sunday without a hot shower.

I slept just about as well that night as the night before, which is to say, hardly. I found out Saturday morning that, while being a homeless refugee is terrifying, it is also boring. Boring, sweaty, and smelly. I did my usual morning text to Mom assuring her I was still okay. She sent back her usual dozen pleas for me to come home. I texted Rody and told him the MIB had been going through our house while they were out. I texted Sioux and asked her if she could bring all my school books over to the house for me. She knows my locker combo by heart. I checked the battery level on my phone—stupid not to have recharged it while I was in the house. Still, I had enough reserve to do some web surfing. First I logged into the school site to check my homework load for the weekend. Figures. There were a couple of big assignments I had to do on the computer. Maybe Monday I could sneak in and get them done and email them in. I didn't know what to do about the ditched math test, which unfortunately, it turns out, I hadn't made up to fool Mom and Dad.

I spent about an hour on the CNN Pipeline site getting caught up with news. The only report on New Flu was that the "canine testing and protective isolation" program was proceeding nicely, but since new cases had cropped up in Oregon, Utah, and New Mexico, they suspected a long incubation period was at work, and the program was being expanded to those states. I wondered whether the expansion was coming from the Feds, not just all the governors' offices. It felt like a stealth roll-out of a nationwide plan.

Cocoa was unusually lethargic this morning. I hoped he was just becoming resigned to lying under a bush all day, but when he barked a raspy cough, I touched his nose. It was warm, very warm. Feverish I'd say. I poured him a bowl of water, but after one lick, he turned his head away. "Come on, Cocoa," I urged him. "You need fluids. They always say that when I'm sick. Push fluids." No use. His eyes closed, and he slipped into a deep, twitchy doggy sleep.

I turned off the phone and sat. And sat. And sat. I watched Cocoa sleep. I listened to the sounds around me. I thought about what a stupid, hopeless position I was in, but I didn't see any alternative. When Cocoa was better (and my mind refused, absolutely refused, to say *if*), I'd come in from the cold. It was just too risky until then.

About noon, I had a terrible urge to pee. Cocoa didn't look like he was going anywhere, but I snugged the leash around a trunk before I snuck out of the creek bed. The Community Center had public restrooms. A woman on the playground threw me an odd look as I passed her, attempting to stroll as if I hadn't a care in the world. Did I smell that bad?

The face in the mirror nearly gave me a heart attack. Hair knotted with leaves and twigs. Huge black circles ringing my eyes, evidence of my three-hour nights. Some kind of insect bite swelling up as a red blotch on my left cheek. I made pathetic repairs with fingers for a comb and paper towels for a washcloth. The woman was gone when I left—probably to avoid the crazy homeless teenager.

Saturday night, I sat up listening to Cocoa's breath

grow wheezier. Taking him to any clinic now would mean a sure death sentence, not sanctuary. But I already knew that. We'd ride it out together, me and him. I stroked his flank, and he didn't even stir. Although he was feverish, I snuggled close to him and covered us with the blanket. Exhausted beyond thinking, I slept with my head on the warm, breathing pillow of his back.

Sunday was bizarre. I felt myself turning feral. My nerves were hypersensitive to the smallest sounds, the slightest shift in the breeze. My nose picked up the mixed scents of dry dirt, sagebrush, eucalyptus leaves, dog, and my own armpits. All through the daylight, I crouched patiently, like a nocturnal animal in my den except for one trip to the bathroom. I was wild, unattached.

A stupid, needy part of me regretted that my parents weren't trying harder to find me, to bring me in, to tell me they'd stand behind me and Cocoa forever. (Wasn't that a bit strange? No search parties? No police cruisers?) I began to see how runaways truly could disappear in this big world, and I was only a quarter mile from home. Maybe the only people looking for me were Turner and Solly. Not Sasha. Not Sioux. Not Rody. Not Mom. Not Dad.

Monday morning rolled around. All I could think about was a hot shower, oh Lord, a hot shower. Cocoa hadn't eaten, drunk, or peed for the last twenty-four hours. I stroked and patted his head. I dribbled water into his mouth the best I could. He licked at my hand in thanks with a dry tongue. I whispered that he had to be a good boy, that I'd be back, and left him tied to the tree. No way could he make the walk home, but just in case he tried.

I let myself into the back of the house and headed first to the kitchen. In the middle of the kitchen table was something that made me stop, and gasp, and ultimately cry. A birthday cake. Beautifully hand-decorated by Mom. We both knew I was too old for a ballerina cake, but still, she had drawn a beautiful pink ballerina in icing on a white background. The tulle of her tutu was made of lacy fondant and poofed out in layers, just like a real one. Big white roses filled the corners, and (without even cutting) I knew that underneath was a pale brown spice cake, made from scratch. She must have spent hours on it this weekend, hoping that somehow I would come home for it today, my sixteenth birthday.

A square yellow envelope leaned up against the cake. My hands shook as I tore it open and pulled out the card, spilling a folded wad of green bills onto the table. The outside of the card pictured a graceful line drawing of a dancer. Inside, Mom's familiar cursive letters filled the blank space: *"Happy Birthday to my darling young lady. I wanted today to be special for you, a day we could spend together doing womanly things."* Womanly things.

I choked down the tightness in my throat and pushed away the tears that smudged my vision. *"I'm so sorry for the misunderstanding that separates us. Please, please come home, and if you can't, if you won't, make the best use you can of this birthday gift. I have the feeling you'll need it. Love ever and always, Mom."*

The money roll caught my eye. I retrieved it and counted out five hundred dollars. Good God. I missed her so much. The cake was proof of just how much she missed me. The gift, well, that was proof of how much she trusted me, after all.

I sat down hard in a kitchen chair and put my face in my hands and sobbed.

A big hand on my shoulder sent me flying into a defensive crouch.

"Whoa, chill, Tor," Rody said.

"Oh hell, Rody, you scared me spitless. What are you doing here?" I asked with a pounding heart.

Another voice answered. "We're wishing you a happy birthday." Sioux slipped into the kitchen. "We ditched!" She smiled conspiratorially at Rody.

"I love you guys," I said, throwing my arms around Sioux.

"You look awful," Sioux announced when I pulled back and she had a chance to look at my face.

"I know. Thanks. Being a runaway teenager is way overrated," I said. "I don't recommend it."

"That's too bad," Rody said grimly. "Because we've got to run farther. You turned on your phone for too long and they traced the GPS signal. This morning, I overheard the cops telling Mom they'd be able to pinpoint your hideout."

So they *were* looking for me. My stomach dived into my shoes. "Cocoa," I whispered. "I left him tied up there. Oh Rody, what if they find him? They'll kill him."

"Tell me where, quick. I'll move him."

I described the exact spot. "One more thing, Rody," I said. "Take a garden mask for your face. Whether the lab tests were fake or not, he's really sick. And you're going to have to carry him."

Rody winced, and his face shifted to an even more determined look. For a split second, he looked like a man. Then he turned back into my little brother.

"Run, Rody. Stay low. Be safe," I said.

For once, I was selfishly glad that I was the one in the house and someone else was doing the running.

Rody reached out to Sioux and touched her face. "Don't worry. I'll take care of it. Can you get the rest of the stuff ready?" She nodded and turned her lips into the palm of his hand. Whoa! What was that all about? Did I miss something here?

Rody slipped out the back door, and I turned to Sioux.

"Whoa! What was that all about? Did I miss something here?"

Sioux blushed. Blushed! I'd never seen that before. "Rody and I were kind of thrown together by this whole thing. We're um. We're together, you know?"

Okay, that was weird. My BFF and my brother.

"He came to me to see if I knew where you were. He told me about...about what really happened to Talisker and the others. It's all so awful, Tor. A couple of those guards went house to house on our street looking for people who still had their dogs. I slammed the door on them."

"I'm sorry, Sioux. I wish...I wish I could have done something in time..."

"For Talisker? No, you couldn't have. It all happened so fast, I didn't have time to think. And at the vets they seemed so helpful and confident. I was totally fooled." She rubbed away a tear forming in her eye before it could fully swell. "Like everyone else," she added with a bitter sigh. "But at least we've started to do something."

"Like what?"

"Rody and I went around and spied on the other vet clinics Saturday and yesterday, just to be sure, and it's just like you said. All those dogs going in and not coming out. And Rody was so smart. He had the notion to take my fancy-schmancy Nikon, and we shot some great video. Zoom, telephoto, the works."

"Not smart, Sioux. Brilliant." I was amazed to find that I could momentarily feel so proud of my annoying brother. "Now we need to transfer that to a flashdrive."

"Done." Her shoulders squared with resolve. "It's safely stashed in my room."

"You guys have been busy," I said with true admiration. "And smart. And productive. Anything else?"

Sioux blushed again. "Well, kissing mostly."

Rody and Sioux kissing? I failed to hide my appalled shock.

Sioux patted my arm. "I know, Tor. Who would've predicted? But, wow, he's a great kisser." She smelled unmistakably like teen love.

I covered my ears. "Not here at the moment," I said. "Please leave a message and I'll get back to you."

Sioux cracked up. Her face glowed. Yeah, teen love.

"So what did Rody mean about getting the rest of the stuff ready?" I asked.

"We need to pack up some clothes for you and cram them in here."

Sioux hauled two of Dad's serious camping backpacks from the family room into the kitchen. They were stuffed.

"What? I can't carry two packs," I protested.

"Only one's for you."

"Sioux-san. Are you coming with me? You're amazing!" I reached out to hug her again.

"Um. No, sorry, Tor. You know I've got my AP classes, and I can't screw up those grades. They actually count, you know?" she said with an apologetic look in her eye. "The other one's for Rody. He's going with you."

"Oh no, he's not," I said. "I can't take care of Cocoa and him both. Besides, one of us in trouble is enough. Mom and Dad will die."

"You need him, he said. He's the one with camping experience. Plus he has half the equipment in his pack."

I rolled my eyes to the ceiling. Rody, Rody, Rody. "Fine. I'll repack it all into mine."

I had started to unzip the pack over Sioux's protests when Rody burst in the back door, breathless.

"Where's Cocoa? In the dog house?" I asked.

"No. I moved him upstream and into deeper brush. They're not going to find him."

"Which way is upstream?" I asked.

Rody shook his head at me and groaned. "Upstream is uphill. Duh."

"Oh. Right. What if he starts barking when they're looking around close?"

"He's not going to bark, Tor. He's pretty much unconscious."

I nodded, throat tight. Couldn't say a word. Luckily Sioux jumped in. "You guys ought to have some cake so your mom knows you were here and got to see it. Tor, you're not going to be able to text us anymore, not now that they're looking for your signal."

"Right." I had to fall off the grid. Disappear without a trace.

Rody handed me a knife and plates and pointed me toward the beautiful cake. "Last bite of real food for a while," he said. "Go for it."

"What's in the packs?" I asked.

"Freaping everything."

"You're not coming," I insisted.

He rolled his eyes toward Sioux as if there was an I-told-you-so in them. "Yeah. I am. Because I packed. Because I have a plan. Do you?" He had me there.

"Not exactly." I cut three corners off the cake with three big fat icing roses. The ballerina danced on, undisturbed.

The cake was pungent with nutmeg and cinnamon. My mouth was dry as dust. I forced myself to swallow as the tears dribbled out of the corners of my eyes. I'm sure it was delicious. Happy Birthday to me.

CHAPTER NINE

NOMADS

I averted my eyes while Rody planted a long farewell kiss on Sioux. Fair enough. It could be a long while before they saw each other again. I gave Sioux a UBF girl hug and dripped tears on her shoulders. "Check in on Mom for me, will you?" I begged. "Tell her I loved the cake. Tell her thanks for doing all my laundry. Tell her I'll be back when Cocoa is well."

"You're sure you have to...?" Sioux looked anxiously between me and Rody. Then her eyes misted over, and I knew she was thinking about Talisker. "Yeah. You're sure. Good luck, you guys. I'll lock up the house behind you."

Rody picked up one of the packs and slid it over my arms.

My shoulders slumped down several inches. "Holy cats. What's in this thing?"

"Hopefully everything we need for a while," Rody answered. "Don't moan. I have to carry mine and Cocoa too."

Spit. I hadn't thought of that. "Sorry," I said meekly. "No more complaints."

Rody opened the back door and peered around.

"Looks good." He stepped back to Sioux and gave her one more last kiss. Sigh. Would I ever be on the receiving end of so much devotion?

It was bright daylight, but everyone was at work. The streets were deserted. Instead of heading toward the creek, Rody started in the opposite direction out the back of our cul-de-sac. Away from Cocoa. I grabbed his arm. "What are you doing? This is the wrong way, cretin!"

He rolled his eyes, shook his head, put a finger to his lips.

I followed him through the tight alleys of the mobile home community backing onto our neighborhood until we popped out way farther down the dry creek. Or, rather, *up* the dry creek. I was glad he had a good sense of direction. He forced his way past the vegetation with me right behind. A branch snapped into my cheek and I swore. At last I made out a motionless lump of brown, well-hidden from the banks. Squatting down, Rody hefted the twenty-five-pound animal into his arms with a grunt.

"Your mask!" I warned him.

"Couldn't find one. Come on. I've got a spot we should be able to reach in a couple of hours."

"Hours!" I squeaked. "How far are we going?"

"Not far. Out to the end of Garden Park, past the houses. It's only about three miles, but we're not going to make good time carrying all this."

I planted my feet. "Hang on, Rody. Think about it. We can't do this by daylight. Some old lady sitting and looking out her front window is going to see us and squeal."

"Okay. Then we'll just get to the end of the creek for now, stay under the trees, and wait for dark."

"Sunset's around 6:30." I knew from my last few days in the wild. "It'll be a long wait."

"Let's. Just. Move," he said between grunts as he shifted Cocoa over his shoulder like a baby.

"Isn't that going to hurt?"

"Who? Me or Cocoa? It's the only way I can carry him, okay? Unless you're volunteering to take both packs."

"Oh, sorry. Never mind."

"Thought so," he muttered.

I stuck my tongue out at him behind his back. Between hiding and ducking and hauling Cocoa, it took us a good hour just to go the few blocks to where we could hole up and wait for dark.

"Now what?" Rody asked.

I took off my pack, rolled my shoulders around, and sat against a tree, arms around my knees. "Now we sit." We sat in silence for twenty-three seconds.

"I'm bored," he complained.

"Welcome to runaway world. Eat lunch."

"Nah. I'm still full of cake."

It wasn't hard for me to settle into my watchful waiting zone, but Rody was restless and fidgety. I finally cracked. "Would you sit still? We have at least another four hours till dark."

"Holy spit, Tor. How can you stand it? I have to move."

"Not till dark." I needed to distract him with conversation. "So...well...here we are."

How stupid. I couldn't think of anything to say to

my own brother. Wait, yes I could. Get him talking. "Did you explain where the flu came from to Sioux?"

"Yep."

"Did she have any ideas? I mean she's the science whiz and all."

"Nope."

I stared at him, willing him to speak.

"No ideas," he said expansively.

Ah, now I remembered. This was why I had no conversations with him. "So, what's all this about you and Sioux?"

"She's cool," he said, avoiding my eyes.

Darn it! What would it take? "She says you're a good kisser."

A slow smile spread across his face, and his eyes brightened. Not exactly the effect I'd been going for, but at least he settled down into his own delightful dream world. Errrrrr. Why him and not me?

I closed my eyes and pretended to sleep. The pretense became real after a while, and I only woke because Rody was shaking my arm. "G'way, g'way," I moaned, only half conscious.

"Get up, Tor. It's dark enough to move," he said.

The street lights glared down, spotlights shining on our stealthy hike. The moon wasn't up yet, but the star wattage beamed exceptionally bright tonight.

"How's Cocoa doing?" I asked.

"Still breathing really shallow, but he opened his eyes a couple of times. I gave him some water."

"Did he eat?"

"Not interested."

I shrugged on my impossibly heavy pack. "Ready."

We were going to have to walk pretty exposed for a while, and I tried to put my bulk between Rody and the passing cars that might notice the burden he was carrying. He had wrapped Cocoa in a mylar blanket for warmth and disguise. I guess I had to give him credit for thinking of that. Oh, and the video.

"Hey Rody. Good thinking about that video evidence," I said.

He grunted.

The walk was easy now, along dark streets with little or no traffic. Just as we got to the end of Garden Road where the houses stop and the horse trail starts into the canyon, the edge of the moon rose over the eastern hills. Behind us lay all of Poway, spread out as a blanket of winking lights. Ahead of us wound a flattened path along a canyon bottom. In a few hundred feet, it would rise up the face of the low mountains that split Poway from the next suburb east. The terrain was hard and rocky, but the horse trail was good.

As the moon rose to illuminate the mountainside, the head-high sage and manzanita bushes stood out in silhouette. The bare upper reaches looked deceptively pale and smooth. I knew that by day, the large white boulders would be more obvious and unforgiving. Where was Rody taking us?

"Rody." I stopped him with a hand. "I can't climb this in the dark, and neither can you. Not with Cocoa. You'll trip and drop him."

"I wasn't planning to," he said scornfully. "I'm heading for that thick bushy area. We'll make base camp there."

Make base camp there. *Big words, little man*, I

thought. Fine, let him act all experienced. I was the one who'd slept out for four nights already.

I dropped my pack in the spot he chose. He lowered Cocoa onto my lap, and I sat there breathing hard, whispering encouragement in his soft doggy ears. His tongue flicked out and hit my cheek. His nose felt a little cooler. I don't think I was imagining it. I wet my hand with water and let him lick it off four or five times. Maybe he'd be able to sit up and use the bowl soon.

I glanced up from my patient to see what Rody was doing so busily. Bless him, he had moved a bunch of rocks into a circle and spread two Insulite pads in the clear next to it. How come I'd never thought of that? Mattresses! Oh my gladness. I nearly swooned in relief. I might actually sleep. Two mylar blankets had been rolled up in the pads. He cranked up our two emergency flashlights and set them down at a low angle so that they lit our little camp but weren't beacons to the houses down the way. Then he set up a cute little camping cookstove and filled a pot with water from a water bottle. Wow. Never knew he was so domestic!

"What'd you pack for my birthday dinner?" I asked.

"Mac and cheese okay?" he asked.

Mac and cheese! YUMMM! I was so tired of peanut butter and jelly I could've hugged him. If he weren't my brother.

"Sure. Fine," I said casually.

"That's good," he said. "Because we've got seven pounds of instant mac on our backs."

"Seven pounds?!"

"Twenty-eight four ounce bags. I figured a two-week supply. If we aren't out of this mess by then, we'll have to go to Plan B."

"What's that?" I asked.

"I'm working on it," he said.

Great. No Plan B.

I know it was only instant noodles and powdered orange cheese-food, but that dinner will go down in history as one of the best I ever ate. "Dessert?" I asked with hope in my heart. Rody tossed me a tiny box of golden raisins. I munched them one at a time, savoring every sweet bite.

Cocoa watched me eat with a bit of shine in his eyes, more than just flashlight reflection. "Where's Cocoa's food?" I asked.

Rody tossed me a gallon Ziploc, and I dropped a couple of kibbles into Cocoa's mouth. He ate about five of them before he stopped and turned his head away.

"He's getting better," I said. I don't think I was fooling myself.

"If you say so." Rody started piling dry brush into the center of his stone ring.

"You're not going to burn that, are you?" I asked, horrified. Good Lord. He'd set the whole hillside on fire. It was the tail end of wildfire season, and we hadn't had rain in forever. "You're insane, Rody."

He looked at me like I was stupid. "We've got to keep the coyotes away somehow. I do know how to control a fire, you know."

"Well, even if you don't set the hillside on fire, you're still totally advertising that we're here. Someone in one of those houses over there will have the fire department on us in minutes."

He crossed his arms and stared me down, his eyebrows tight with annoyance. "So what do you suggest?"

To be fair, I couldn't expect Rody to admit he'd been the dumb one. "What about the flashlights?" I suggested.

"They run down every thirty minutes. Duh."

"Are there really coyotes? In this canyon?"

At that moment, with the moon sitting nearly full on the mountain crest, a low and lonely howl split the night. A short barking howl answered from another direction.

"Nope. Those are just big crickets," Rody said sarcastically. Then his tone changed. "I make it at least two."

"Oh spit," I whispered. "How about if we take turns keeping guard?"

"Don't look at *me* that way. I'm exhausted."

"Fine." I huffed. "I'll take first watch. Moron. Wastrel. Troglodyte."

Rody glared at me. And I was just getting warmed up. "Martinet. Slugabed." As I ran out of nifty invectives (curses on his character), he lay down on his Insulite and pulled the mylar blanket all the way over his head. Fine.

I covered myself up, put Cocoa's head back in my lap, and leaned against a lumpy boulder to keep me awake till the end of my shift. Which was when? I couldn't check the clock on my phone. It was powered down. A long ghostly howl echoed across the canyon. A cold shiver ran down to my toes. Cocoa lifted his head and growled. Maybe I wasn't alone on this watch after all. I patted him. "Thanks, buddy."

I lost track of how many times I cranked the flashlight. All I know is that eventually my heavy eyes refused to stay open and, boulder or no boulder, I fell into a dream-filled sleep. In my dreams, I ran and ran, searching for my suitcase which wouldn't stay packed, searching for a flat place to sleep in a field of rocks, searching for a toilet that wasn't standing out in public. All the time, and out of sight, the looming and invisible presence of men in black followed me.

The freaping birds woke me again. It was official. I hated birds. I opened my eyes to the dawn gray light. The mountains blocked the rising sun from view. There wasn't a cloud in the sky to light up in brilliant color. But the fading stars and suggestion of light promised that morning was on the way. Rody remained a silver lump, buried in his bed. At this point, I decided to let him sleep on.

I stood up and stretched as high as I could reach, then bent double and hugged my knees. Everything hurt. Cocoa rose wobbly to his feet and stretched with me. He yawned and gave a vigorous shake. "Good boy," I whispered. "Oh, good boy, Cocoa." My eyes filled with tears. He lapped the first bowl of water I poured for him, emptying one of our water bottles, and asked for more, which I gladly gave him. I put a few kibbles to soften and swell in the water.

The sounds of pouring reminded me I had to deal with something urgent. That toilet dream was a message from my body, and unfortunately, there wasn't a handy Community Center near this hideout that my stupid brother had chosen. I wandered off, looking for a dense bit of brush to squat behind. By daylight, the houses up on the ridge were too easy to see, and the shrubs that had looked thick and protective by night were revealed as incredibly sparse. We were way too exposed here, especially if a horse or hiker headed up the same trail we had used. I made do with the best spot I could find to pee. I hated hanging there, trying to miss my feet, feeling the breeze blowing on my exposed butt. No paper either. I hated camping with a passion.

When I got back to base camp, Rody's silver cocoon was twitching, and in moments, his head poked out. "It's morning," he announced. "You watched all night. Uh, thanks."

I shot him a bleary nod. If he wanted to think that, no way would I confess to sleeping on the job.

He stood up, turned his back to me, unzipped, and did his guy thing with a roaring splash. He turned back with a grin.

"I hate you," I said. "You're enjoying this. Just wait till it's number two."

I plopped down on my heels and glowered at him, but I couldn't keep it up. The moment he waved a packet of instant cinnamon bun oatmeal in my face, I caved. With his mad outdoorsman skills, Rody boiled some more water on the camp stove, and we made oatmeal in our macaroni bowls, which we'd licked clean the night before. Cocoa watched our every spoonful, wagging his tail, before he ambled to the nearest bush and lifted a leg.

"Look at that good boy." Rody smiled. "He's a lot better, don't you think? Should we break camp and head home?"

"No!" I yelled, then covered my mouth as the sound bounced around. "No," I said normally. "I'm kind of afraid. Don't you think they'll come take him even if he's better?"

Rody shrugged. "Why should they?"

"Remember the door to door thing? They might be taking all of them," I reasoned.

"Tor, we can't live out here forever. We need a plan."

"I thought *you* had a plan."

"This was it," he said. "You said we'd go back when Cocoa was better."

"We can't go back till we know for sure it's safe. Till they stop."

Rody's cheer of a moment ago was drowned in bitterness. "They won't stop till all the dogs are rounded up."

"But there are over *sixty million* of them!" My mind quailed (that is, shrank fearfully into a small, cowering, feathered heap) at the picture of sixty million dead lumps of fur in trucks. "It's going to take a long time."

His voice went flat. "They seemed quite efficient, from what Sioux and I witnessed."

My imagination wept at the idea of a dogless United States. How fast were they wiping out our best buddies, our companions, the only creatures (besides moms and dads) that gave us unconditional love? I glared with total frustration at my inert cell phone. The temptation to web browse was overpowering. "I wish I could get some news. I feel so freaping isolated, not knowing what's happening."

"Oh. Here. Try this." Rody pulled Dad's hand-crank emergency radio out of his backpack.

"OH!" I grabbed it and hugged it to my chest. "I take back hating you. Thank you, thank you, thank you." I danced around with the electronic appliance in my arms.

"Sure. Whatever," Rody said, subdued.

In a state of bliss, I cranked up the radio and tuned it to the CNN simulcast band. In a moment, I was grounded, reoriented. It was 7:03. It was Tuesday. The so-called protective isolation had been in effect for a whole week. I wondered how many states were doing it by now. I wondered how many Americans were keeping their dogs safe at home in spite of the orders and the marauding (roaming, thieving, plundering) National Guards. I wondered how many vets were passing sleepless, guilty nights and whether any of them were fighting back and refusing to participate. I listened greedily for information.

After half an hour I realized with growing alarm that there was a giant hole in the news, a page that had been skipped. Of course, I had expected a lot of talk about the upcoming election in two weeks. The popular President was up for re-election and everyone assumed it would be a straightforward victory. There was speculation about how some money scandal was going to affect the Governor's race in Virginia. The pundits pontificated (pundificated?) about various tight races across the country. But the only mention of New Flu was some propaganda piece about how swiftly and responsibly the administration had responded to the potential crisis, unlike some paralyzed and incompetent administrations of the past. Swiftly and responsibly? Did that mean the spread was contained and everything was going back to normal? Was it yesterday's news already?

In the distance, hawks wheeled in the morning light. Beside me, a lizard snuck out from under a rock and darted off. It was peaceful. Then a chopping sound from far off became noticeably louder, and I turned up the volume on the radio.

Rody leapt up and scanned the sky. "Get under cover now, Tor," he ordered. "There's a search chopper out."

Silhouetted near the hawks, the heavy black bulk of a helicopter hung in the sky. Oh, come on. They weren't looking for us. Were they? As if picking up on my thoughts, the chopper turned and headed up the creek bed, then over toward the mountains, weaving back and forth in a pattern.

"Can they see us? Can they see us from the sky?" I asked Rody.

"I don't know. I can't tell. Make sure your mylar is rolled and stowed. That silver glint could definitely catch their eye."

I packed everything away with frantic haste. Then I noticed the unused fire pit, a perfect circle of stones. Spit. The next time the chopper was headed away from us, I dived out from our bushy cover and scattered the rocks and twigs, and dived back under again.

"Good idea," Rody said. "Sorry I missed that." He squared his shoulders. There was something touching about his trying to take responsibility for me, but the soft morning sun on his smooth cheeks showed he was just a boy. Guilt swamped me, for dragging him into this, for tempting him away from safety. Not that I'd forced him to come along. To be fair, he'd forced me to bring him. So why should I feel guilty?

"What did you do, anyway?" he asked. "Why are they so after you? It can't just be Cocoa."

"I know," I said with a sinking feeling. "I guess I really pissed someone off."

Rody turned a worried face from the sky to me. "I'll say. Well, we can keep you out of sight at least until the food runs out. And I brought a lot of cash. If they're not looking for me, I can do re-supply runs…somehow."

The chopper continued a thorough search pattern until it passed right over our camp. My toes curled so tightly, they cramped. My teeth clenched in fear as the chopping sound became unbearably loud. Then the helicopter swept past and moved methodically over the bare hillside, eventually cresting the mountains and heading off down the other side.

"As soon as they leave for good," Rody said, "we've got to get going. We'll have a window of time when they think this area's all clear."

"Where are we going?"

He pointed to the mountains, a red sliver of the sun just easing above the top. "Up and over."

"What's on the other side?" I asked.

"Safer terrain, I hope."

"That's your plan? Safer terrain *you hope*?" I sized up the long, steep, rocky slope facing us. "That's stupid. It's probably just the same on the other side."

"Stupid?" he gasped. "Who's the stupid one who ran away to a ditch with no food and no clothes? No flashlight, no radio, no camp stove?"

"At least it had a stupid bathroom." I growled.

He glared at me in silence.

"Fine," I said. "But we're not carrying these stupid packs and then find out it's no better. We'll hike up and look over before we make a commitment. Then we'll move if it looks good."

"Fine. We need more water first, though."

I gestured ironically at the dry, rocky creek bed. "Good luck, Scout Leader."

"No, no. Not from there, you idiot. The last house we passed had a pool in the backyard."

"Gross. I'm not drinking pool water, no matter how thirsty I get. I totally refuse."

Rody gestured to his pack. "Camping filter…"

Oh. Maybe he did think of everything.

"I'll go back for it," he said. "You stay under cover." He grabbed our four empty water bottles and set off. I reached for the radio and started cranking.

CNN was rerunning excerpts from the President's prime time news conference yesterday. Spit. Wish I'd caught it live. His familiar voice was saying, "And economic indicators are returning to normal as the danger has been placed under control. Our protective isolation policy is working. I continue to encourage all Americans to return to their usual routines now that the quarantine period is behind us. Quick action on the part of the Federal Government, in cooperation with State and local agencies has averted the potential pandemic crisis. People of America, you may rest easy knowing that the situation is almost fully contained in the western states."

A cold, cold feeling settled on me. The protective isolation policy was working? Read between the lines— the slaughter is progressing ahead of schedule. No more dogs equals no more flu. Sure I'd saved Cocoa from a fate just about equal to death, but how many other dogs had been taken already? And why had they lifted the quarantine so fast, after only two weeks when it was just starting to work? It couldn't all be about holiday shopping and the election. Could it?

I wished at that moment that I was a member of the White House Press Corps. These follow-up questions were obvious to me, but no reporter stepped forward to ask them. Typically, they went for the clever sound byte over substance. The next question was, "It is true, sir, that you are the first President in over a hundred years, since Woodrow Wilson, not to own a dog?"

The President replied, "Jack, I confess, I'm more of a cat person myself." A light chuckle sounded in the background. But perhaps it explained a lot. Perhaps.

The rest of the press conference quotes were reruns of basic campaign talking points. Here we were in the home stretch of election season. Imagine how people would react if they knew what was really going on.

CHAPTER TEN

OVER THE TOP

"You know how to work that thing?" I asked.

Rody ignored me with restrained silence. Bent over the camping filter in concentration, he appeared to know what he was doing. I have to admit, reluctantly, I was impressed.

After he had filtered four pints of lovely, fresh, eighty-degree, chlorinated, body-infested swimming pool water, we packed two of the bottles into the backpacks in the shade (not that they could get any warmer) and kept two in hand for our short reconnaissance hike up the mountain.

"Hey Rody, you forgot a daypack. You negligent lummox."

"So did you, belligerent termagant," he shot back.

"Oooh. Well said. Touché." I bowed to his quick riposte. (That's a fencing term. I think it means a quick return thrust.) "Do you think Cocoa can make it up the trail with us? I don't want to leave him behind."

Cocoa was busy exploring his new environment with his whiskery nose. He had found an interesting hole in the ground and was pawing gently at some poor unsuspecting rodent's front door. Rody slapped his own leg twice, and Cocoa came to stand beside him. He laid a hand on Cocoa's head. "You up for this, faithful hound?"

Cocoa yawned, his long pink tongue curling. He licked his whiskers.

"He says, yes," Rody translated. Then he read the worried look on my face. "He'll be fine, Tor. You're right. He's getting better. Maybe that booster shot helped him fight it off faster."

At first, the horse trail was smooth going (for a dirt path strewn with small rocks), and it was easy to make our way through the scrub and up the face of the mountain. In twenty minutes, I looked back and down, amazed at how far our gradual climb had taken us. The mountain face sloped away to the creek bottom, lots of feet below us. Don't ask me how far. I'm no good at judging distances. I surveyed the lay of the land due west, across Poway, which by day formed a red sea of tile-roofed housing developments as far as the eye could reach. I knew the ocean was somewhere over there, past the next bit of coastal range, but the air was too hazy to make out a line of blue. It was such a beautiful day, with a breath of cool autumn breeze. We were far from the madding crowd, and if it weren't for needing to pee again, wondering when it would be safe to go home, and trying to figure out how to thwart the evil government, I would have been totally at peace.

Cocoa had no trouble keeping up, but the thing about recovering and moving was that his body decided to purge itself of all the mucus and other evil humors. Every minute or so, he sneezed violently, cleaning out his sinuses, and occasionally, he stopped to make the most alarming hacking, coughing sounds followed by licking and slurping as he sent the phlegm down to his stomach for disposal. Gratifying to see these revolting signs of progress.

No matter how far down our starting point receded (that is, faded into the distance), the mountain peak itself appeared no closer, like those nightmares where you are running in place as fast as you can for your life. On top of that, the path grew steeper and more slippery with rubble. Cocoa's little paws were sure-footed, but I hadn't put on the most practical shoes. The treads of my sneakers were worn smooth. No help at all. If I broke something, my dance teacher would absolutely slay me. Rody, of course, had thought to wear his well-broken-in hiking boots. Of course he had.

"How long?" I asked.

"We've only been hiking for forty minutes," he answered.

"You're kidding. I'm almost out of water."

Rody turned an exasperated scowl on me. "Idiot. I thought you said you wouldn't drink it under any circumstances. Don't think you're getting any of mine."

"Oh shut down. I don't want any of yours," I grouched. We climbed and climbed till the trail petered out entirely. I squinted at the bright granite boulders still looming above us. This whole hike was starting to feel like an exercise in futility. We'd spent an hour getting seven-eighths of the way up. The remaining eighth looked so hazardous, it would take at least that long again. The autumn breeze had disappeared under the blazing late morning sun. My shirt was now plastered to my back with sweat, and all I had to drink was a dribble of warm water that someone had been swimming and possibly peeing in.

We were scrambling over and around boulders now. Every large step felt precarious, as my stupid sneakers slipped on the weathered granite. Cocoa was having a harder time, too, but we had gone past the point of no return. We had to make the summit or admit that we'd wasted the entire freaping morning.

With a yell of triumph, Rody hit the pinnacle twenty feet ahead of me. "Dazzle view," he called down. "Come on!"

I breathed hard, not bothering to answer. I just kept putting one tired foot in front of the other tired foot until I pulled up beside him and looked over the top. And, like the proverbial bear in the infinite loop song who went over the mountain, what do you think I saw? Another freaping mountain—that's what.

"Rody, you pernicious dolt. Plan B?" If I hadn't been terrified of falling down the hillside, I would have stamped my feet. "You call this plan B? Your dazzle view is a wasteland." All I saw was miles of more scrub, not a drop of water in sight, and a couple of highways heading off into the murky distance.

"At least no one would think of looking for you here," he said with a half-hearted smile, all teeth, no eyes. His tone told me he was as dumped as I was.

"Great. So they'll never find our desiccated corpses after we die of exposure, starvation, and dehydration." I wasn't sure of the exact order, but our odds of succumbing (dying in a very sucky way) to one or more of them were pretty high if we kept on this route.

Rody's shoulders slumped. "Okay, what do *you*

want to do?"

Good question. What *did* I want to do?

"Retreat. Run away." I said lightly.

I stood precariously on the top of the mountain, my damp hair lifting with the new breeze. I turned my head from side to side evaluating the options in either direction. To the west were armed National Guards, vets who'd gone over to the dark side, Federal Agents, and canine corpses piled high; but also to the west were civilization, my parents, ample food and water, school, and my friends. To the east lay wild, open spaces, a vast horizon, uncalculated possibilities; on the other hand, to the east lay parched barren terrain, pathless miles, uncounted shrubberies. So what did I want to do? I knew Rody would follow me, either way. An awful responsibility.

Retreat? Run away? My own words echoed in my ears. Which direction was retreat, though? Was it going back or going ahead?

I waved my fists violently at the sky, like Charlton Heston playing Moses or something. "What am I supposed to do?" I yelled. "What am I supposed to do?"

Even without burning bushes or other special effects, it worked. It came to me in a brilliant flash that no one else could see.

"For creeps sake, be careful," Rody said. "If you fall off the mountain, Mom'll kill me."

"You know what, Rody?" I asked in a completely new, happy, purposeful tone of voice.

"What?"

I laughed at the perplexed look on his face. "I've *got* it. The answer. I have to go to the library."

"You're nuts," he said.

"No really. The library. I've been acting and thinking locally. I've wasted a ton of time. **Now!**" Echoing shout. "**Is the moment!**" Wagging finger. "**To take a stand!**" Arms thrown up to the sky.

Of course, at just that point, to match my dramatically delivered speech, I gestured dramatically, lost my balance, and fell painfully between two rocks. My right arm was grazed and bleeding when Rody helped me extricate myself.

"Break anything?" he asked without an ounce of tenderness.

"No." Creeps, it hurt, but I couldn't let him know that.

He muttered under his breath as we slip-slided our way down the mountain. It's probably just as well I couldn't hear what he was saying since it was all about me. Never mind. I was busy composing emails in my head. I just needed a safe place from which to send them.

Why the library? I couldn't turn on my phone without drawing unwanted attention. I had a strong suspicion that Turner and Solly had put a key logger or other spyware on my laptop at home. They'd had an easy opportunity when they broke in. What I still couldn't understand was, why me? What were they after? What or who did they think I knew that I wasn't supposed to?

We got back to base camp by mid-afternoon. Cocoa collapsed in the shade after downing two bowls of water and a full bowl of chow. My heart warmed to see his appetite in action. He'd turned the corner on the road to recovery.

"So what's Plan C?" Rody asked as he devoured a protein bar.

"We need to spend one more night hidden out here," I said. "Then early tomorrow morning, we'll go back to the house. If you don't mind missing one more day of school, you can watch Cocoa, keep him out of sight while I go to the library. I need to contact some friends in high places. And then we'll throw the spotlight on this whole thing and end it."

"Spit, Tor," Rody said. "I suggested going home this morning. Before the climb of death, if you'll recall."

"Well this morning, that sounded to me like going backward, but now that I have my sense of direction, I figured out how to go forward. So it's different."

"Whatever. That means I can have two of these bars, anyway. You want one?"

We ate our late lunch in a lighter mood. No doubt Rody was thinking about getting back to Sioux. I was giddy with the fantasy that I could do it. I could put the brakes on this slaughter of the innocents. It wasn't about saving Cocoa anymore. It was about saving all of them—all of them who hadn't already fallen, that is.

I wish I could say that morning dawned bright and beautiful, filled with hope and optimism. It didn't. For the first time in weeks, months even, morning dawned dark and rainy. We were soaked. We were frozen. We were miserable. I wished for a tent and a campfire. I closed my eyes and clicked my heels together three times and said the magic words, "There's no place like home." I opened one eye. Spit. Still in the canyon with

Rody and Cocoa looking like a pair of drowned beavers. Actually, I don't think you can drown a beaver.

Rody's mouth was turned downward in a grim scowl. "It doesn't work without the ruby slippers."

I knew there was a loophole. Soggy sneakers just couldn't perform that kind of magic. "Since you didn't pack the hot air balloon, I guess we'd better get going."

"Aren't you worried about being seen?" he asked.

"You know, somehow, I'm not." I held my head high, water streaming down my forehead.

We plodded along the street in the rain. Cocoa tailed immediately behind us, smelling like, you'll never guess, a wet dog. The packs sagged like they'd gained ten pounds of water, but even so, my feet stepped lighter as we squelched toward home.

"I get first shower," I said, staking my claim by right of seniority.

Rody grunted unhappily in response. He'd only been out two nights. I was three nights filthier.

The closer we got to home, the bouncier my strides. The drivers that passed us hunkered down over their steering wheels, concentrating on driving in the rain. No one turned their heads and stared at the strange sight of two drenched hikers and a soggy mutt. We all tumbled into the house—the cold, dark house.

Well, what had I been expecting? A welcoming reception? Mom and Dad couldn't take a leave of absence to wait at home for us, all day, every day, wondering when we might show up. But was this a good thing or a bad thing? I couldn't decide.

Cocoa shook his tight coat, ears flapping madly, and sprayed water all over the walls. Rody and I dumped our packs to drip near the garage door. It was then I noticed that he was shivering, and his teeth were chattering like crazy. I had no choice but to be the responsible big sister. "You take first shower," I said generously. "Just save me some hot water, please."

Rody didn't argue with my magnanimous (amazingly generous) gesture. He nodded by way of mute thanks and headed up the stairs. The water blasted on seconds later. While the rain dripped out of my clothes, I boiled water for a huge mug of lavender tea and turned on the instant gas fire. Cocoa curled up in front of the hot artificial logs, put his head down, and was instantly asleep. I swear, I could've done the same, but I had work to do first.

Now that we were home, I didn't care if they traced Rody's phone, so standing and leaking on Mom's clean floor, I texted Sioux: *we're back.*

Two seconds later, I got a return message: *bro!!!!!!* I assume that meant *be right over,* not some reference to my brother. I also assumed that meant she'd bro after school, not now. She could get all of the unspeakable happy reunion kissing with Rody stuff out of the way while I was working.

I also texted Sasha: *hey T here what's new.* I'd missed only two ballet nights. It felt like a year.

While I waited for the shower, I did a thorough news scan on my computer. I searched all my favorite sites, both network and alternative. Not a hint of what I was looking for, hoping for. No reports of any citizen uprisings. No protests lodged by the American Veterinary Association. No ASPCA picketers in front of the White House.

What was wrong with everybody?

I couldn't find any sort of report on the protective isolation policy with numbers attached—how many dogs "released to owner"—how many dogs "taken in for protection." I couldn't find any more updated numbers on the New Flu—how many dead, sick, or recovered. There was a huge black hole where the information should be. Why weren't people demanding it? Why wasn't the press living up to its name and pressing for answers?

The water stopped in the bathroom I share with Rody, one of those goofy Jack-and-Jill ones with a door into each of our bedrooms. He unlocked my door from inside and poked his head into my room. "All yours."

He was pale and shivery, even after all that hot water. Kind of pathetic. It roused my protective instincts. "Rode, I turned the fire on downstairs. Go warm up for a while." He shuffled off to dress.

I leapt into the shower and turned it on full volume. "Yes! Yes!" I sang into the hot spray. "Yow!" I shrieked as the blast hit the huge scab on my arm. I soaked and soaked and washed and washed until the hot water ran out. I was clean. I was warm. I was bright pink. I glowed like a brand new human.

When I came downstairs, Rody was asleep in front of the fire with his head on Cocoa, both of them snoring lightly. I didn't have the heart to disturb them, so I put a quilted down vest over my sweatshirt to hold in the warmth, found a pair of dry sneakers, grabbed a large umbrella, and took off for the library. The door snicked shut behind me. I was off to wreak havoc in the halls of power. I hoped.

CHAPTER ELEVEN

SHAKEDOWN

An impenetrable dome of silence has fallen over all of us, and I despair.
- www.governmentsecrets.us
Posted October 26

It was only one walking mile to the Poway Library, no big deal except that we'd already covered a lot of ground this morning. I rehearsed the three-part plan in my head and found myself on the steps of the library in no time. Ready to execute plan C, I sat down at a vacant computer to create a brand new free email account under the name Joe Citizen. I was bold. I was ruthless. I used tons of big words from the online thesaurus. And I bluffed like crazy:

> *Dear Governor (fill in name here) of (fill in state here):*
>
> *I am sure you are aware of the spate of dog killings taking place around your state as a "protective isolation" measure by the authorities. The National Guard would not*

have been deployed in this effort without your consent. I am sure you are also aware of the false information being given to your citizens to lure them into turning over their pets willingly. Veterinarians have been coerced into falsifying test results and euthanizing indiscriminately. We both know that dogs are not human, and that you are "acting under orders," as they say, but I wonder how your constituents would feel about your role in silently allowing this to happen under your own roof, on your watch. I am aware that you (are/are not) up for re-election in two weeks. News of your complicity may affect the outcome of all the races in your state. I am willing to hold my peace about your role until after the election if I have your written guarantee that you will testify to the source of your instructions if called on to do so. You may reply to me via email.

Yours very sincerely, Joe Citizen.

Over the next three hours, I sent that email to the governor's office in every state except Hawaii, which already quarantines incoming animals. I wanted to spread my net wide. Because of the cone of silence clamped around the neck of the neutered press, I had no idea how far the outrage had spread. All I needed was one or two governors to confirm my suspicions. Call me an optimist. I didn't even wait for replies before I created the next email.

Dear Alex:

It's me again, your reliable informant, writing under an assumed identity. The Federal Government has tried to silence me with a duo of brutal agents, but I will not be silent. I realize that your investigation into my allegations of canine genocide must be ongoing as you have not reported this atrocity to the world. Let me assure you, it is true, and the orders derive from the highest levels of government. I have several governors willing to tell us just how high the orders originate. The American public may feel very grateful to you for breaking this story prior to the November 8 election. Very grateful indeed. Please contact me at this email to let me know if you are further interested in my information.

Yours as ever, Joe Citizen.

I couldn't put the third part into effect quite yet. That was too gutsy even for me.

"Oh sweetie, oh my little girl, you're safe. You're safe." Mom practically throttled me when I got home from the library. She squeezed the breath out of my lungs then held me at arms' length to scan me with her mother radar. Even though I was wearing a sweatshirt, she held my left arm gingerly. "How's the scrape feeling? Did you wash it well? We don't want it to get infected."

How did she do that? "How—"

"Rody told me, sweetie. He told me everything."

Over her shoulder, I made brief eye contact with Rody, and he shrugged. I wasn't sure what *everything* included. Whatever it was, though, she seemed remarkably calm. Good job, Rody.

"Mom, the most important thing is that Cocoa's just about well again. He's way past contagious. So you're not going to take him anywhere, right? And you'll defend him if they try to take him away, right?" I waited for her all important answer. Cocoa glued himself against my right leg and knocked against my hand with his head. I crouched next to him with my arm around his neck and we both implored Mom with sweet, hopeful, brown eyes.

Mom harrumphed in her throat, which meant Cocoa was safe. I was safe. Maybe even forgiven.

She stroked Cocoa's head, then kissed him between the ears. "That was a very silly thing you did taking off like that. You had me worried, worried, worried. Look at these gray hairs." She pulled a strand of hair from her forehead.

"Mom, it's blonde."

"Well, it would be gray if I didn't dye it."

I knew this was one of those discussions I could never win. So I caved. Gotta know when you're beaten. "Sorry, Mom. It was extremely…impulsive and hasty of me. I weep with penitence."

She shook her head with a twisty, laughing smile and hugged me again. "Your father has been absolutely beside himself. It was all I could do to keep him from turning the entire suburb into a search party. You'd better look a whole lot sorrier than that when he sees you."

"Should I practice my forlorn, contrite daughter face? Oh my gladness, what's that totally amazing smell?" My stomach acknowledged with a growl that I was famished.

"I just threw together some steak and mushroom pie and a green bean casserole."

"Wow. I feel like a prodigal, um, daughter. I should run away more often," I joked.

"Don't even think it, Missy." The hug tightened.

"Yeah, don't even think it," Rody said hoarsely. "I'm still trying to get warm." Then I noticed how overdressed he was, even in front of the fire.

"Oh, honey." Mom turned to Rody. "You caught a bad chill out there, didn't you?"

"S'nothing, Mom. I'm fine. Just a cold."

Mom was convinced. I wasn't. My head burst with images of Rody carrying Cocoa, being licked by Cocoa, being breathed on and sneezed on by Cocoa. A terrible foreboding settled in the pit of my stomach. Why had I let Rody talk me into taking him along? I was the one who'd taken the full course of antivirals—he'd had only one dose. I was the one who gladly signed on for the risk, not him. He had come along out of some misguided sense of having to organize me. I crossed my fingers and toes that he was just chilled from the rain. Yeah, right. After six hours in front of a fire.

"Punkin!"

I whirled toward the garage door to see a bear hug waiting for me. Dad spun all of me around, as if I were still five, knocking my legs into the wall. He's pretty nimble on one and a half legs. He put me down with a laugh. "I'm extremely glad to see you all in one piece. I imagine I have your brother to thank for that."

"Gonna spin me too, Dad?" Rody asked without getting up.

"You should be locked in your room for a week for encouraging your sister." Dad's face turned stern just long enough for me and Rody to know how close he was to being dead serious.

Mom came to Rody's rescue. "After all, honey, he couldn't just let Torrance run off on her own again. At least he packed appropriately and kept her safe."

"And I kept in touch," Rody put in.

"We appreciated that, sweetie," Mom said. "Very responsible."

No way. They were giving him credit for being responsible? "Rody, what did you do? Responsible? They could have traced us," I protested.

"Nah. No one was spying on my phone. I knew what I was doing."

"Of course, he did," Dad said. "I had full confidence I him. I trained him, didn't I?" He pointed an accusing finger at me. "You're the one I worried about."

"Hey!" I protested. "I took care of myself just fine before Rody came along."

"You could've been eaten by mountain lions," Rody said.

"Oh spit. Were there really mountain lions?" I asked. "I thought I only had to worry about coyotes."

Rody took a look at the expression on my face and laughed his head off. Brute. He was forced to stop when he was overcome with coughing. "Not where we were camping out," he admitted between gasps. "But a little ways down by the bird reserve behind the lake, there are definitely cougars."

"I am so glad I didn't know that," I said. "So glad."

"Oh dear. Me too," Mom added.

Dad patted her on the back and kissed the top of her blonde head. He winked and made some sort of *we-da-men* gesture to Rody.

After that, the atmosphere lightened. We were jolly and frivolous all through dinner. We even tossed bits of expensive steak to Cocoa. We were just so happy to be alive and together. All five of us.

Of course after dinner I had to break up the happy reunion. I dashed upstairs, well, lumbered up, to be honest, with a stomach full of real food. When I reappeared in my ballet stuff, Mom dropped the pot she was washing. It clattered against the stainless steel sink. "Torrance Olivia, don't tell me you're going out tonight. Aren't you exhausted?"

"Of course I'm exhausted," I said. "But if I miss another night of dance they might not let me do the Christmas show. Don't want to risk it. So can you drive with me?"

Mom made a great dramatic show of pulling off her wet dishwashing gloves, sighing heavily, and finding the car keys. But I noticed the trashy paperback romance tucked into the side pocket of her purse. She was more gruntled than she let on. (Yeah, it's a real word. Coined in the 1930's when people were funnier.)

My ID card still worked, so they hadn't kicked me out of the studio for going AWOL during rehearsals. I burst through the studio doors, anxious to stretch out at the barre and unkink all the muscles that had been tortured over the last week.

Sasha flew across the floor to greet me, with an odd gleam in his eye. "Tor. You are *so* just in time." He swung his eyeballs to one side, gesturing for me to check behind him. Oops. There was Felicity, warming up at the barre, holding on with her right hand. On her left was a bright pink cast.

I looked back at Sasha, a question in my eyes.

"Yep," he answered. "Miss Trudeau said the dance would be yours if you were here tonight and didn't miss any more rehearsals. Shhh. Let her tell you. Act surprised."

I beamed at him. Then I put a genuinely fake-sympathetic expression on my face and went over to Felicity. "Hey, Feliss. What happened?"

"Freaping gymnastics happened. Stupid balance beam."

"Been there, done that," I said. "Remember how I broke my foot before the recital two years ago?"

"Yes I do, Tory. But it wasn't as if you had an important part in that kiddie recital. It's not remotely the same."

"Well no, it isn't," I said as graciously as possible to the little tabby. "Accept my condolences, will you?"

I turned back to see Sasha following this little exchange of hisses. He glided over to me and whispered, "You can put your fur down. You won this round." He ran his hand down my spine and patted me on the butt. And the weird thing was, it didn't send my hormones into a spiraling frenzy or my pulse to dangerous, heart-attack levels. It was just Sasha. My best friend. What a relief.

The teacher watched my beauty and precision closely with a raised eyebrow and an appreciative look. "Well, Ms. Maddox. Very nice. Maybe you just needed a little vacation to get your groove back."

I laughed inside. Vacation?! Maybe standing on top of a desolate mountain with the wind dancing in my hair had given me a new image to hold in my head as I whipped through my chaînée turns. Maybe scrambling unsteadily over boulders had given new elevation to my leaps. Whatever the reason, I knew I was dancing at my best and beyond. At the end of class, Ms. Trudeau pulled me aside and offered me the *pas de deux* spot. I joyfully accepted. Oh yeah.

"Mom, mom, mom, mom, mom! Guess what?" I yelled, throwing myself into the car.

"You got the part?" she asked.

How does she do that? "How..." I started.

"Sasha told me everything," she said.

Everything?! Dear God, I hoped not. "When were you talking to Sasha?"

"He called over to the house Monday night, when you weren't at rehearsal. He wanted to know if you weren't there because you were disappointed about the audition results and couldn't face it. What a nice, thoughtful boy he is, Tor. I like him."

"I do too, Mom. He's a great *friend*." I emphasized the word for her benefit as I started the car.

"Anyway, he wanted me to tell you about Felicity breaking her arm, but at that point, I had no way to get in touch with you. Ahem.'"

Somehow she filled the word "ahem" with as many meanings as the dictionary. And it's not even a word. More of a long, drawn out throat clearing.

"I didn't want my phone to be traced." I squirmed under her accusing eye.

"Yes, I know sweetie. But you surely didn't think I wouldn't worry night and day."

Guilt, guilt, guilt. Change the subject. "Yay. I got the part. You have to make sure Rody comes to watch me this time."

"He's not much of a dance fan, Torrance. Why do you specially want him to come?"

"I don't know. I just want him to see me doing something I'm competent at. Extremely competent. Just tell him Sioux will be there."

"Sioux?" Mom asked.

Ha! She didn't know. There was something she didn't know. Hee hee. As casually as I could, I said, "Well, yeah Mom, since they're together and stuff. You know."

Mom's eyebrows flew high. "Really. Rody and Sioux. Hmm. Fancy that." And then she added a comment that truly surprised me. "Well, it's about time, I must say."

I wanted to go to sleep so badly, but I had tons of work to make up, and I didn't want to get farther behind. I did all the homework due the next day; then I started working from the first day I missed, last Friday. Look at that. It wasn't even a week. Felt like a million years. By two a.m. my eyes were blurry and streaming.

I went into the bathroom to splash another round of cold water on my face. Rody tossed and coughed loudly in the next room. I sat down in front of my books again to work and passed out. I guess I could sleep in any position by now.

Sioux was waiting at my locker in the morning. "I missed you!" she yelled.

"Oh, you're sweet. I missed you, too," I replied. "But we saved Cocoa. Did you see him? He's so much better."

"No, I mean I missed you yesterday afternoon. Rody said you were at the library or something."

"I had some serious work to do," I said evasively. By light of another day, my confidence that I could pull off the Master Plan was evaporating. Come on, really. Would anyone higher than an intern staffer read my emails before they spam-tagged them? Would CNN really listen to the ramblings and accusations of a sixteen-year-old girl? Okay, they didn't know I was a sixteen-year-old girl. But I wondered how much crank mail they got every day.

"Anyway, it sounds like camping was a great adventure, searching for your own water, and cooking out over a camping stove, and that death defying climb, and holding off the coyotes and cougars. I mean, wow."

I guess Rody didn't have any trouble being conversational with Sioux, but my gladness! He must have made himself the hero of this great camping drama. An entirely new side to the boy. Who was I to crush his fantasy or his reputation?

"Oh yeah, it was a great adventure," I said. "Rody was a rock. If he hadn't been there, I would have been toast." Sioux's eyes glowed with Rody-worship. And that, folks, was my good deed for the day. As if a little white lie in the cause of love could make up for what I hoped to pull off next.

After school I bused home. Rody was fast asleep, the sound of congested snoring leaking from his room. I snuck three extra doggie treats and a marshmallow to Cocoa, who looked 105% perfect by now. Then I walked over to the library to check Joe Citizen's email account on a nice, safe, neutral computer. Just like a terrorist. And I was on my way to threaten the President of the United States. Go figure.

I stared at the email login screen, trying to hold my hopes at bay. It was a shot in the dark, right? I'd be freaping lucky if I heard from even one.

Joe Citizen logged into the email account. Joe Citizen had thirty-seven messages. Thirty-seven! I started at the top and read down one by one. Okay, twenty-three of them were auto-responses which read something like "Governor Blank appreciates the concerns of all the citizens of the great State of Blank. Rest assured that he will give your letter due consideration. Thank you for your participation in this great democracy of ours." Blah, blah.

Ten of them were more personal letters basically asking me who the hell I thought I was to be threatening them. But four of them, FOUR (!), were real answers. They all pretty much confessed that their hands were forced by "the highest level of executive authority" (and we all know who that is, Mr. P!) and even against their better judgment, they were told to cancel quarantine and institute a purge under the cover that CDC would provide with the "protective isolation" policy. They asked to meet personally to discuss the appropriate time and place for revealing this information, code words for "after the election, please."

This stuff was so hot, I was afraid the computer would melt.

I had to have a backup in case the Feds found and trashed my account. I sent two copies of each letter to the library printers. With the change trapped in the lining of my wallet, I paid the librarian, who didn't even glance at the pages. One set of letters, I folded in thirds and placed in my purse. The other set, I folded and slid between the pages of the biggest, most dusty, boring tome I could find on an almost unreachable shelf. Even if I got mugged on the way home and lost my copy to the muggers, these pages would stay hidden until I needed them.

The other thing was, I had to save a digital copy, at least one. My family was too obvious, so I forwarded a copy to someone that no one knew I was connected to—Sasha.

I had two more jobs for the day. First, I copied the body text of the memos, leaving off the names of my sources, and emailed the four of them to Alex. I enclosed a personal note:

Dear Alex,

I hope your investigation is wrapping up soon. I enclose this testimony from the original sources, but I am prevented from revealing their identities at this time. Was Narlee in on it from the start or was she a dupe of her own agency? Player or played? I'm curious.

Yours very sincerely, Joe Citizen.

The second job was the hardest, but it was what I had come here to accomplish in the first place. I had to write a memo to the President that would get passed up the line as quickly as possible, not end up in the bulk folder. Sure. No problem. Right.

I sat there in the library, head in my hands trying to recompose my thoughts. All my earlier mental drafts seemed inadequate. This one had to be perfect.

I remember back in third grade when our class was studying citizenship and we all wrote a joint letter to the President saying something that amounted to "Have a nice day." If I did everything right, if I had guessed right, my letter would give the President a really lousy day. It had to be right. I didn't have a Plan D.

Dear Mr. President, Sir:

I am writing as a concerned citizen, just an average Joe with a dog, to demand on behalf of all thinking and feeling people that you rescind your order to drain the animal reservoir, to sacrifice sixty million animals to a sense of fear. You may have thought it politically expedient on the eve of the election to create this imaginary program of benevolent "protective isolation" as a symbol that this administration was responsive; you see it as a

161

quick and cheap alternative to an extended quarantine and vaccination program. I doubt it will prove so when, on the eve of the election, I shine the light on your betrayal of our trust and reveal publicly that you abused your executive power to authorize and order what amounts to the wholesale slaughter of a species. Is that any way to treat man's best friend?

Quarantine was working. It will work better with mass distribution of canine vaccines and human antivirals in the hotspots, as well as masks for pet owners.

If within eighty hours, I fail to see evidence that the quarantine is restored and the deaths halted, I will come forward with the entire story on national news. Numerous governors are prepared to support my story. You see, it will be politically expedient for them to do so.

Thank you for your prompt attention to this matter. And have a nice day.

Sincerely, Joe Citizen

My hands were shaking as I pressed the send button. But it was done. For better or worse, it was done. I'd given it my best shot. The President had until nine p.m. Eastern on Monday to meet my demands or meet the press.

Up to this point, I'd never actually posted to *www.governmentsecrets.us*. Now, I gave in to a dangerous impulse to let the blogger know there was hope, that something was on the move. I couldn't do it as myself, of course. I'm sure Turner and Solly had that angle covered. So, as Joe Citizen, I posted, "Don't despair. I'm working on the outside. But very soon, I'm going to need someone on the inside. Will you be there for me?"

CHAPTER TWELVE

EVIDENCE

Yes.
- www.governmentsecrets.us
Posted October 27

I exited the library with hope in my heart. I wondered when I might get a response and what form it would take. My head was awhirl with my own loud thoughts, and I was too preoccupied to notice the familiar scary black car lurking in the library parking lot. Then the passenger door snapped open and a familiar figure stepped out.

"Ms. Maddox? May I offer you a ride?"

"No thank you, Steve," I said, all atremble inside but cool as a refrigerated melon on the outside. This was not exactly the response I'd been hoping for. "I'd rather walk. It's a lovely day." Actually, the sky was an ominous gray, heavy thunder clouds gathering on the mountain tops. A rumble shivered the air. Did these guys bring their own special effects?

Agent Turner took my arm firmly, not painfully, but definitely firmly. Let's put it this way. I couldn't pull loose. He opened the back door with his free hand and helped/pushed me inside. The door closed and locked electronically. Spit. He ended up holding my purse.

Turner got back into the passenger seat and nodded to his partner. "Go get it," he said.

The second man in black got up without a word.

"That's not Solly," I said. "What happened to Solly?"

"He's on paternity leave. His wife was just discharged from the hospital yesterday."

"Girl or boy?" I asked. A baby? Somehow that made Solly seem a smidge more human. I shouldn't have kicked him.

"One of each." Turner chuckled and mimed pulling his hair out.

I knew what he was thinking. Solly would be lucky to have any left in six weeks.

Being in the position of a prisoner at his mercy, I decided to take the offensive. "Hey, it was nice catching up with you, but I'm expected at home. Where's the handle on this thing?" Who made cars with no handles on the back doors?

Out the window I had a clear, if dark-filtered, view of Agent Two carrying a desktop computer out of the library. "What's he doing? You can't steal library property," I squeaked. "I paid for that computer. I'm a taxpayer."

Turner glanced back with a quirk to his mouth. "Hardly."

"Well, I would be if I had any income," I grumbled.

"We have a warrant," Turner added for good measure.

The second agent dumped the computer into the

trunk, slammed it shut, and came back around to the driver's seat. He turned to me with a hand extended. "Ms. Maddox? I'm Agent Turner."

Sure. Right. Then I studied him closely. He was. Holy spit. He was a thirty years younger version of Agent Turner. I gasped. "Oh my God. Is this some secret government cloning program? You're the prototype and they're churning out hundreds of you in secret labs? I can't believe it. The government is mass producing Agent Turners."

And I had thought that the cloning conspiracy theorists were crackpots.

Both Agent Turners laughed. But it wasn't an evil, maniacal laugh as I'd expected.

Agent Turner Two said, "Good one Ms. Maddox. Very good."

Steve added, "This Agent Turner was developed in the usual fashion. He's my oldest boy."

"You never told me you had kids, Steve," I said in wonderment. Maybe these MIB were semi-normal people, after all.

"Steve? She calls you Steve?" Turner-the-son asked.

Agent Turner-the-dad shrugged. "Apparently so."

"We go way back," I said. "Which reminds me, Steve, why are you still following me?"

"Give us the identity of your person on the inside, and we'll leave you alone."

"I don't have a person on the inside. I don't even know *what* the inside is," I insisted.

"Who are you trying to contact secretly then?" he persisted.

"None of your beeswax. I know my rights."

"No, you don't," Elder Turner said.

"Aha!" I exclaimed. "That's true. Because you haven't Mirandized me. So let me go this instant."

When Young Turner started reciting, "You have the right to—" his father cut him off.

"We're not arresting her. We're buying her a…what do you want? A burger? Arby's?"

"Ooooh. Arby's. How about a large jamocha shake?" I'm so easily bought, I'm pathetic.

"You heard the lady, Rick. A jamocha shake."

He pressed the power and the dashboard lit up. "Whatever you say, Agent Turner."

Oh, come on. "Rick. You actually call your dad Agent Turner?"

"Only when I'm working," he said.

"Not to be judgey," I said, "But that's really weird. I would still call my father Dad even if I were working with him, which isn't likely since I don't have any interest in pharmacy. I've been thinking more along the lines of professional ballerina."

"You're too tall," Rick said. "Ballerinas are more petite. Not to be judgey," he added.

I wasn't ready to face that ugly truth yet, thank you very much for forcing it in my face. "Maybe I won't grow any more," I said in denial.

"Too late," he said, rubbing salt in the wound. He let off the brake and slipped away from the curb.

As we bumped down the library driveway, an identical sleek black car passed us, heading into the parking lot. Steve followed it with his eyes.

"Reinforcements? For picking up little me? Isn't that overkill?" I asked.

Rick shook his head. "Nah. They're not with us." He smiled at his father. "A day late and a dollar short again, huh?" He stepped on the accelerator and jerked away while the other car was busy turning around.

Agent Steve made a hmming noise. He held up the governors' letters he'd pulled from my purse.

"Give me those," I yelled. "You can't go through my purse!"

"Yes, I can. Reasonable suspicion. And I've got a warrant," he said automatically. "From the looks of these printouts, I'd say you should be thinking more along the lines of espionage, intelligence, covert-ops. Young lady, you seem to have a flair for stirring up a mess of trouble. I think we'd rather have you on our side. Maybe you should consider the Academy."

"Which Academy would that be?"

"If I told you, he'd have to kill you," Turner said, pointing to his son. "Don't worry. When it's time, rest assured, we'll find you."

I harumphed. "Why does that not surprise me? How'd you find me this time? Follow me from home?"

Rick jumped in. "Nope. As soon as you were ret-scanned at the library, we got an alert. We had a bunch of systems tagged to watch for you."

"Wait," I argued. "There's no ret-scan at the library."

"Sure there is," he countered. "All public computers have that built in to their vidcam. How do you think we track the terrorists who bounce around from library to library?"

"What? When did this happen?" So much for the sanctity of the public library. Now it was just another lens in the great national security spycam.

"Last time the Watchdog Alert Act was renewed we slipped it in."

Turner Senior cleared his throat. "Rick, don't you think that's enough state secrets for today?"

The car pulled to a stop in front of Arby's.

"Well ain't that ironic," I said. "They're killing all the real watchdogs with one hand and installing electronic ones with the other. God bless America. Let freedom ring." I was going to become as cynical as Rody at this rate. "Are you going to cuff me?"

"What are you talking about?" Rick asked. "We're getting dinner, not arresting you."

"Dinner? What time is it? My Mom's going to totally freak if I'm not there when she gets home."

Rick smiled at me. "Relax, Ms. Maddox. Tor. It's only quarter to five."

I suddenly had an idea. "Are you sure? I'd better check." I pulled my phone out of my pocket. "Yeah. Okay." As soon as they turned to exit the car, my thumbs started flying. I texted Sasha: *help rescue @ new arby now now now.* I stuffed the phone back in my pocket and prayed.

We sat at a booth in the back, me sipping my hard-earned jamocha shake, the men digging into their trays of food. I had to ask. "Do you guys always wear those glasses? For creeps sake, we're in a restaurant."

"Sorry," they said together, and pulled them off in a perfectly synchronized gesture, like a chorus line of two. I stared across the table at four of the bluest eyes I'd ever seen, deep turquoise and long lashed. My heart skipped a beat. It took me a moment to catch my breath.

"Holy spit! Are those registered weapons?"

Turner crinkled his beautiful eyes with an inner laugh, and Rick blushed and looked down. Woohoo. I made a man in black blush.

"No, seriously," I continued. "If you guys really were clones, maybe those could be bionic eyes that shoot lasers or conceal cameras or zoom lenses or infrared detectors."

Turner whistled tunelessly, innocently, and looked away.

"Not really?! That is so cool. Which is it?" I asked. Then I caught the twinkle in his twin pools. "You're mocking me, aren't you?" I turned back to my milkshake in exasperation. Men. In black.

Rick made a peace offering, sliding his curly fries halfway across the table. "You sure you don't want any?"

"No, thanks," I said, but he left them there.

In spite of my resolution not to weaken, I couldn't help noticing one perfect golden-brown coil, a monster in the middle of the short spirals. I had to have it. My hand darted forward to snatch one end of the curly fry. By some hideous coincidence, Rick's fingers reached the same one, and it sproinged like an overstretched slinky between us. I shot him a glare through my eyelashes.

He deflected it with devastating smile that would have turned hostile missiles back along their paths. "You know, one of us is going to have to give or it'll break," he warned softly. "And I want it all."

I lost my grip. Literally. The prize dangled from his hand. He devoured it with a blissful expression that made my toes curl.

Well, two could play that game. I plunged a salty curl into the sweet depths of my milkshake, swirled it around, and raised it to my lips. Rick watched with an expression that was no doubt calculated to look innocent, but I caught a flicker of a laugh deep inside.

A fleeting thought dashed through my head—wasn't he way too young for an official government agent? But then again, his father was what they call well-preserved. Even without cloning, it probably ran in the family. Maybe he was older than he appeared.

Turner took the lead. "Okay, Ms. Maddox. To business." What game were they playing now? Good cop, good cop?

"To business," I echoed, lifting my milkshake in a toast. Rick laughed and clinked it with his soda. His dad glared at him.

"Ms. Maddox. If you please. Be serious. You're in over your head. Someone is using you to make some rather unpleasant allegations about the government, which poses a serious degree of risk. We'd like to get you out of the loop now, for your own safety."

He said it so nicely, like he was honestly concerned, that in fact, I did feel a tremor of fear. "Why did you guys send that search copter out then? It scared the living creeps out of me."

The Turners exchanged a look. Steve rubbed his clean-shaved chin. "I'm sorry. If you saw a helicopter, it wasn't one of ours. Ms. Maddox, I'm trying to be nice and friendly and non-threatening here, but it's very, very important that we get the information we need before...before the copter people do find you and take you out of your home for questioning in a more serious and scary environment. I'd rather you told us here and now who is leaking information to you. We're the good guys."

"No one." I was a rock.

"Who told you which governors to contact?" He waved the letters at me. Rick grabbed them and looked at them for the first time.

"No one. I swear. I emailed all of them. All fifty. Minus Hawaii. Those are the four who replied."

"Our analysts will be able to take apart that computer trail and trace your correspondence. We can check your story."

"Check away," I said. "It's the truth."

He jumped as if he'd been bitten then pulled a buzzing cell phone out of his pocket.

"Turner. Hmmm. Mmmm. Hmmm. Ninety-six? Okay. Will do. Yeah? Right. Hmmm. Really? Okay." He placed the phone on the table in slo-mo.

"Who did you correspond with today, Ms. Maddox? We've got the library wireless records and the computer in the trunk, but you'll save Rick a very late night if you just tell me."

"And I'd really, really appreciate it," Rick put in.

He was so cute and earnest, I was almost convinced. I'd be helping him. He'd be grateful. Maybe very grateful. I might as well. He'd figure it out anyway.

But then he said, "I was hoping to be up for the Georgetown-Penn game tomorrow. So if you're willing to cooperate—"

Spill my secret plan? So he could watch football? Seriously? I snapped in the heat of the moment. "Why should I? You never believe me. I plead the second."

Steve intervened. "Ms. Maddox, that's the right to bear arms."

"Oh, spit. I plead whatever is the right not to tell you anything."

"Self-incrimination? That's the fifth. But we're not accusing you of anything except being a pawn in someone's political game. That someone is using you as a conduit to get to some people, to tell people some things that our boss would rather handle more delicately."

"He would rather not have everyone know about the dog slaughter? Well, no spit," I said boldly. Could they really trace everything I did today? I decided not to give anything away for free. "All I did was collect my mail, the mail you are still holding, by the way..." I glared at Rick pointedly.

He looked up from the letter. "Huh? I'm sorry. Did you say something to me? Agent Turner, have you seen these letters?" His father nodded. "This is...this is appalling if true."

"He doesn't know?" I asked Turner. "You didn't know?" I asked Rick.

"Is it true?" he asked his father.

"That's not the point," the senior agent responded. "The point is that someone in a government office has breeched confidentiality to blow the whistle on a massive scale. We need to bring in that person."

A light bulb suddenly came on inside my head. So *www.governmentsecrets.us* wasn't a conspiracy nut. He was someone within the government, maybe at the CDC or in the West Wing. Oooh. This was very interesting.

"But Agent Turner, Dad, you don't understand. I took Springer to the vet last week. He tested positive, a flu carrier. They told me—"

"They told you to keep your claim check in a safe place," I filled in. "They told you that ninety-five percent get better, and they'd call when you could pick him up."

He nodded, his mouth grim.

"I'm sorry, Rick. I am *so* sorry." It's true. I was. "But think about this. If they could fool you, how many other people have been fooled? Who's really the dupe? Me, or everyone else?"

Rick's face turned red, but he didn't say a word. I couldn't tell if it was embarrassment, anger, or grief. Maybe all three, a painful combination.

"One more chance, Ms. Maddox." Turner said patiently. "Who's Sashay96? Is that the person posting the antigovernment blog?"

Behind him, the restaurant door opened. My heart leapt. "Sashay96? He's my dance partner. We were supposed to practice tonight. Weren't we Sasha?" Thank gladness his clothes—a tight black tank and loose gray sweatpants—matched my hasty fabrication.

Sasha took in the scene in one glance, slid into the booth next to me, and rested his arm on my shoulder. "I waited and waited for you, Tor," he improvised. "What happened?"

"Oh dear," I said innocently. "Didn't you get my email? I was unexpectedly held up at the library," and at the words held up, I stuck a finger into his waist, like a gun, "and then these two gentlemen" (extra emphasis) "offered me a ride home in their shiny black government car. Didn't you guys? Except they wanted to stop for a bite on the way."

"You guys don't mind if I steal Tor away now, do you?" Sasha asked without really asking. "We've only got the studio for another hour."

Steve's eyebrows lowered in concentration. "You're a dancer, eh? Ballroom?"

I could tell Turner was sizing up Sasha with his experienced eye and dismissing him as the possible government turncoat. Sasha was sizing up Rick. Rick was staring at me. What a cat's cradle of looks we were all giving each other across the table.

Sasha slid out from the booth and stood. Then he oh-so-elegantly raised his foot over his head and balanced in a vertical splits stretch, toes pointed to the ceiling. Rick's eyes went wide, and Turner scrunched up his face as if in severe pain.

"Not ballroom," Sasha replied. "Ballet." He lowered his leg and reached out a hand to me. "Shall we?"

I smiled at Turner. His glower promised I'd pay for this soon, but for now he wasn't going to make a scene. I left the restaurant on Sasha's arm, and anyone watching should have known that at least part of it was true—we knew how to move together.

Here I was again in Sasha's car. All I could think of was how grateful I was to be rescued. "Thank you, thank you. Thank you for saving me from the evil federal agents."

"They didn't seem evil," Sasha commented. "In fact the young one was rather pretty."

"Hey. I saw him first," I said, punching him in the arm. "Don't even think about it."

CHAPTER THIRTEEN

NEW YOU

"So what's really going on?" Sasha demanded.

"Did you get my email?"

"Email? No, I thought you were just making that up. I haven't been home yet. In fact, I was heading that way when you screamed for help."

"Well, when you get home, you'll find I forwarded you four letters from state governors willing to back me up when I go up against the President. Hey, watch the light!"

Screeech. "Sorry. I was distracted. I thought you said you are going up against the President."

"I did."

"Uh, which president?" Sasha asked.

"THE President. Of these United States. Hail to the Chief. You know." I hummed a few bars. "Dun dun da dun dun…"

Sasha absorbed this confession in silence for a moment. "So that's why those Feds were buying you milkshakes?"

"Well, no. They don't even know about me threatening the President with exposure. At least, I don't think they do. Yet. They've been after me ever since I started talking to CNN." Screeeech. "For creeps sake, Sasha, would you watch the road?"

He swerved back into the middle of the proper lane. "Sorry. But if you're going to keep saying such outrageous things, you can't expect me to drive. Start at the beginning."

So I did. I ended up finishing the story in my driveway. "I don't know what kind of serious and scary interrogation room Turner had in mind, but I'm really glad you came, because they weren't happy with my answers."

I don't even know if they could secretly interrogate a minor anyway, but who knew anymore? Obviously a lot of the protections I took for granted didn't actually exist. Maybe they would keep me awake till I broke down or deny me chocolate when I had PMS. Something hideous and cruel. I had no idea whether to believe Turner when he claimed to be a good guy looking out for me and the "inside person."

The other problem was, I really didn't know who *was* on the inside. Or even what the inside was. All I knew was that he'd promised in front of the internet and everyone that he'd be there for me when I needed him. That time was coming up fast.

Sasha came around the car and opened my door for me. "Why don't you get your dance bag and come back to my house? No one's there. We can download and make new copies of those letters for you. Tell your mom I'll drive you to class tonight."

"Sounds like a plan," I said. Mom was surprisingly agreeable even though it meant I would miss the chicken pot pie she was fixing. She really liked Sasha.

"Rody will be happy to eat your share," she said in answer to my apology.

"Does that mean he's feeling better?" I asked with great hope.

"Yes, it does," she said. "A good long day in bed is the best thing for a bad cold."

I sighed with relief. A bad cold. Not deadly flu. Praise be. I didn't have to go forward in life as an only child with fratricide (brother killing—that's the special word for it) on my conscience.

"Love you, Mom. You're the best. You'll be there at pick-up time, right?"

She uh-huhed and gave me a peck on the cheek. "Dance pretty."

Cocoa bounced around my legs, holding his leash in his teeth, anxious to be out and about in a hostile world. Who could blame him? His internal clock still told him it was past walk time, and he didn't follow the news. "Hang in there, boy," I told him. "I'm doing what I can."

Sasha drove like the wind to his house. I'd never been there before, and it was weird to actually pay a visit to Sasha-land. It was extremely tidy and carefully decorated. His folks weren't home yet, working late again in their lab at the university. He put a couple of frozen enchiladas in the microwave to heat up while we checked his email.

"What's the subject line I'm looking for?" he asked, scanning the list, while my eyes went down the sender column.

That was weird. There wasn't anything from Joe Citizen's account. "I didn't use one," I answered. "But it's not there anyway. Here, check the bulk folder. Maybe it hit a spam filter."

We both looked down the list. Nothing.

"Sorry, Tor. Are you sure you sent it to me? Maybe you sent it to Sioux-san."

"No. It was definitely to you." My shoulders sagged. The long arm of the Feds had somehow reached into Sasha's host server and grabbed his mail before he could see it. That wasn't right. That was totally out of line. That was a serious violation of our sacred right to communicate in private. I hoped my big, dusty, unreachable tome was safe. Surely they wouldn't tear apart the library looking for copies. Would they?

I didn't say anything to Sasha. I didn't want him to feel as creeped out as I did. I wondered if *www.governmentsecrets.us* was aware of the intense scrutiny, aware that his every word was being scanned for clues, aware that his account was being traced. Whoever he was, he must be really good at covering his own tracks or they wouldn't still be trying to find him through me.

"Can I check my mail here?" I asked Sasha. "I'm afraid my computer's bugged."

"Sure thing."

I went to my host site and tried to log in as Joe. *User id and password do not match.* Oops. Must have typed too fast. I tried to log in again, typing very carefully. *User id and password do not match.* I entered the email address and clicked *Forgot your password.* Instantly the mail host returned *User id unknown.*

All right, now I was freaping furious. Someone, not me, had closed Joe Citizen's account in the last couple hours. I wouldn't be getting any more responses to my letters. They would bounce back. The recipients would think I was a stupid prankster. My face glowed hot with helpless anger and embarrassment.

I wasn't expecting an email response from El Presidente, obviously, but I had really been hoping for one from Alex Fletcher. Only one thing to do. I opened up two new accounts with a different provider, using new names.

Through one of them, I sent: *Dear Alex: it's me again, Joe Citizen, but the Feds are monitoring and shutting down my communication channels. I have to find another way of getting through to you. I have really important information to deliver, proof of involvement at the highest level. I don't know whether you even got my last email or whether it was intercepted. Don't respond to me at this name. Use gadfly@hushmail.net.*

"Think that'll work?" Sasha asked.

"I hope so." I sighed. "I really hope so."

When I got home from dance, Rody was scarfing down a bowl of popcorn in front of the TV. Mom and Dad were nowhere in sight. Cocoa snoozed next to him.

I grabbed a handful of sweet kettle corn. "Hey, Rode, can I borrow your phone a minute?" At the sound of my voice, Cocoa sat up and pawed the air, his sign for *Please feed me*. I tossed him a fluffy kernel, which he snapped out of the air.

"Use your own," Rody said, holding the popcorn bowl closer on his lap.

"I can't. I'm pretty sure it's tapped or bugged."

"Yeah, right," he said.

"No, really," I protested. "Know why I was late this afternoon and why I missed dinner?"

He grunted, which I took as a request to go on. "I was waylaid and dragged off by the men in black. They questioned me ruthlessly for hours." I tossed Cocoa my last popcorn and dusted my hands on my jeans.

Rody turned and looked at me with a little smile. "Yeah, right. So why did they let you go? Did you hi-yah-wheel-kick them unconscious?"

"Ugh. Imbecile. No. Sasha rescued me."

Rody's eyebrows quirked up. "Sasha rescued you? What, he disabled them with a grand jeté?"

"Oh, shut down. He just waltzed me out from under their noses. They couldn't make a scene in a public place."

"Which was where?"

"Arby's."

"Arby's? They interrogated you ruthlessly at Arby's? Did they threaten to burn your eyes out with horsey sauce or something?"

I blushed. "No. They bought me a jamocha shake, actually."

"Sounds scary," he said.

"Puhleeese! Just let me use your phone. You don't know what these guys are capable of." Even Rody's silent smile was sarcastic. I huffed. "Technologically, I mean."

"Fine." He pulled the warm phone from his pocket, and turned back to the TV.

I connected to check the hushmail site. There it was. Hallelujah. The answer to my prayers. A letter from Alex himself: *Dear Joe, can you come into town for a meeting/interview? I want to see what you've got and hear what you've got in mind.*

Using the gadfly account, I sent back: *Yes, I can come. But probably not until Sunday. It will take me a little while to arrange things here. Send next communication to snoopy@hushmail.net.* So that was fabulous. But now, how was I going to get to Atlanta from San Diego?

"Are you done yet?" Rody asked.

"You can use my phone," I offered. "I can't risk it."

"What are you doing now that's soooo top secret?"

"If I told you, I'd have to kill you." Spit. I would have told him if he hadn't asked that way. Why did he have to be so...so like that?

I fumbled around for a while, trying to figure out how to use Expedia and nearly died when I saw the cost of a flight. Eight hundred dollars! That would totally use up my birthday money and the twenty I had in my wallet and I'd still be short.

"Rody, can I borrow about three hundred dollars?" I asked.

Popcorn sprayed out of his mouth. "What? Why?" Cocoa dove for the crumbs.

"I need it," I said.

"Not good enough. Why?" he insisted.

Groan. So I had to tell him, which ended up saving me a lot of trouble, actually.

"Why don't you just ask Mom or Dad to take you?" he asked.

"Are you nuts? Can you imagine in your wildest dreams that they would say yes? If I tell them anything, it will all end in tears (Mom's) and violence (Dad's)."

Rody snorted with laughter.

I didn't see what was so funny. "Right. You agree. This is something I know I have to do alone. All alone....So will you help me?"

He stared at me for a moment. Then he closed his eyes and mumbled.

"What?"

"They will so kill me," he said sadly.

"And? Your point?"

"I'm trying to decide if it's worth it," he said with exasperating calm.

Taking a cue, I answered just as calmly. "Rody, *no one* else is doing anything. It's just going on and on, every minute of every day. Think how many Taliskers per hour that might be. Think how many other girls like Sioux have had their hearts broken."

I had struck the right nerve. He saw my point. And although he pretended to be totally unimpressed with the idea that I was going to Atlanta to meet with Alex the announcer to reveal my evidence against the Chief Executive, he did make a good point: "They should pay for it." Made sense.

"So how do I—?"

"Just write back and ask him to make all the arrangements."

"Oh. Okay."

Simple enough. Sort of. I went into the new Snoopy account and found there was already a letter waiting for me. It was after one in the morning in Atlanta. Alex kept awfully late hours.

Dear Joe: my staff will make all the arrangements, but we'll need your departure city and a name that matches your photo ID.

Oh spit. Identification. Somehow I didn't think my Poway High Student ID or my dance studio ID was going to get me on an airplane by myself. I was going to have to look eighteen and have documentation to prove it. Hmm. What would Joe Citizen's real name be? Got it. T. Oliver Maddox.

I sent Alex the information he needed and a new email address to contact me at. This jumping accounts thing was working out great. I couldn't imagine how my darkly dressed friends would ever get a handle on me this way. Serve them right for stealing my letters and my secondary backup. Tomorrow, I needed to fetch my real backup from the library.

"Do you think it's too late to call Sioux?" I asked Rody.

"Naw. We were going to facetime at eleven anyway, after this show's over."

My brother? Facetiming a girl? Wow. Will wonders never cease?

I hit the call button on Rody's phone. Just as I suspected, her number was right on top of the recently called list. She answered breathlessly, like she'd just run to get it. "Hey Rody! I thought we were on for eleven? What's up?"

"Hey Sioux," I said. "I'm up."

She giggled. "Tor! What are you doing on his phone?"

"Mine's bugged," I said. Probably. "Look, I need some serious help."

"Anything." Sweet girl, she didn't even hesitate.

"Can you help me find an outfit that makes me look

at least eighteen? And do you know anyone at school who can get me a fake ID?"

"A fake ID? Torrance Olivia what are you trying to pull off?" she whispered into the phone.

"I'm going to Atlanta on Sunday," I said calmly. "I'm going to CNN headquarters to tape an interview with Alex." At least I hoped that's what I was doing.

"You're going to be on CNN? With Alex Fletcher? I hate you!" she whisper-screamed. "Okay, I'm on the job. The mall opens at ten Saturday but my Mom has dibs on the car. How are we going to get there?"

"Sasha will give us a ride," I said confidently. Thank gladness I had best friends I could count on through thick and thin.

Sasha, good old dependable Sasha, was on my doorstep at nine thirty sharp. Blade was waiting in the front passenger seat, so I slid into the back.

"Hey, Blade," I said, determined to be nice since he was going to be a regular factor in my friendship with Sasha. I wasn't going to create some stupid "he's my friend," "No, he's my friend" contest. I despised girls who played that game. I wasn't going to be one.

"Hey, Tor. Sasha told me about your aging project. At school I'm chief costume tech for the drama department, so he pulled me in as a consultant. I hope that's okay with you."

"Hey, I'll take all the help I can get," I said. "I put myself into your expert hands."

He turned around, studying my face while Sasha drove. "Eighteen, huh? That's definitely doable. You want to shoot for older?"

"Why not? Let's see what you can do."

So Sasha and Blade and Sioux, who would normally be voted "least likely to play Barbies" spent an hour with me in the "Professional Dress" section of Macy's. They finally settled on a gorgeous dark brown pantsuit with a copper-colored silky blouse underneath. It was very autumn. It was fabulous (even though I could feel the spirits of Valaree and Sophe whispering in my ears, *Not brown and orange!*). The price tag was unreal, but I wasn't paying for my own airfare, so I was still ahead. Sort of. The sales clerk looked a little surprised when I paid with a fistful of twenty dollar bills. "Birthday cash," I explained.

Blade pointed to the escalator. "Make-up counter," he ordered.

I automatically covered my cheeks with my hands. "Make-up? Do I have to? I hate putting stuff on my face." I really did. For dance recitals, we had to goop up with foundation, powder, blush, liner, lips, lashes, lids, the works. It made me feel plastic.

"Trust me, Tor," Blade pleaded. "We'll age you ten years."

I had this awful vision of added wrinkles and bags under my eyes, a sagging chin, a splash of gray. But Sasha stole my baseball cap, and Blade gave the make-up lady at the counter instructions, and I sat there and took it. Finally they turned the counter mirror so I could see myself. Except it wasn't me. Some college girl stared back at me, her head mysteriously transplanted to my body.

Sioux bit her lip. "I hate you. You're gorgeous. If your dad sees you, he's going to lock you in the stone tower and throw away the key."

I smiled. My friends made me feel pretty. Even in my scruffy jeans and brown t-shirt.

But Blade wasn't done with me. "Okay Rapunzel," he said. "Let's buy this stuff then go to Heads Up to take care of *this*." He let my long, long pony tail slide through his fingers.

"My hair? No, no, no. Don't touch my hair."

"Trust me, Tor," Blade said again. It was his refrain for the day, apparently. They dragged me kicking and screaming (well, in my mind anyway) to Heads Up. Just my luck, there was an unoccupied chair and an unoccupied stylist who introduced herself as Tami. Blade picked up a style book, leafing through it while my hair was washed.

Tami the stylist wrapped a warm towel around my head. "Pretty hair," she said. "What did you have in mind today? Trimming the split ends? A long layer cut?"

Blade held out the open book to her and pointed.

She looked back and forth between me and the picture, like an artist studying a blank canvas. "You sure?"

Blade nodded.

"Lemme see," I begged.

Blade slammed the book shut. "Nope. No peeking."

Sioux had one hand over her mouth, a stunned expression on her face.

"What?" I said. "What? Tell me!"

Blade laid a finger across his lips. "Shhh. It's a surprise. Close your eyes, Tor."

I sighed heavily. For twenty minutes, there was a

horrifying sound of snipping all around my head, then some brushing and blow drying action. Maybe a smidge of mousse. I couldn't see, but I smelled vanilla and almond.

"All set," Tami said at last. "Ready for the new you?"

"No," I admitted. I opened my lowered eyes. All around the base of the chair were long snakes of wet brown hair. My hair. *Blade, what have you done?* Very carefully, I raised my eyes to the mirror. I stared in silence, hardly breathing. Then I screamed.

"Do...do you hate it?" Tami asked, her eyes welling with tears.

I jumped out of the chair and hugged her. "I love it. I can't believe it. That isn't me!"

Sioux fist bumped Blade. "That was the point, wasn't it?"

"Sasha? Opinion?" I prompted, grinning from ear to ear.

"Oh, chica. You are unsafe at any speed," he said. He and Blade high-fived.

"Thanks, Blade. You're brilliant," I said. "Of course, I never doubted you."

I gave Tami a ten dollar tip and hugged her again. She gave me her card for next time. I carefully ran my fingers through my short, soft-feathered hair. It was so fluffy and it curved around my cheeks, ending in irregular spikes at chin level. As we walked toward the five dollar photo booth, I glanced in the store windows just to bask in the sight of my new reflection.

We took a whole strip of my pics, then we all crammed into the booth in various combinations for some memory shots. Blade kept my face shots so he could make me a genuine fake California driver's license—a man of many talents, it seemed. I was feeling so happy and generous, I bought everyone lunch. What the hey. It was only money.

They dropped me and Sioux off together at my house. Sioux walked in first, mischief on her face, to make sure Rody was there. At first, he didn't see me, and he greeted her with a slow kiss. I watched, terrified and fascinated. It was so weird, yet stirring at the same time. Then she said, "I brought someone with me..."

I stepped into view and Rody got his first look at the new me. The seconds ticked by in his eyes as his brain tried to register what he was seeing. Hee hee. Perfect. He laughed and said, "Good God, Tor. You've been busy."

Understatement. I laughed, too. "Do you think Mom and Dad will approve?"

"Mom possibly. Dad—I wouldn't count on it. I don't think he can call you his little *punkin* looking like that."

I was strangely flattered. "Where are they?" I prompted.

"Still playing tennis."

Cocoa bounded into the kitchen at the sound of our voices. I swear, if dogs could do a double spit-take, Cocoa would have. He ran toward me with a happy bark, looked up, skidded to a stop, feet scattering everywhere, reversed course, dashed behind Rody, and gave a warning "stranger" bark.

"Cocoa, you silly," I said, holding out my hand. He sniffed suspiciously, gave a doggish shrug, and retired to his cedar bed to glare at me with one open eye. I'd have to bribe him later with a gingersnap.

"Hey Rode, can I check my mail?" I asked.

He tossed me his phone without protest, and I logged into my current account.

Alex had written back: *There will be an eticket in your name for a morning flight on Sunday.* He listed the flight details. *You'll be met at the airport and we'll take it from there. Looking forward to it.*

I had a nine o'clock in the morning flight to Atlanta on Sunday that got me in after six p.m. (curse the time change) and a return late Monday afternoon. Boy, they didn't mess around.

I released the breath I'd been holding for weeks. Wow. It was really happening. It was all really happening.

"Sioux," I said in a shaky voice. "It's really happening. Can you do me one more favor?"

So she and Rody walked over to the library hand in hand to collect my hidden evidence while I stayed home and texted Sasha (since his email was being watched by my shadows): *Time for the next step. I'm going to Atlanta tomorrow. I'll need a ride. Can you pick me up at 5:30 a.m. on the corner? And bring my ID?*

I hadn't told him about the whole CNN thing yet, just in case the MIB picked him up for questioning. All he knew was that I now had a second identity as T. Oliver Maddox.

Sure thing, he texted back immediately. I loved him. No questions asked, just ready to help out.

Mom and Dad got back from tennis a little while later. The front door rattled, and I hurried to pose myself in the front hallway. The door swung open, and Mom and Dad froze on the threshold, staring at me open-mouthed. Mom's racquet slid from her hand and clattered on the floor. Dad dropped the can of balls he was holding. The top popped off and they rolled away. He cleared his throat.

"Sunshine," he said to Mom. "I think she's growing up. Too fast, if you ask me."

Mom dashed a tear out of her eye and collected herself. "Torrance, you look lovely. Very grown up indeed. What brought all this on? Your birthday present?"

Dad smiled knowingly. "I'll bet it started with that Homecoming dance. Didn't it, punkin?" He called me punkin. Cheers. "I guess it was coming sooner or later, but I'm sure going to miss that pony tail of yours. May I?" He stroked my new hair, smiling a dadly smile. "Very cute," he said.

"Make-up?" Mom asked. "I thought you hated it."

"Um. I do. I did. But you can't fight progress." I smiled helplessly. Taking a cue from Dad, I added, "All the sophomore girls wear a little make-up. I figured I'd better start blending in."

"That's not exactly—" Dad started.

"Well, it's quite effective," Mom said. "I'm just not so sure I want my sweet sixteen-year-old daughter having that effect, if you know what I mean."

"Oh, Mom. Don't be silly. I'm still me."

She looked at my Dad telepathically, but neither one said what they were thinking.

Cocoa nudged a tennis ball into my hand and licked my knuckles.

I excused myself as soon as I could. "I already ate lunch at the mall, so I think I'll go up and get started on my homework."

Ditching yet another day of school was not going to help my academic record at all. I wanted to make sure I got everything done today for Rody to turn in for me on Monday. Plus, I had to pack an overnight bag. My stomach fluttered with nerves. Spit. It was really *happening!*

I might look twenty-something and have the paperwork to prove it, but I was still freshly sixteen inside, let's face it.

Rody woke up early to send me off in the morning. I was touched. Even Cocoa got out of his dog bed with a huge yawn and a stretch when he heard me sneaking down the stairs. Nothing gets past him. He padded quietly over to me and flumped down across the toes of my high heels, pinning me in place.

"Say hi to Alex for me," Rody joked.

I guess to him this was all some abstract adventure. I was the one living it. "Hope this works," I said tremulously.

"It will," he confirmed. "You'll make it work."

Wow. I think that was the nicest thing he ever said to me. All choked up inside, I couldn't reply. Just nodded.

He handed me a tiny flash drive. "Here. Don't forget this. I hope it helps."

Good gladness, his evidence video. I had completely forgotten. "Of course. Thanks. I was just about to ask you for it," I said. No sense in confessing, not while he had so much confidence in me.

He gestured upstairs. "You better leave before they get up. I'll cover for you as long as I can, tell them you caught my cold or something."

"Okay then." I slid my feet out from under the dog. "Bye, Cocoa. Wish me luck." I kissed him on the top of his fuzzy head. He flapped his ears and trotted back to bed.

I tiptoed out of the house. Didn't look like anyone was surveilling me this early in the morning. Sasha's car was standing at the corner, water vapor from the exhaust pipe condensing in the cool morning air. My brown high heels click-clicked on the sidewalk. I walked with confidence, head high. Blade hopped out of the passenger seat and opened a door for me. These guys were real gentlemen.

"Tor, my masterpiece!" he said. "Your chariot awaits. Don't snag your pants on the suitcases."

"Suitcases?" The back seat had two suitcases on one side. "What are the suitcases for?"

Sasha shrugged. "You said you needed a ride to Atlanta. That's not a one day trip, you know. I figured we'd need some luggage."

"Oh, Sasha, Blade. I don't believe it. I love you guys. You dropped everything to drive me to Atlanta? But I just need a ride to the airport. I'm flying. Didn't I say that?"

They looked at each other. "Oh." "Oh."

"But a road trip would have been fun," I said meekly. "Sorry. Maybe next time I run away."

CHAPTER FOURTEEN

ON THE FLY

I had flown plenty of times for vacations, so I knew the routine. Being all carry-on was easy. I typed my faux-name in at the eticket machine and out came my boarding pass. Like magic. Security barely looked at the freshly printed driver's license that I held out to them with shaky hands. My overnight bag and I went through x-ray without any holdup. So there I was, at the gate, incredibly early, ready to fly. Should have brought a book. My head was spinny.

Now that it was crunch time, I had to figure out how I was going to get Alex to agree to my deal—we would tape the interview including my evidence for their special report, but hold running it while the clock counted down on the President's deadline. I glanced at my watch. Thirty-six hours to go. I needed a drink. A good stiff Coke with all the sugar and caffeine.

After watching planes take off through the window for fifteen minutes, I broke down and wandered over to the bookstore. I grabbed a soda out of the fridge and a spy thriller from the best seller shelf. That wasn't my usual kind of reading, but somehow it fit with changing my identity, sneaking off in the early morning, flying across the country alone, and holding secret meetings with hot evidence in hand. Well, spit. My life was probably more interesting than the story I had just paid $14.95 for.

But I didn't want to think about my life. For a few hours, I needed a break. I started reading and didn't look up till they announced boarding. My purse and carry-on clutched tightly to my side, I held out my boarding pass for the flight attendant. She studied it far more carefully than security had. I gulped.

"T. Oliver—that's an unusual name," she said in a friendly voice.

"My Mom's maiden name, uh, it's Oliver," I improvised. "I go by Tee, though."

"Cute. Have a nice flight today, Tee." She scanned the boarding pass and handed it back to me. "Next, please."

Whew. Another hurdle cleared. I headed down the jetway to the clump of people waiting to board, made it back to my row, and placed my purse and carryon between my feet. Taking no chances. Ah, a window seat. How nice of Alex's people to arrange that at such short notice. I pulled out my book, which had become quite gripping by this point, and started reading. The plane gradually filled around me.

The intercom crackled. "Please take your seats, everyone, buckle up, and stow your tray tables in preparation for pull back. Please pay attention to the important safety instructions on the monitor."

I didn't bother looking up. I could recite them by heart. I knew that in the unlikely event of a water landing my seat cushion could be used as a flotation device and that if there were a sudden drop in cabin pressure, an oxygen mask would drop out of the compartment above my head. The instructions didn't say anything of more immediate concern, like what to do if an air marshal suddenly pulled me off the plane before take-off.

As the flight attendants went down the aisle, slamming the overhead bins shut, I relaxed. I was in the clear. *I did it, I did it,* I congratulated myself. And it looked like I was going to have the whole three seats to myself. Hallelujah. My heart raced. *And so, the adventure begins,* my internal documentary narrator announced. *Not really,* I corrected. *It began weeks ago. We just didn't know it.*

I was still paying attention more to my book than to my surroundings when a dark-suited man slid into the middle seat next to me. I turned to suggest that he take the aisle seat to give us both more room. Then I had a heart attack and died. Holy spit.

"Good morning, Ms. Maddox," said Agent Rick Turner. Pocketing his traditional dark glasses, he looked me over in a half-second assessment and nodded as if he'd figured something out. They must train them to do that. Make snap judgments based on observation, I mean. "Nice suit," he said. "Are you going to tell me why we're going to Atlanta?"

"We? WE?" I hissed. "I didn't invite you along, you know. If you have a problem with it, get off the plane." Cornered cat, spitting and hissing at large, friendly-looking dog with sharp white teeth. If I could have made my hair stand up on end, I'm sure I would have.

"Don't go all stro on me," he said, whatever the

heck that means. "I'm just along for the ride. Curious, that's all."

"I so don't believe that," I said. "You're not here to stop me?"

"My instructions are only to follow and observe. So that's what I'm doing. Observing." He paused, observing. "I like what you've done with your hair. Very spiff."

"Thank you." There was a long silence, the kind they call pregnant because it's heavy and feels like it lasts for nine months. "If you don't mind my asking, how'd you find me? I thought I was extremely careful."

He laughed, and his turquoise eyes lit up like sunlight sparkling on the warm Hawaiian ocean. I imagined throwing on a bikini and diving in for a swim. Whoa.

"You did a creditable job, for an amateur," he said, "but we were already watching Alex Fletcher's mail for any more communication from you. It was a cinch to pick up your new accounts."

"Spit. Never thought of that."

"No. But they'll teach you to think like that at the Agency."

"Which Agency would that be?" I asked.

He arched an eyebrow. "Just let me know if you're interested. The summer internships are still taking applications."

"You're kidding, right?"

"Only half," he replied. "That's how I got started in intelligence. You should consider it. You've got potential."

"Potential intelligence? Gee, thanks." I expected

him to laugh, but his eyes went all soft and serious on me.

"Tor, you've got a rare and precious quality—certainty that the world can be a better place, and you're going to help push it there, come hell or high water."

An incredible warm feeling spread through me, and I relaxed. He wasn't here to drag me off to prison or a secret interrogation gulag. In some strange way, he was in my camp, even if the Oval Office considered me some kind of junior enemy combatant. Or a disobedient civilian. I still wasn't quite sure what his role was here, though. A thought occurred. "If you read Alex's mail, then you already know why I'm going to Atlanta. And you know I still have my letters in spite of your best efforts to steal them." A small victory, but I gave myself a mental pat on the back.

"Where did you keep them, anyway?" he asked. "We knew there was another set somewhere."

"How?! How'd you know that?"

"From the printer log."

Man, these guys were smart. "In the library," I said. "Inside a dusty old out-of-date atlas."

"Good thinking." The approval in his eyes made my insides all woozy again, in a good way. "What are you reading?"

I tilted the cover toward him. He laughed, a friendly, casual chuckle. "So that explains it. Your burning interest in cloak and dagger work."

"Not really," I said. "I usually read chick lit. Believe it or not, this is my very first attempt to overthrow the government."

"Hmm," he hummed thoughtfully. "You're not doing a half bad job of it. Who's your guy on the inside?" he added off-handedly.

I sighed. "You still don't believe me. I have no idea. No one told me about H3N1. I just figured it out from reading a few websites. No one told me about the slaughter. I figured it out from what I saw at the vet. Plus I may have inherited my Mom's intuition."

Rick raised a questioning eyebrow.

"She just seems to know things, without anyone actually telling her. She reads between the lines."

"That's an excellent trait to have in intelligence work."

"Geez, are you a talent scout for the mystery agency?" I asked.

He smiled hugely. "We all are. Part of our job description. That and teach people the secret handshake."

"Secret handshake?! You're kidding, right?"

"Only half." He took my right hand in a firm grip and tickled my palm with his pinkie. It made my toes curl. I giggled.

"I'll remember that," I joked.

"That way you'll know when you're talking to someone safe, one of us."

"What do you mean?" I honestly couldn't tell if he was kidding or not.

"We're the good guys, remember?"

You know, I'd been hiding and running from them for so long, I'd sort of forgotten that. At least in theory they were the good guys. Defenders of liberty and all. Who was their boss? What was their goal? Did they report to this President or did they transcend the four-year administrations, see them as passing scenery on a long distance trip.

As an invisible hand pushed me back into my seat, I realized that we had taxied and taken off without my noticing. "We're on our way!" I said.

"To what?" he asked.

"I don't know," I confessed.

"Well, I'll enjoy observing." He winked. Winked! Zap went my toes.

I let the roar of the engines and the steep climb mold me to the cushion. I tilted my head toward Rick. I could feel my eyes smiling at him. I was awfully glad that if someone was going to follow me across the country, it was him, not Turner (much as I liked him) or Solly.

"Did you really kick Solly down on your front lawn?" he asked.

Ack. How'd he do that? Another mind reader? "I did," I said. "But I honestly didn't know he was expecting twins. Now I feel awful about it."

"Really?" His eyebrows lifted in a skeptical tilt.

"A bit. Yeah, a bit." However, in spite of myself, I savored the memory of unleashing that powerful kick and having it work so well. I knew I could have disarmed him if Turner hadn't grabbed me.

"I didn't think so," he said lightly. A tiny smile turned up the corners of his mouth. It made me want to kiss him. His eyes flew wide. Oh spit. I had to control my thoughts better. This was ridiculous.

"Excuse me, folks," the flight attendant broke in as she slid to a halt next to Rick. "What can I get you, sir?

Ma'am?"

Saved by the drink cart! "I'll take a ginger ale, please," I requested.

"Make mine a double," Rick said. The flight attendant gave him a dimpled, flirty smile. She served us and pulled away to the next group. "May I see your ID?" Rick asked me.

"For ginger ale?"

"No. For Homeland Security. I want to know what it takes to get on an airplane these days."

"Is that your department? Homeland Security?" I burned with curiosity.

He gave me the standard answer. "If I told you…"

"Yeah, yeah, yeah. I get it. Here. What do you think? Will they let me rent a car?"

The look on his face was priceless. Like I would really try to rent a car. "Listen here, Ms. Maddox. I would no more let you get behind the wheel—"

"Kidding!" I interrupted. "Geez. I've only got my permit. You think I'm nuts?"

"Well…yes. Sometimes," he answered. (Fair enough. I thought so, too.) "This isn't a bad job." He critically eyeballed the ID Blade had made for me. "Hmm. Twenty-two might be pushing it a bit."

"How old are you anyway?" I asked.

"Twenty," he replied. "So if you're going to be older than—"

"Hang on. Twenty? Are you a super-genius? Graduate from high school at fourteen?"

He blushed. "Not quite. Seventeen. No, I'm doing a co-op year between sophomore and junior year at Georgetown."

"Oh. That explains it. A co-op year." I drained my ginger ale and crunched an ice cube while I tried to puzzle it out. "I have no idea what that means," I finally confessed.

"Sorry. Keep forgetting how young you are," he said. (I flinched inside.) "Co-op is paid work experience in the middle of college. I'm normally based in D.C. doing analysis for the Agency."

"When you aren't shadowing criminal suspects like me, you mean."

"Right." He refilled my plastic cup from the can the flight attendant had left on my tray table. "Congratulations. You're my first field assignment."

"I feel special," I quipped.

"You are special," he said in a tone that made my breath catch. "So what's with T. Oliver? How'd you get away with that at security?"

"I told them Oliver is my Mom's maiden name and that my name is TEE. But anyway, there are so many girls floating around out there with boy names like Randall and Tyler and William, it isn't much of a stretch." I blathered on with my neck pulse banging fast and loud against my eardrums. "There's probably a cute little Oliver in pink out there somewhere."

"Probably," he agreed. He reached under the seat ahead for his briefcase. "Mind if I read a little? I've got some casework to catch up on."

"Go ahead. You don't need to entertain me. I've got my book."

So during the rest of the hour that it takes to go three hundred miles by air, we read quietly until touchdown in Phoenix. At least, he read. I was distracted by the way he scanned and flipped a page every fifteen seconds, and by the faint scent of bodywash that wafted from his shoulder beside me, and by the way his nostrils flared just slightly every time he breathed in and relaxed when he breathed out.

And the math. That distracted me as well. Twenty minus sixteen was four years. Four very long years. Twenty-five percent too old for me. Totally out of my league. Way. Don't even go there. But the little calculator in my head clicked and said, sure, that's *now*. But in five years, that'll be only nineteen percent. In eight years only a sixth. And by the time you have grandchildren, it'll be like down to nothing, no difference at all.

His head tilted just a smidge, and his eyes swerved over to catch me staring.

I stammered. "Did I...did I say something?"

"Grandchildren?" he asked, his eyebrows practically touching.

"Grand...grand journey!" I snapped out. "Look, we're landing." Ack. And we were, thank gladness, or my idiocy would have been complete.

Our connecting gate was only a few doors away, but we were late enough that boarding had already started.

"See you at the other end," Rick said as I found my seat near the front.

"Oh." I was faintly disappointed. "You aren't, you didn't...?"

"Your row was already booked when I made my reservation."

"Surely someone with your super secret powers

could have rebooked them," I suggested.

"Gotta draw the line on abuse of power somewhere," he said. "Have a good flight."

When they finally told us to make sure our tray tables were stowed and our seats were in the fully upright position in preparation for landing at Atlanta airport, I was almost done with my book. My eyes were blurry. I began to question what I was doing so far from home. I began to worry that Mom had run around crying when she inevitably found out I was gone again. Had Rody caved yet and told her how far away I really was? They'd go all stro, whatever that meant.

I didn't have a good plan for getting to CNN Central except for hailing a taxi. Being a San Diegan, of course, where the average household has one point three cars per person, I had no idea how to hail a taxi or how much one might cost. Imagine my delight when a guy in a chauffeurish suit was hanging just past the secured area with a sign that said *Mr. Maddox.*

I bounded up to him. "You must be my ride."

"*Mister* Maddox?" His voice rang with doubt.

"It's an assumed identity," I whispered.

His eyes slid over me in a rather strip searchish way. "I'll say," he said. "Do you have checked luggage?"

I shook my head. He held out his hand for my small carryon. I swung it over my shoulder. "That's okay. I've got it." I wasn't going to risk letting those printouts out of my hands ever again.

"You can call me Bill," he said. "Please come with me, *Mister* Maddox." He lingered again on the word Mister. I suppose he considered himself funny.

I followed behind him, a good four inches taller in my heels, attempting a graceful, confident stride. The bald spot on the crown of his head bobbed at my eye level. When we reached the sliding exit doors, I glanced back over my shoulder to see whether I was still being shadowed. Two unfamiliar men in black stood with their backs to me. Rick was talking to them, pointing back toward the gate area. With the raised hand, he ever so subtly waved me away. The two strangers took off toward the gates. My heart filled with joy. He was letting me go.

Then a suspicion entered my mind. "Bill. Are you with CNN or the Agency?"

I pictured myself stepping innocently into a black car without door handles which would drive me off to God knows where. Knowing Team Turner, they might have arranged this second ride for me, straight to the Agency's dark, secret interrogation rooms where they would threaten to torture me with strawberry smoothies or something. My real driver might be lying bound and gagged in a broom closet in the airport.

Bill snorted. "Agency? Alex Fletcher's office at CNN booked transport to your hotel. Were you expecting a different arrangement?"

"Not if you weren't," I said in a voice filled with mystery.

"Very well, *Mister* Maddox."

"That's getting old," I complained. "How about just calling me Tee."

"Very well, *Miss* Tee."

I sighed. Not much better. But I was spared the necessity of listening to it repeatedly in the car. A privacy window separated me from Bill, and even though I tried to focus on the view out the tinted windows, my eyes were so heavy that I gave in and let them close. I catnapped while the car sped quietly along the highway. The sound of my door opening startled me awake. I glanced at my watch. Almost seven. The President had twenty-six hours of sand left in his hour-glass.

Bill helped me out of the back seat, not that I needed it. Oh, spit. Was I supposed to tip him? I had only twenties and a couple of singles. Too much or too little. So no tip. Save us both a lot of embarrassment.

The building in front of me was immense, with *Omni Hotel* in big letters to the right side and *CNN* on the left. My heart skipped a beat. I was here.

"Miss Tee, this is your hotel. The room is reserved in your, ah, assumed name. Please feel free to charge any legitimate expenses to the room. I'll pick you up at eight tomorrow morning and take you to your meeting."

Bill pulled away, leaving me on the doorstep of the Omni with an overnight bag on my shoulder. Even at six foot something in my business-like suit and heels, I felt very, very little. I wanted my Dad to check us in. I wanted my Mom to figure out where we were going for dinner. I wanted Rody to nag me to put on a swimsuit and help him find the hotel pool. It wasn't the same without them. Shoot. Even a Turner would be welcome company. The huge lump in my throat made it hard to swallow.

A doorman coughed into his white glove, and I realized he'd been holding the door for me. "Check-in is over there, ma'am." He pointed across a huge, absolutely gorgeous lobby awash with highly polished hardwood. The gleaming floor included an inlaid compass design, which I took as an omen. I was right where I was supposed to be.

"Any more luggage?" the doorman asked, looking at my dinky shoulder bag.

"No," I said. "Er, the airline misplaced my suitcase."

"I'm sorry to hear that," he said. "Our concierge will be happy to provide you with a complimentary emergency kit." I bet they would in a swish place like this.

Check-in worked like magic. I passed inspection. No one demanded to know what a sixteen-year-old was doing masquerading as a legal adult. The desk agent handed me the keycard, explained about the restaurants, and pointed me toward the elevator.

I clicked across the polished floor, overwhelmed with splendor, and elevated to the fifteenth floor to find my room. It was huge, with picture windows providing a panoramic view of the city and Olympic Park down below and the color streaked sky above.

I tossed my bag onto one of the double beds and sat down. Shoes and knee highs came off first. I stepped out of my grown-up clothes and hung them up carefully for tomorrow. From the bag I retrieved my black dance leggings and a t-shirt from last year's Nutcracker show. I reached for the ceiling, flopped over to touch my toes, and automatically reached for my hair to gather it into a bun. My hands closed on air. Oh, how my dance teachers would kill me! Well, it was entirely too late for haircut remorse, and, anyway, I liked it this short. Ceiling, toes. Ceiling, toes. My travel-weary legs gradually loosened.

In spite of the time change, the coming night fooled my stomach into believing I had skipped dinner. The idea of dining alone in a fancy restaurant was rather bleak, so I pulled out the room service menu. Holy spit. The prices! Continental breakfast was twenty dollars! Dinner would be at least forty. I suppose I could charge CNN for a salad—chicken Caesar—and a diet cola. I had barely hung up, when a knock and muffled "Room service!" penetrated the silence. Amazing! You sure get what you pay for in these fancy places.

I had two dollars ready for the tip as I opened the door.

My surprised face reflected back at me from a pair of sunglasses.

"Thanks, Ms. Maddox, but that's not necessary," Agent Rick said. He was standing in my hotel, in my doorway, holding a pizza box.

"What…what are you doing here?"

"Bringing you pizza," he said. "I didn't think you'd want to go to a restaurant tonight, plus my expense account doesn't go that far."

"I just ordered a salad," I protested.

"Good thinking. We can have it with the pizza. So are you going to let me in or keep me here with my hands burning?"

I stepped back. "Oh, sorry. There's, um, a table over there." Well, the man had pizza. It wasn't like I was going to send him away. Not immediately. Plus it appeared that he had saved me from the other guys at the airport, so it was only polite to share my salad.

Rick proceeded to make himself annoyingly at

home. He carried only a briefcase on a shoulder strap, which he tossed onto the empty bed. Then he pulled off his necktie, rolled it up into a spiral, stuffed it into a pocket, and shrugged off his jacket. His glasses and a rental car key he set on top of the TV cabinet. It appeared that he was moving in.

I was trying to formulate an appropriately biting comment when real room service arrived with the salad. Rick tipped the server.

"Hey, I was going to do that," I said.

"My treat," he offered. "Actually, your tax dollars, so don't worry about it."

"I don't pay taxes yet," I said, just to be fair and honest. "But my parents do."

"So that's okay, then." Rick smiled in the nicest way and took a water from the mini-bar. "I guess this one's on CNN. Cheers." He clinked my soda can.

I smiled back. This could be fun, sitting at our little table, sharing pizza and salad. I felt much better than I had in hours, ever since he'd waved goodbye in Phoenix. After dinner, he broke out a Toblerone candy from the mini-bar and split it, handing half to me.

"Dessert," he explained. "You have to end a meal with chocolate."

Much as I agreed about chocolate, I was a little worried about racking up a mini-bar bill. Dad never lets us get anything from them, says they're like an overpriced convenience store.

Rick smiled as I hesitated. "CNN won't mind," he said, reading my thoughts again. "Really. What do you want to watch?"

"How about CNN? The founder of the feast," I

suggested.

"News?"

"Yeah, I've been out of touch since yesterday. I need to know if I missed any important announcements."

"Are you expecting one? Has it gotten that far?" he asked, studying me closely. His face changed in an instant from the friendly guy bringing pizza to the agent who was surveilling me.

"No. Why do you ask?" I snapped. Drat the man. He was just too perceptive. I wondered how they trained up clairvoyance or if it came naturally to him.

"Just some crazy notion, I guess. So who would be making this announcement you aren't expecting? Maybe I can get some advance notice on it. I've got other sources."

I stared him down for a half a minute. Okay. It was more like he stared me down. Like for ten seconds. I broke first. "The CDC. Or the President. I hope." I glowered at him, mad at him for making me want to tell.

Must be those stupid cerulean eyes. Which twinkled.

"You aim high," he said.

"No sense aiming too low," I retorted. 'You'll just hit the ground."

"True enough," he said. "True enough."

"True enough," I echoed. "So are you going to tell me who you really work for and why you aren't dragging me back to San Diego?"

"Nope." He perched on the end of the second bed with the remote.

"Not fair." I pretended to pout, which had no effect.

No effect whatsoever.

"CNN it is." He clicked the TV to the right station.

"Thanks."

Out of the corner of my eye, because I certainly wasn't watching his every move, I saw him unbutton his shirt cuffs and roll up his sleeves. His forearms, which I'd never seen before come to think of it, were surprisingly tanned and athletic. Did he lift? Play tennis? Swim? Alligator wrestle?

He continued to perch, elbows on knees, chin in his hands, studying the screen.

We watched a full cycle of news till the repeats started with no hints that something big was about to break. "I guess...I guess not," I said in a low voice. "I guess that's it for now."

"Are you okay?" he asked.

"Yeah, of course." I stuffed my disappointment down. Why did I ever let myself hope this would be easy? "Let's watch something else now."

Rick convinced me to switch to a pay-flix, mentioning a movie I'd been dying to see.

"What about the bill?" I asked. "You know what they charge for those?"

"I'll pick it up," he said with an unexpected smile. "I'll have the desk separate out all the extra stuff. Will that make you feel better?"

An unexpected burst of guilt and gratitude floored me. I nodded.

Facing the movie, I flopped on my stomach on my bed, feet bent up behind me. Rick leaned back on the second bed's pillows and kicked off his black loafers. I noticed a hole in the toe of one sock. It made him seem more ordinary somehow.

It was a good movie, but parts of it kept disappearing into mini-dreams. Even with the three-hour time change, my brain demanded sleep. I drifted in and out of the plot, in and out of consciousness. One time I reopened my eyes, I noticed Rick watching me instead of the movie.

"What? Was I snoring?" I asked groggily.

"Nope. But you look all done in. Why don't you catch some real Z's. You've got a big day tomorrow."

I didn't try to play dumb. I guess by now I took it for granted that he knew all my secrets.

"Kay." I slid off the bed to go wash my face and brush my teeth. When I came back to the room, he had the covers turned down. "You can...go now," I said warily. "Bye."

He shook his head, no. "Can't. I've got orders to follow."

"You don't need to surveille me anymore today. I'm going to be asleep in three seconds. Nothing interesting is going to happen. I promise."

He crossed his arms and rolled his eyes ceilingward. "Tor, you're a sixteen-year-old girl three thousand miles away from home in a big city. I'm going to stay here to make sure nothing bad happens to you. I'm quite sure your father would appreciate it."

"How sure are you?" I had a terrible suspicion.

"*Very* sure."

"Yeah?"

He nodded, tight lipped.

"You already talked to him, didn't you?" I mentally cringed at the tense conversation I imagined. "How did you calm him down?"

"I used the words *national security matter* and I gave him my word I'd watch over you like a *brother.*"

"That's not very reassuring," I said. "I have a brother. I know brothers." I admit that was doing Rody an injustice, but it had to be said.

"Yes, well, it seemed to reassure your father. Under the circumstances."

"Circumstances?" I thought about it for a hot second. Combine college guy, hotel room, three thousand miles from home, nubile teenage girl (that is, potentially tempting in a way I couldn't really let myself imagine in case he read my mind again). Gulp.

"Hmm. I can see that it would. Okay. Good night. *Brother Rick.*" I slid between the sheets, which were deliciously warm from lying on top of them. "Why are you being so nice to me?" I murmured drowsily.

He sank down on his ankles to my eye level. "Remember? My old Springer was an early casualty. Poor old guy was already ten, on his last legs, but I had him since I was in fifth grade. Now I can't help feeling that I lost him through carelessness. I didn't ask enough questions. The questions you *did* ask. So you see, I'm kind of rooting for you. Is your dog okay?"

"Yeah. Cocoa's great. Thank gladness." I sank into the pillows. "He was sick for a while, but he threw it off. He's a strong little mutt...resilient...feisty."

"Good. Glad to hear it. He takes after his owner."

Through heavy lids, I thought I saw his hand move toward my cheek, my hair, but he was only pulling the blanket up to my chin. "Get some sleep. I'll try not to disturb you."

"Why? Do you snore at night?" I asked.

"No. I type. Lots of analysis reports to catch up on."

"S'okay. Won't bug me. M'already asleep," I muttered. That's how tired I was. This amazing, nice Federal Agent-in-training with azure eyes just bought me dinner and a movie and tucked me into bed, and I fell asleep without another thought.

Well, just one. If Sioux could see this, she would scream.

CHAPTER FIFTEEN

GOVERNMENT SECRETS

The waft of coffee and a strange buzzing woke me. My eyes cracked open. A hotel room? Where was I? Oh yeah. CNN. Atlanta. Omni. What time was it? The clock on the TV said seven. I had only an hour to prepare myself. I hit all the clock radio buttons, but the buzzing droned on.

A warm buttery smell demanded my attention. Two silver pots, two cups, and a basket of flaky croissants over on the little table beckoned me. Lots of food, and I was starving. I slid out of bed. On my way to the bathroom, I tripped over a pair of men's shoes. Oh spit! How could I forget? That's why there was a strange vibration coming from the bathroom. That's why there were two cups. I knocked. "Are you almost done?" I called in.

Rick cracked open the door. My heart skipped a beat. His white shirt was unbuttoned, and his hair was towel damp and crazy. "Hey, you're up. Good. I was just about to wake you."

How? I wondered, and immediately clamped down on my imagination.

He made a stretchy face as he swiped the electric

razor across his upper lip. "Did you help yourself to a hot drink? I didn't know if you drank coffee, so I ordered some hot chocolate as well."

Before I could stop myself, I blurted, "My dossier doesn't say that I take three heaping teaspoons of sugar and lots of milk? You mean there's actually something the government doesn't already know about me?"

He smeared some goop on his hands and ruffled his dark hair, watching my face in the mirror. "I know it seems that way sometimes," he said. "It's the times we live in, I guess. Anyway, the government doesn't know that your hair sticks straight up in the morning."

My hands flew to my head. "Now it does."

He grinned. "Tell you what. I'll leave that out of the official report." He pulled a comb through his hair and handed it to me. "Okay. Bathroom's all yours."

I'd never shared a comb before. Not like this, in the morning, with someone half-dressed and freshly out of the shower, where only moments before he'd been entirely—I swallowed hard and found my voice. "Hey, thanks for thinking of the hot chocolate. Didn't you get any sleep?"

He was bleary-eyed and dark-circled this morning. Not that it was a bad look for him.

"Not much," he said. "I've got a lot going on."

I followed him back to the table, where he poured a cup of black coffee and gulped it with a grateful look on his face. His shirt still hung open over his black suit pants, and I tried not to stare by concentrating all my attention on pulling apart a croissant. Crumbs fluttered everywhere.

He plonked down the empty coffee cup and started

buttoning. "I'd better leave so you can get ready."

I kicked myself for the flash of disappointment. "What are you going to do now?" I couldn't help asking.

"Oh, this and that." He tucked in his shirt tails and reached for his jacket.

"Hmm. This and that. Sounds like a crazy day then. Will I, uh, will I see you later?" I had been ready to do this trip all on my own, but I was big enough to admit that there was definite comfort in a familiar face. Especially his familiar face.

"I think that's going to depend on how the day plays out," he said. His arms disappeared into the sleeves. "That's about all I can say."

"Whew. You guys are secretive. Okay. Um." I held out my right hand. "Bye, I guess? Thanks for everything—for calling Dad. For guarding me." Somehow my intended handshake turned into a longer hand hold. I loosened my fingers with regret, to be honest, and let my hand drop.

Rick patted my vertical hairdo. "Seeya, Spike. Good luck with your operation."

I had this momentary flash forward—like reverse déjà vu—like one day he'd say those words again and I'd remember this moment. Weird.

Now I had only forty-five minutes to get myself down to the lobby, so I showered as fast as humanly possible. Seems like they hadn't heard of low-flow shower heads here in Georgia, and the cascade of water was like swimming under a hot waterfall. I yearned to lean against the wall, close my eyes, and enjoy it, but I needed time to blow dry my new hair and figure out how to do my make-up. I was downstairs in the lobby right on time, looking like a million bucks on steroids. Hair was moussed and coiffed, cheeks lightly tinted, lashes long and dark, lips shimmering to match my bronze blouse.

It was wasted on Bill, who was standing there frowning at his watch and tapping one polished shoe.

"Hey. I'm right on time," I said.

"So you are. Please walk this way with me."

"We're not driving?" I asked. Bill's stolid face cracked into a dubious smile. Now I knew how far from home I was. If this had been California, we would have driven next door.

I followed Bill to the lower level atrium of the CNN Central complex. For a news junkie like me, this was my hajj, my pilgrimage. The main floor was just starting to bustle for the day—shops were opening (of course coffee had been available for hours). The live stage was being set for the afternoon show. The world's longest free standing escalator was a conveyor belt to my personal heaven, leading from the main floor to the upper atrium level where the studios and offices began. It all happened up there.

Security guards were hanging out at all the exits, as well as at the top and bottom of the escalator. Pretty much everywhere. Made me wonder. "Hey Bill. How many guards are there in this building?"

His eyes narrowed. "Is there a reason you ask?"

"I'm making conversation. I'm curious. What? You think I'm a security risk?"

He looked me over, from my high heels to my little

pearl earrings, the ones I got for my thirteenth birthday. "Nah," he concluded. "But I still can't tell you. Rules."

Soon we reached a security checkpoint into the office area. I flashed my fake ID and signed the log with my assumed name. The attendant compared me and the picture, which obviously matched. He didn't run the fake card through any kind of mag-reader device, thank gladness. Blade wasn't that sophisticated—the stripe was a blank. Then only the final barrier loomed, the retina scan. Please don't let it be hooked up to an alarm, I prayed. I had no idea if these things did real time feedback. But I didn't see any kind of attached screen that would announce my real name and flag a mismatch. Heart thumping, I let myself be ret-scanned and hoped that it would just end up in a computer somewhere. I counted to ten. No alarm bells. No nets falling out of the ceiling.

I was in.

Still, my heart raced. It was actually happening. When I first set this plan in motion I only half-believed I could pull it off. Now here I was, bearing the weight of responsibility for millions of dogs. No one else had stepped forward to speak for them in the two weeks that the protective-isolation-murder-plot had been in effect. Time was running out on man's best friend. If I didn't blow the dog whistle, so to speak, who would?

"This way, Miss Tee," Bill said.

Eventually, I found myself in the small waiting room of an office suite. Bill exchanged a few quiet words with the receptionist, who buzzed in to pass the word along.

A moment later, Alex Fletcher stepped from his office. He looked almost exactly like himself, only smaller. His welcoming smile turned to puzzlement. "T. Oliver Maddox? Really?"

I stuck out my hand and shook his. "Torrance Olivia. Tor for short," I said.

"For short?" He laughed. So I outsized him by a couple of inches. Story of my life. But he had a friendly grin that helped calm my nerves. "Let's talk in my office for a few minutes before we do the real interview on camera," he suggested.

Alex's office was furnished with two dark green leather chairs and a small cherry-wood side table at one end, a bookcase on the wall behind. The opposite wall was all window. It was arranged subtly like a set, and I spied around for hidden cameras—not that I'd see them if they were hidden.

"Can I offer you coffee? Or a Coke?" he asked.

"A Diet Coke would be great, thanks." Anything to keep my hands from fidgeting with nerves.

Alex opened a section of paneled wall to reveal a well-stocked mini-fridge below and a shelf of glassware above. He handed me a glass and a cold soda. "Please. Make yourself comfortable." He pointed to one green leather chair. From the other, he studied me wordlessly. Was that a journalistic technique? A waiting game? Was I supposed to break down and confess?

I broke. "I have the governors' letters," I said in a rush. "With names. And a video showing the terrible truth behind 'protective isolation' at several veterinary clinics. But I have one condition before I turn them over to you."

"What's that?"

"I've given the President a deadline to respond with a change of policy before I go public with this information. I want you to honor that deadline. And I want final say on whether to run or kill my interview."

Alex frowned. "Ms. Maddox, without your evidence, our story has a one-hour half-life. I've rounded up a couple of veterinarians willing to talk about coercion, but no one inside the conspiracy willing to talk and no one to point the finger upward. I'd be going out on a limb to cover it at all. The government has plausible deniability. You know what that is?"

"Yeah, yeah. They can claim the veterinarians were rogues acting on their own. I know. I'm sorry. But I promised the governors I'd wait until after the election if they agreed to cooperate. If I'm going to break Joe Citizen's word and totally screw these four governors, I've got to have the utmost reason."

"How old are you, Ms. Maddox, if you don't mind my asking?"

"Would you believe twenty-two?" I asked. He shook his head. "Would you believe sixteen?"

"Holy cannoli." He steepled his fingers under his chin. His eyebrows bounced up and down, reflecting the inner workings of his mind. "Fascinating. *Sixteen-year-old girl calls President to account.* Now that's got some teeth. I like it. And I *want* to run it. What exactly are you after, Ms. Maddox? Publicity? Your fifteen minutes of fame?"

Fame? That was the last thing on my mind. In fact, up until this moment, with everything falling so perfectly into place, I had myself convinced that I'd never have to run this interview. The President was supposed to fall for my bluff at the last minute, see reason, pull back, and step down to quarantine again. Now I had this sickening feeling that it might actually end up that I wasn't bluffing after all. Truly, I'd never expected the story to run. It was the rudder I was using to try to redirect the ship of state, the lever I was applying to the immovable object.

"I just want to save the poor dogs," I replied frankly. "The ones left to save, that is. Do you have any idea of the casualties so far?"

"No. But I'll find out." He jotted himself a note. "All right, Ms. Maddox. I'll agree to your terms." He held out his hand to shake on it. Either that, or to get the letters from me.

"Can I get that in writing?" I asked, not offering either my hand or the letters.

"Suspicious, aren't you?"

"Yeah, well that's why we're here today, isn't it?"

"Fair enough. We'll work it into your release." He called to the outer office and gave the receptionist a few quick instructions. Then, "Yes, sure. Send her in." He gave me a half-apologetic smile. "I hope you don't mind, but Dr. Wave is here to meet you. She wants to know who independently cracked the H3N1 source mystery. I told her you were...I mean, Joe was coming in today."

"Narlee? For real?" How great was this?

"This should be fun," Alex muttered under his breath.

Two seconds later, there she was, larger than life.

Public voice and face of the CDC. She stared at me. Her face squeezed in on itself, as if something sour had burped up into her mouth. "Joe Citizen?" she asked. "You're Joe Citizen?"

"Yep. Yes, I am," I said. I sat up ballerina straight and fixed her with my most serious and steady gaze.

She squinted back. "Oh, Chrisicles. This must be some kind of joke. Are you sure?"

"Of course I'm sure. What do you mean?"

An unflattering look of disbelief crossed her face. "Don't try to tell me you have a virology lab."

"Of course I don't," I said. "I'm a freaping tenth grader."

"Then who else was doing viral analysis? Who told you the results?" she demanded.

I crossed my arms and sighed. "How come no one believes that this wasn't so hard to figure out?" And why was she being so weird about it?

Narlee just stared at me, and the realization eventually sank in. They must have spent months running test after test to reach the same conclusions that I had. But was that why they were so slow to announce the results? Or were they just trying to slip it in under the radar, hoping it would stay invisible until after the election? I didn't want to believe that.

A strangled laugh sounded from the outer office, and a smallish, gray-haired woman appeared in the doorway behind Narlee.

"Hey, who's she? Who let her in here?" Alex asked.

"I hope you don't mind, Alex," Narlee said. "My admin assistant. She's a huge fan and has been begging to get a glimpse of you. She insisted on coming today."

"I'm sorry. This isn't a good time—" Alex began, but the woman strode forward in her tidy white blouse and brown skirt and comfortable maroon loafers. She stuck out her hand.

Not to Alex. To me.

"This is the one I really wanted to meet," she said in an odd tone. I shook her hand politely. She fixed me with a pointed stare. "Milly Baxter at your service. I said I'd be there for you. When you asked."

"Holy spit." This was rather unexpected.

I mouthed: *Government secrets dot u s?*

She nodded.

"Holy spit." I could hardly believe it. I squeezed her hand extra hard, for support.

"Mildred, what are you talking about?" Narlee demanded.

"Dr. Wave, enough is enough. I can't keep quiet any longer."

Narlee's chest rose as she drew a furious breath. "Mildred, you are my confidential assistant. Got that? *Confidential.* Do you know how high they hang whistle blowers in this government? And how deep they bury them afterwards? I've worked damned hard to get where I am today, and if you screw it up for me, so help me, I'll provide the shovel."

Yikes! "Well, that answers one of my questions," I interjected.

"And what's that, Ms. Maddox?" Alex asked. He was watching the interplay as if it were a three-way tennis match.

"The one about whether Narlee was ignorant, incompetent, or evil."

"How dare you…" Narlee raised a hand as if to slice me with her manicured nails. Then she noticed Alex watching her and turned the gesture aside, pretending to sweep a hair out of her face. "Alex, I'm quite prepared to answer any ridiculous, laughable allegations these two may care to bring."

"On camera?" he asked. Narlee nodded emphatically.

Alex's mouth twitched like a cat's whiskers, just before the pounce. "Ms. Baxter, are you in, too?"

She patted her blouse smooth and squared her shoulders. "Yes, I believe I am," she said. "And I'm sorely ashamed that I hid behind an anonymous website for so long."

"Mildred, you may consider yourself fired, effective immediately," Narlee said, her jaw tight and eyes narrowed.

Milly smoothed the sleeves of her blouse again. "Dr. Wave, my letter of resignation and early retirement papers are already signed and on your desk."

The only reaction from Narlee was a loud huff.

"Okay ladies. Now that the formalities are out of the way, shall we get started?" Alex looked strangely amused by all the drama. A small chuckle escaped him.

"What?" I asked.

"I was all prepared for Joe Citizen, not this." He gestured to the three of us.

Ha. Me neither. "Roll the camera and start the questions, Alex," I said, aiming a hard look at Dr. Wave. "I'm ready." I glanced at my watch.

The President had less than twelve hours.

We sat behind one of those official news desks.

Make-up people patted our faces with powder so we wouldn't shine. Camera men clutched venti cups of Starbucks like life preservers. Production assistants with clipboards threaded tiny lapel mics up inside our shirts.

"Good to go?" Alex asked me. The muscles in my back and neck clenched with nerves, but I managed a tiny nod. He gave the cameras a sign, and the red recording lights came on.

He paused for three seconds, putting on his anchorman face. "My guest, Ms. Torrance Maddox, is a remarkable young woman. Working only with a computer and her powers of observation, she figured out and tipped off the CDC about the source of the New Flu infection over a month ago. Now, she brings some serious criticism of the protective isolation policy the CDC has imposed in thirty states to combat the New Flu strain of canine influenza. Ms. Maddox, please tell us about these allegations."

I took a deep breath, swallowed the lump that had suddenly invaded my throat, and began. "Mr. Fletcher, from my internet research, I know that in farming, outbreaks of deadly diseases like avian flu and mad cow are controlled by what they call *culling*, that is, killing any flock or herd that contains sick animals. They do that when quarantine just won't work. I guess that in the back of my mind, I realized the easiest way for the government to stop the new epidemic in its tracks is to kill all the dogs. Eliminate the carrier. Shoot the messenger. But I never imagined that our pets would be treated so drastically. Then when I took my own dog to the vet, I saw that it was actually happening—someone at the highest levels of government had developed a plan to pretend to test the dogs, tell everyone their dog tested positive, take them away, and kill them in secret. That would guarantee an end to the spread of disease. Mr. Fletcher, I was horrified, and I had to speak out, no matter what."

Alex gave me a little nod that said I was doing fine. "So Ms. Maddox, you suspected that dogs were being secretly eliminated as part of a widespread plan. What proof do you have in support of your allegations of a government conspiracy?" He gestured subtly to the four pieces of paper I held in my hand as props (the real ones were locked in Alex's office safe along with my video). I took that as my cue.

Carefully avoiding any mention of their names or states, I told him about the four governors who were willing to testify that they were ordered to hoodwink their citizens into surrendering their dogs for slaughter.

Alex turned to Narlee for the rebuttal. "Dr. Wave, you claim the CDC ordered protective isolation for canines, not mass destruction. Am I correct?"

Narlee smiled demurely. "Of course you are. Goodness, we'd hardly send out soldiers in the night to slay people's pets. This is America. Many people voluntarily brought their pets to the humane society or to vets' offices requesting that they be destroyed. This is precisely the type of panic we are trying to avoid with universal testing. All the animals who have been temporarily removed from their owners have paperwork proving they are flu carriers."

"But the paperwork is faked!" I protested.

Narlee gave me a pitying look. "Honey, I know you personally found it hard to accept it when your dog turned out to have the New Flu—so hard that you ran away with him. You dragged him through your locality, exposing people and other dogs to the disease, breaking both the quarantine and protective isolation policies."

How did she know all that? "Okay, I did run away. But Cocoa recovered from the flu. It's not highly deadly to dogs. And I didn't catch it, and neither did my brother Rody—we had taken antiviral medication. It probably protected us."

"Oh really," Narlee said. "Now you're a medical expert?"

I raised my eyes to Alex, pleading for him to intervene. He didn't fail me.

"We have an accusation and a denial. Let's hear from the last person on this panel, an administrative assistant at the CDC. In fact, Dr. Wave's right hand woman. Milly Baxter, can you shed some light on these conflicting accounts of the protective isolation policy?"

Milly gave me the thumbs up sign. I realized she didn't know about my deal with the President, or with Alex. This was it for her career. She had laid it all on the line. I respected her hugely in that moment.

Her voice was soft, but controlled. "Mr. Fletcher, the CDC, under orders from the Chief Executive, ordered a plan called Protective Isolation which, in fact, consisted of removing dogs from their owners, under false pretenses if necessary, and destroying them."

Alex's eyebrows shot up. "Including healthy dogs?"

"Yes, Mr. Fletcher. Including healthy dogs. As a CDC insider, I was aware of the order, and I attempted to get this information out by leaking it through a blog site. It was cowardly of me, and I should have blown the whistle much sooner. Thank goodness Ms. Maddox was clever enough to read between the lines and had the gumption to do something about it. Her courage in stepping forward today brings this deception to light."

Oh great. She was calling me courageous. She didn't know that my greatest hope was *not* to have to air this interview.

Narlee broke in with her first honest reaction, a gut wrenching cry of, "Why, Milly? You knew the political realities. You knew we had to keep the country safe and the populace calm."

Milly shook her head sadly. "Dr. Wave, you know how much I've always admired you. But you're fooling no one but yourself with this talk of keeping the populace calm. How calm do you think people will be when they take their claim tickets back to their vets and find that, mysteriously, there are no survivors? You told me yourself that the quarantine was working well— dog owners were even more cooperative than your models had predicted. In three months we could have let the disease run its course and be back to normal. That's what you told all of us. Then you changed. What happened?" She let the accusing words hang in the air.

Dr. Wave remained speechless.

"I have the answer," I interjected. "Low pre-holiday sales in a shaky economy. Low election turnout predicted in a presidential election year. It wasn't about pandemic control. Am I right? It was about money and politics."

Narlee stared at me with a queer look. She had nothing to say, so I continued. "Mr. Fletcher, did you know there were sixty million dogs in this country a few weeks ago? How many are there now? Dr. Wave, how many are left? Can you tell me? Do you even know?"

She had the grace to look shamefaced.

Milly reached over and rested her hand on Narlee's arm. "Dr. Wave. Please. Don't cover for them any longer. It's beneath you. You're a scientist, a doctor, a healer."

"Narlee," I added gently, "don't underestimate the power of the light side. Tell Alex what's been going on. Tell him we don't need to kill any more dogs. You're the voice and face of the Centers for Disease Control. It's time for honesty."

Narlee looked over at me and Milly with large wet eyes. She took a deep, shuddering breath. "Okay then. Crisicles. Here goes everything. It's true. It's all true, Alex. The idea for protective isolation came from above. It made sense, the way it was presented, as a temporary vet-hospital sponsored quarantine. By the time I realized that it was a cover for eradication of the animal host, it had already begun in California. I told myself that we could always start over afterwards, repopulate California with new pets once the danger was past. Then the program spread east to other states, rushing ahead of the disease to completely healthy populations."

"Is it working to contain the New Flu?" Alex asked.

"Of course," Narlee answered with a sad shake of the head. "No dogs equals no flu. But as a protective measure it is inhumane and extreme and unnecessary. There is no reason for a single healthy dog to be destroyed as long as careful quarantine is observed. The government can protect pet owners by releasing the stockpile of antiviral medications that have been hoarded in preparation for a bioterrorism attack. Alex, there are tens of thousands of cases of N95 surgical filter masks in storage that could be distributed. Homeland Security has spent a lot of effort and money preparing for a man-made attack. Now, Nature herself is mounting an attack through random chance and mutations. We already *have* the tools to respond, Alex. We just need the go-ahead to use them."

"Thank you," I whispered to Narlee. Her eyes were wide and staring, her expression shell-shocked, like she couldn't quite believe what had come out of her mouth.

Alex cut the recording and thanked us sincerely. I bet he couldn't wait to get into the editing room to put it all together. The camera operators, who had, of course, been silent through the whole thing, gripped my hands and told me I had done a great service for the country. Milly gave me a big hug around the waist. Narlee shook my hand limply with a sad look that said, *Chrisicles. How did I let myself get talked into this?*

The last I saw of them, they were headed out the studio door together, not exactly speaking to each other, but at least together. Maybe Narlee would forgive Milly when she saw how much good could come out of this. Maybe she'd sleep better at night, too.

In his office, Alex gave me an autographed picture (I got another one for Sioux) and asked me how I wanted to spend the next few hours until my flight.

"Can I take the official tour?" I asked.

"Of course you can. Want to see the final version?"

"Um, sure," I said. "If I can. Will it be done before I have to leave?"

"Ah. Probably not. I've got a lot of editing to do as well as shooting all the connecting pieces. You'll just have to wait till it airs and be surprised."

Till it airs. Spit. I didn't want it to air. I didn't want to ruin Narlee's career. I didn't want Millie to resign. I didn't want to break my deal with the governors. I tried to smile back, but my cheeks wouldn't cooperate.

My voice shook a little when I reminded Alex of his promise not to run with it. Not yet. I had given the President until prime time tonight to respond (and he had to respond to this threat, didn't he?).

Alex nodded, but I could tell he was already taping, cutting, and editing in his imagination. It would have been a great special report. I hated to disappoint him with my caution. I hated to hang Millie and Narlee out to dry. But if the rest of the dogs were saved, I figured the ends justified my means.

"How should I get in touch with you later?" I asked.

He whipped out a cell phone and shared all his contact info with mine. I gulped. How many other people had Alex Fletcher's private line?

So. It was done. Almost. I felt exhausted and relieved. I felt like it was over.

Silly me.

CHAPTER SIXTEEN

THE TIME BARRIER

I left the building a little after eleven in the morning, wondering what to do with myself. The car was supposed to come for me at 2:00 in the lobby, and until then I was all dressed up with no place to go. The ups and downs of adrenalin had left me shivering and shaky.

I wandered across the street to see the Centennial Olympic Park, a welcome oasis of green in the middle of the city. I sat down on a bench, and for some reason, my eyes filled with tears until the park blurred into an Impressionist painting. I let them puddle until they broke free and ran down my cheeks.

A hand appeared over my shoulder proffering a white handkerchief. I turned a tear-streaked face to see Rick Turner. "Thax," I wept, applying the handkerchief to my stuffy nose. "How'd you find me?"

"GPS," he said simply. Duh. My phone was on. "Rough morning?"

"No. No, everything went perfectly," I said. "Better than I imagined. I'm just...I'm just tired, I guess. I want to go home." Another batch of tears broke loose.

Rick smiled ruefully and sat down beside me. He

put a comfortable arm around my shoulders and patted me.

"Why are you consorting with the enemy?" I asked with a sniffle.

"Who says you're the enemy?"

"I imagine your boss the President is thinking so right about now."

"Who says *he's* my boss?" Rick replied.

"Okay. *That's* a mysterious comment," I muttered, patting my face dry.

He smiled innocently and whistled three notes. "You want to get some lunch now or go standby on the 1:15 through Denver? It'll get you home a little faster."

"Way to change the subject, Rick." But it worked. "Do you think we could?"

"Hang on." He flipped open his phone and murmured to whoever was on the other end. "All set," he said. "I got us both seats, but we'll have to dash. Better?" He flicked the last runaway tear off the tip of my nose.

My heart melted. "Yes. Thank you. I'm beginning to think you can do anything. You know I've never seen you and Superman in the same room at the same time…"

"Shhh." He put a finger to his lips and pretended to look around covertly.

I whacked him with the damp handkerchief, which had no effect whatsoever. So I threw my arms around him and gave him a huge hug, which did. He hugged me back for about a millionth of a second, then gently peeled me off him and said gruffly, "Come on, little sister. We've got a plane to catch." Even after he let go,

I still felt the impression of his arms. I wondered if he still felt mine.

Rick watched with amusement as my fake ID got me through security twice. We bought banana-peach-mango yogurt smoothies and French fries for lunch, and sat in our gate departure lounge waiting for boarding.

"I knew he'd get around to torturing me with smoothies," I said to my spoon.

"Oh?" Rick's eyebrows arched all the way up to his hairline. "Someday, you're going to have to explain that comment to me."

He took his laptop out of its travel case. I'd bought another spy thriller, but I couldn't read. My mind was too tired. My brain jammed with static. My eyes rested on the CNN monitors running silent in the waiting area. I tried uselessly to read the announcer's lips.

The clock ticked. The sand ran down. When they called boarding, I was still waiting to see a late breaking announcement from the CDC or maybe even the President himself.

Rick kindly left me alone with my anxious thoughts as I turned page after unread page through the long flight. Perfect gentleman to the end, he drove me home from the airport through the hideous evening traffic and spectacular California sunset. It wasn't until we got to my freeway exit that he broke into my mental safe-room.

"So, mission accomplished, Tor?" he asked.

"Spit. I hope so. Watch the news tonight."

"You going to be on?" he asked in an innocent voice.

"Spit. I hope not. No, I definitely hope not."

He quietly mulled my answer over. "In real life, there are no bloodless battles," he commented and fell silent again. I could hear the gears of his busy mind whirring. I wished I could tell what was going on in there.

The sky was dark violet by the time we pulled into my driveway. The kitchen door flew wide, and Mom and Dad blasted out of the opening. They squeezed the breath out of me, pumped Rick's hand, dragged us inside. Dad was all over Rick with thanks for watching over his wayward daughter. Whatever he'd said to Dad on the phone had clearly made a good impression.

Mom wore a sort of hysterical version of her all's-well-that-ends-well face. She clenched one hand around mine to keep me from vanishing. Dad alternately beamed and glared at me, relieved at my independent (sort of) survival, furious that I'd set off without talking to them yet again. Honestly I was a little scared to lose sight of my bodyguard. He might be all that was standing between me and my parents and belated infanticide. I begged him to stay with my eyes. He smiled invisibly and leaned back against the kitchen counter.

Cocoa suddenly shot out of nowhere, ran straight past Rick, and tensed in front of the door, growling.

"Come here, boy," Rick called in a calm, commanding voice. Cocoa spun round and jumped up to greet him like an old friend, the door forgotten. Rick hooked a finger inside Cocoa's collar as he roughed up the scritchy spot behind his ears.

The doorbell rang.

Mom handed me a huge bowl of Milky Way bars. "You can get it," she said.

What? I opened the door to a tiny witch, a pirate, and an astronaut. "Twick a tweet," the witch said. Ah. I'd completely lost track of time. With the sudden onslaught of pint-sized candy-seekers and constant interruptions, Mom and Dad didn't grill me or Rick about the trip.

Rick kept the conversation fun, light, easy. My parents were dazzled and distracted, as I'm sure he planned. He handled them brilliantly.

Just as the doorbell dings slowed down, the kitchen timer dinged. Mom peeked into the oven, and a wonderful garlicky tomatoey smell filled the house.

"Rick, you will stay for a bite, won't you?" Mom asked.

Why he chose this moment to abandon me to my fate, I don't know, but he refused Mom's offer of lasagna, saying he had a lot of work to catch up on. Didn't he always? His eyes beckoned me as he headed to the door.

"Mom, Dad, I'll be right back. I'll, uh, see Rick out to his car."

I stood eye to eye with him, under a dark moonless sky, in front of his MIB-mobile. The stars reflected on the highly polished black roof, a parallel universe. We were only inches apart, and I could hear the even tempo of his breathing.

The pitter patter of the last little goblins ended as they disappeared inside with a joyful yelp, to count and trade their loot.

"That was fun," Rick said.

"The kids? Yeah, they're awfully cute."

Then I realized he wasn't just talking about handing out candy. He was talking about everything. For him, the mission *was* accomplished and over. He had protected and observed, and now he was going to vanish, as quickly as he had appeared only three days ago.

Three days? How could it be three days? I felt like I'd known him all my life. Or did my life really begin when I met him?

"Oh spit," I whispered. "This is where you drive away and disappear forever." My eyes filled up with regretful tears. Inches away, his face blurred.

Wrong place. Wrong time. Wrong age.

He reached out and cupped my head between his hands. A million seconds passed. Maybe it was only a millisecond. I lost track, drowning in the depths of the look in his eyes—a look that said, *Yeah, sorry, I know.* Then he lost, or won, some battle with himself and leaned forward to brush my lips with a feather light touch of his. Hello and goodbye, all in one.

"Not forever," he whispered back. "It'll just seem like it. But I'll keep track of you, Torrance Olivia Joe Citizen Tee Oliver Maddox. No matter how many times you change your name."

I laughed shakily. My lips trembled on the verge of a sob. But I held it together. "What should I do now?" I asked.

His fingers still cradled my cheeks. "Go back inside. Finish your homework. Get good grades. Kiss a few high school boys. Go to a wonderful college. Challenge yourself. Remain vigilant. Be faithful."

"To you?" I asked stupidly.

"To yourself, Tor."

Cold air rushed in when he lifted his hands from my face. I suddenly felt untethered, a lost astronaut spinning in the darkness, losing warmth and light.

He turned away, reaching for the front door handle of his car. I slipped between him and the window and glued myself toes to chest against him. So close I could feel his heart drumming a little too fast. "Just one more, please," I begged, my lips less than a breath away from his. "One more to remember."

"Oh spit," he said. "This is so outside the rules." He held both my hands in his and whispered across the gap, "Make it memorable."

I did.

CHAPTER SEVENTEEN

LIAR'S POKER

Sometimes life refuses to give you time to catch your breath. And, I admit, I was completely breathless watching Rick's car disappear into the night. I needed at least three weeks of uninterrupted pondering (not to mention dwelling, cogitating, ruminating, and brooding) to figure out what had just happened between us, and I wasn't going to get it. Part of me wanted it all to be a foolish, tantalizing dream so I could wake up and laugh at my uncensored imagination. Part of me wanted to hang on with all my strength to the most real moment in my entire life. And the awful part was that I had to keep it all to myself. The potential trouble index was off the charts. Higher than code red. No one could find out that Rick and I had crossed this time barrier. Blown through it, actually. Left it in smithereens. Not even my best friends.

I took the kind of deep, centering breath that I always take before an important performance. Then I went back inside.

As I came into the room, Dad was lifting a square of lasagna with the spatula, Rody was grabbing a piece of garlic bread, and Mom was putting a pile of salad onto my side plate. They turned toward me, a perfect family tableau. Mom's gaze flicked across my tell-tale face, my dilated pupils, my flushed cheeks, my tingling lips. Her own eyes went soft and crinkly at the corners, and her eyebrows pulled together with worry, reacting to the story she had read there. "I'll say grace," she offered.

I had trouble being devout, my mind a seething foam of thought bubbles, and I missed the heartfelt prayer she uttered, no doubt earnestly and cryptically asking for my protection in between saying thanks for the bounty of bread and lasagna. A single large bubble floated to the top of my mind and popped.

"Amen. Has anyone seen the news?" I blurted. It was almost two hours past the President's deadline to call off the slaughter.

"Sorry, Tor. Didn't know we were supposed to be on alert," Rody said. "Plus I'm grounded from everything for life," he added.

"What? Why? When?" I stammered dumbly.

Dad put a firm hand on my shoulder. "Your brother is currently serving a life sentence for (A) aiding and abetting your escape, (B) lying to us, and (C) continuing to refuse to tell us what's going on. And if it weren't for knowing that a trustworthy and reliable government agent was watching your every footstep, I'd be in a mental hospital for violently insane fathers right now." Thank gladness he was too busy scolding me to notice Mom flinch when he mentioned *trustworthy and reliable*.

"Rody?" I asked.

"My head is bloodied but unbowed," he quoted.

"Anyway, it wasn't my story to tell. But if you can get me some time off for good behavior, I'd certainly be grateful."

"Who are you and what have you done with my pesky little brother?" I said.

He acknowledged the compliment with a shrug and a head tilt, not a kid, but a young man just coming into focus.

Dad growled. "This sibling loyalty is touching as hell," he said, "but I think it's about time you started explaining. The most I could get out of Rick was a vague answer about a mission involving national security and reputation. And since I don't recall signing you up for the junior spy league, that explanation is far from satisfactory. So perhaps you'll begin with where you've been for the past—" he glanced at his watch "—forty or so hours."

"Atlanta," I said.

"What!" Dad's fork crashed and his salad flew everywhere. Under his controlled exterior, he'd stored up more voltage in the last day and a half than a human battery can possibly hold. I wanted to hide under the table until the inevitable explosion blew over. "Do you mean to tell me the government put my daughter on a plane and flew her out of state? Without my knowledge or permission?"

"Sorry, Dad," I said meekly. "Actually, I'm the one that put myself on a plane and flew out of state without your knowledge or permission. *They* followed *me*."

"Don't be ridiculous, Torrance," Mom said. "You're not old enough to buy a ticket and get on a plane by yourself."

"Duh, Mom," Rody burst in, obviously glad to be able to spill it. "CNN bought her ticket, and she had a fake ID."

Dad's face turned a dangerous purple and his hands clamped firmly onto Rody's two shoulders. "Oh, this gets better and better. CNN. False ID. So you knew all of this Rody?"

"Um, yeah."

"And you didn't think this rose to the level of importance that an adult should be involved?"

"There were adults," I broke in, valiantly trying to prevent Rody's premature death by strangulation. "Alex Fletcher was running the whole deal. And there was Rick, of course. And Narlee Wave and Milly."

Dad released Rody and pushed his plate away from him. "Start. At. The. Beginning. **NOW.**"

So, as our food got cold, I started over, back to when they refused to believe the dogs were being killed. Back to when I had asked them to help me and they hadn't listened. I made the most of that, believe me. Mom and Dad exchanged a guilty parent look across the table.

Mom turned shiny wet eyes back to me. "Honey, I'm sorry I didn't believe you."

"I'm sorry I ran away," I said in response, which was polite, but not entirely true. Dad remained quiet, subdued, listening.

I told them about the emails, about the interview, about turning Narlee against the Dark Side.

Dad shook his head in wonder. "I can't believe my little girl did all this. I mean," he hastily corrected himself, "I *do* believe it, but even so…"

"Now what?" Mom asked me, ever so practical.

"Now the President's deadline was three hours ago and I really, really need to check the news." We left all the dirty dishes and food on the table and went to the living room to watch and learn. I tried to imagine how he would announce the pull back to quarantine.

But he didn't. There was nothing. Not a word.

The evening anchors didn't even mention the New Flu. All the lead stories were either election-related or about a missing child in Iowa or a four truck pile-up in the freak storm outside Chicago. Nothing at all about the pandemic. At eleven o'clock, Mom said softly, "I have to turn in. Work tomorrow." Dad dropped a kiss on my head and went up with her. I don't think he knew what to say.

"You going up, Tor?" Rody asked.

"I'll just wait a little longer."

"It would probably be tomorrow, anyway," he offered. I could tell he was trying to boost my sagging spirits.

"You're probably right," I said. "But even so, I'll watch a little longer. You don't have to." I grabbed a throw pillow and made myself comfortable on the carpet. Cocoa trotted over and put his head in my lap. He yawned widely. I couldn't help copying him.

"That's okay," Rody said. "I'll hang with you." He stretched out on the couch, keeping me company. But when I peeked back at him a few minutes later, he was asleep, the light from the screen flickering across his closed eyes. I think I passed out around two.

The third stair creaked when Mom came down at seven. My head popped up from my arms. "Have you two been up all night?" she asked.

"Nah," I answered groggily. "I get first shower."

Rody glared at me with cushion stripes on his cheek. "Fine. Whatever." He thumped back down, instantly asleep again, which was most unlike him. Maybe he *had* been awake during the night.

"Any news?" Mom asked tentatively.

"Nope. Nothing yet."

I stood under the hot water thinking, thinking, thinking. Sure it *might* be announced today. Should I be patient? Give it a little longer? But I'd carefully planned the President's deadline so that he could announce a change on the prime time evening news, Eastern time zone. I'd given him plenty of time to decide whether he was going to meet my terms. The roar of the shower crashed around me as I faced the obvious. It wasn't a matter of time. The gaping silence last night *was* his answer—a resounding, "No."

Rick's words came back to me, complete with meaning this time. In real life, there are no bloodless battles.

Then I thought of Rody's favorite card game, Liar's Poker, where you call bullspit on your opponent and he has to stop bluffing, lay down his cards, and show you what he's got. Yeah, I got it now. The President had just called bullspit on me. *Show me your cards, Joe Citizen. Then we'll see who wins.* He didn't believe I held a good hand, a freaping good hand. But I had a pair of whistleblowers and four-of-a-kind incriminating emails, Ace high. He'd soon be sorry he ever messed with me and my dog.

I sat on my bed in my bathrobe, my toweled-off hair porcupining every which way. Since Mr. President refused to cooperate, I *would* do it—run the report with all the damning evidence. It was exactly one week till the election. I probably couldn't have hit a better time in the news cycle to break open the conspiracy.

I cheered myself on. I could do it. Sure, it wasn't Plan A, but then what plan survived the first encounter with the enemy, as they say.

Creeps, it was only one little phone call. Narlee and Milly had already made peace with this decision, had already peered over the precipice and jumped willingly. Why was I still standing on the edge? What did I have to lose, compared to them?

But could I do this to the governors? They'd kept their part of the bargain. What business did I have breaking mine?

Then the answer came to me. We-The-People's business. That's what. The People had a right to know before they voted next week. Something tickled the back of my brain and I turned to my computer to check it out.

I was right. I had another president firmly in my corner on this one—Thomas Jefferson. My quote site said, "Enlighten the people generally, and tyranny and oppressions of body and mind will vanish like evil spirits at the dawn of day."

Okay, Thom, I said to his ghost. *It's time to enlighten the people.*

I whipped out my cell phone and speed-dialed Alex Fletcher. He answered immediately, in a confused, breathless voice like I'd roused him out of a deep sleep. Did I get the time change backward? No, it was after ten in Atlanta.

"Whoozzit?" he asked while I was gathering my thoughts.

"It's me, Tor," I said. "Tor Maddox. I just called to tell you I'm ready to run it."

"Tor? Ms. Maddox? Thank goodness you called me." He sounded weird, kind of panicky. "I didn't know how to get in touch with you. You didn't leave me *your* number."

"Oh, I'm sorry about that," I said. "But anyway, are you ready to run the special report? I'm totally go."

There was a slight delay. Then Alex answered gruffly, "Tor, I'm sorry. I can't."

"What do you mean you can't?" I yelled.

A voice floated up from downstairs. "Are you okay Torrance, sweetie? It's time to leave." Ack. Mom. Bad timing.

"It's uh...there's uh...let me put it this way. Someone powerful is putting the kibosh on the whole thing."

"Someone at the network?" I asked. My voice trembled with anger. "They can't do that. They can't suppress the truth."

"No. Not the network. It's bigger than that. They took it all. Everything."

"What do you mean? Who did?"

"Government men. After you left the studio, a bunch of toughs came in like storm troopers and confiscated all the recordings."

I pictured guys in riot gear or high tech hazmat suits blasting their way into the studio. "Oh my God. That's unreal. But don't you have backups?" I asked in disbelief.

"No. We hadn't even downloaded from the cameras to editing yet. And they walked out of the building with the cameras. I've never seen anything like it."

My mind raced. "What if we just reshoot? Or do it live?"

"Couple problems with that," Alex said. I wished I could see him. His voice was dull, stunned, like he'd been drained of all his life's energy. "First of all, I just got re-assigned and sent on-location for the next three weeks."

I hated to ask. "What location?"

"Egypt. I just got in a few hours ago. Anyway, that's not all."

"It gets worse?"

"Oh yes. The same group that pulled the cameras also pulled Dr. Wave and Ms. Baxter out of the studio just as they were leaving. And I haven't been able to reach them since. I've been trying every half hour I wasn't in the air. I just hope they're…safe."

"This is insane! This is unbelievable," I shrieked. "What happened to my First Amendment? Where's my freedom of speech? Freedom of the press?"

"Damned if I know," Alex said. "At least I still have my job, but I find myself wondering what it's all worth it if things like this can happen."

I hated the defeated tone in his voice. "Oh spit. Let me think. Narlee and Milly have disappeared into custody, you're banished to Cairo, the tapes are gone. There's no backup. Lemme think. Lemme think. What about the camera men? They heard everything we said. They're witnesses."

Alex moaned so loudly I could hear him 8000 miles

away. "Tor, that's not going to play. Interviewing cameramen about what they heard in an interview? I think there are enough people in trouble already without widening the noose."

"Okay. Still thinking," I said. "What about surveillance cameras? Were there any of those security cams on in the studio when we were recording?"

"Damn. Good idea, almost. They're all over the place. But they're video only. I don't think lip reading plays well either."

"Spit. Then I don't know what to do." I didn't.

"That makes two of us," Alex agreed.

"Who did it? Did you get any names or anything? Department ID? I have some friends in the government who might be able to help us."

"No. Quite honestly, I was stunned, off guard. When ten guys muscle their way past internal security and come in flashing badges and papers..."

"Papers?" A sudden gleam of light pierced our shared darkness. "Hey, what about the letters in the safe? We've still got that proof. We can get those governors in to—"

"Sorry. They knew about them. Somehow. They broke open my safe when I refused to give them the combination. Of course they found your flash drive, and the letters are gone, too. There's no way the governors are going to stick their necks out a week before the election without those letters to hold them to it."

By this point, I was nearly speechless with fury—for Alex and for me and for Truth, Justice, and the American Way.

"Who were those storm trooper guys?" I asked.

"Don't know. They didn't stop to chat. Just your typical government agent men in black types. Quiet and capable. Black suits, sunglasses. Just like the movies. Except no automatic weapons."

"Oh…my…freaping…"

"I'm sorry. Let's give things a little time to settle down. When I get back stateside, we'll figure it out. There's not much I can do from here. As they obviously planned."

He hung up, but my mind was already off and running. Didn't even stop to say goodbye.

Men in Black. Friends in the government. What kind of idiot was I?

Here's the scenario that unfolded in my brain, like a movie you're watching where you want to scream at the person on the screen, "Look behind you, you idiot! Don't go down the dark alley alone!"

In the movie theatre of my brain I see Rick taking off from the hotel before me. He pulls out his phone, calls the other guys, says, "She's on her way to the studio. Let's give them a couple of hours. We'll see who the net pulls in." Then he sees me leave the building, calls his guys, says, "They're done. Go grab it all. I'll take care of the kid." And while the goons are grabbing my whistleblowers, my documentation, and my interview, he dries my tears, takes me to the airport, buys me smoothies (because he knows how easily I am bought), takes me home, acts all nice and normal so I'll never suspect anything.

I scream, *Turn around, you idiot*, to the girl on the screen.

"That was fun," he'd said to me. Fun. Was it fun? Was it all an act? An operation? Is mission accomplished when the naïve girl is totally duped and putty in your hands?

Then I realize I'm in the wrong theatre. That isn't my Rick. He is wonderful, kind, clever, sweet. He charms my parents. He charms me. He leans me up against his car in the starlight and steals my senses. He promises me without words that in a parallel universe the future waits for me to catch up.

Now showing on screen one: Get real. You've been played. Sucker.

On screen two: No. I refuse to believe that. Not yet.

"Torrance! Your father's ready to leave! Come on." Mom's voice takes over the soundtrack. "You are not missing one more day of school this year, young lady."

So clinging to the tiniest thread of hope that I am not the world's worst judge of character, that I am not the world's biggest gull (as in gullible), I had no choice but to get on with what was going to continue to be the worst day of my life.

CHAPTER EIGHTEEN

REMIX

"Punkin, I know you're disappointed about last night."

I sat next to Dad in the passenger seat of the car, staring vacantly ahead and trying to figure out where to go from here. He read the desolate expression on my face and tried his best to be comforting. "You did an extremely brave thing, but you can't always expect an ant to move a rubber tree plant."

What was he talking about? "What're you talking about?" I asked.

He started singing in his scratchy, out of tune way: "Next time you're found, with your chin on the ground, there's a lot to be learned, so look around..." He paused as Rody and I stared at him blankly. "Don't you know this?" He sighed and launched into the rest: "Just what makes that little old ant think he'll move that rubber tree plant? Anyone knows an ant can't move a rubber tree plant. But he's got high hopes, he's got high hopes, he's got high apple pie in the sky hopes."

Rody patted me on the shoulder from the back seat. "Corny. So last century, Dad."

"So do you think I was trying to do the impossible?" I asked Dad. "Doomed to failure? Misguided and inappropriate?"

"Well, realistically...." He trailed off, leaving the "yes" unsaid. "Did you honestly expect...?"

"Forget it," I snapped.

"Hang on," Rody said. "Doesn't the ant succeed in the song?"

"Oh. Well, yes," Dad admitted. "But that wasn't my point. My point is that no matter how high your hopes are, if you tackle something that's just too big for you, you can't expect to win. You need to pick your battles. You saved Cocoa. You tried to warn others. You can find satisfaction in that."

But I didn't. I couldn't. "You know Dad, if a whistle blows in the forest and there's no one there to hear it, does it make a sound?" Even to my own ears, my voice dripped bitterness.

"Tor, that's just an old joke," he said as he pulled up to the curb in front of school.

I dragged my backpack onto my shoulder. "No it isn't." I slammed the door and ran into school. How could he not understand?

With two of the scanners on the fritz, it took forever to get through ret-secure and into school. The guards weren't doing anything to hustle the lines along, and by the time I got through pack search, I was late for first period. And not only had I forgotten to get an excuse note from my parents, in all the rush, I completely forgot to stop by the attendance office to get a re-admit after my unexplained absence yesterday. Had I done that, I would at least have found out privately about being in detention after school. However, my first period science teacher pointed it out loudly and publicly, choosing that day to make an example of me. ME! Who hadn't gotten in trouble since the fourth grade water balloon incident in the staff restroom. Then he handed out a chapter test for which I was rather unprepared, as in I didn't even remember being assigned to read the chapter.

I walked zombie-like from class to class until lunchtime. It was a good thing I had no appetite, since it smelled like they were serving onion and cheese burritos today. I was trying to decide what might be palatable, or at least not entirely revolting, when I was grabbed from behind.

"Oh my God, Tor," Valaree squealed. "Sioux told me about the new do, but I didn't believe her. No baseball cap? Is it really you? Oh my God, Sophe. Look at her."

I couldn't help smiling at their joy. Like their little furry caterpillar had burst into a short-haired butterfly. "It's no big deal," I said, tucking a short strand behind an ear. "It's a lot easier to wash."

Sophe and Valaree exchanged a disgusted look. "She has no idea," Sophe said. "She's a natural for prom queen and she has no idea."

"Yuck," I said.

Sophe took a step back and cast a critical eye over my faded jeans. "We still need to work on the wardrobe, makeup, and manicure. But it's doable."

"Definitely doable," Valaree agreed.

"Have mercy," I pleaded. "One step at a time."

Valaree grabbed Sophe by the arm. "Oh my God, I just had the greatest idea for a yearbook spread. Before and after makeovers. What do you think?"

I let their happy chatter sprinkle over me like a refreshing spring shower. It was nice to talk fluff, even if it was only for a little while.

Those two hours in detention were a new low for me. While the kids who'd been mouthing off to teachers or fighting or smoking zinged wadded up paper balls around the detention room, I kept my head down and scribbled away furiously in my English notebook, getting ahead with the poems due next week. Somehow, they were all turning out dismal and dark. We were released at five, long after the bus was gone. I figured on calling Sasha to bail me out. Otherwise, it would be a very long walk home.

The sight of his car pulling up in front of school gladdened my heart. "Thank you, thank you," I said, sliding in and giving him a totally sisterly hug.

"So was it amazing? Was it an adventure?" he asked. The bottom half of his face was smiling, but not his eyes. His voice was a little off, too.

"It started out amazing and went...went downhill from there." My voice trembled a little, enough for him to catch on.

"This sounds like a long story," he said. "You want to grab a milkshake on the way?"

My stomach realized it had skipped lunch and growled out an answer. "Sure, okay."

Sasha pulled into the Arby's where the Turners had interrogated me, where I'd called Sasha for help the last time, where I'd first met Rick. My chest clenched. I reminded myself to breathe.

"Come on, Tor. I'll buy," Sasha offered.

"Uh oh," I said. "The last time you bought me ice

cream it was to prepare me for bad news." He turned a stricken face to me, wordless. A hundred dire thoughts ran through my head. "Oh spit. What now?"

"Prepare yourself," he said dramatically.

"What?"

"Oh Tor, I'm sorry. Remember the no missing rule? When you didn't make it to dance last night, they took your part away. I tried to tell them you had a business trip, but it wasn't any good. For some reason, they didn't believe me."

I was shocked at how little the news affected me. Shows how much perspective I'd gained over the last twenty-four hours. "It's okay, Sasha," I said. "There'll be other recitals."

"Really? Really? I thought you'd be completely dumped."

"Yeah, it's funny. I'm okay. I guess I've got more important things on my mind right now. Can I still get that jamocha shake though?"

"Duh." He laughed with obvious relief that I hadn't gone hysterical on him and ordered two shakes. "Hey, I saw that interview just before you called."

"Saw what interview?" I took a long, cold sip of milkshake.

"Duh, Tor. Yours. On CNN. It was, um, different from what I expected."

I choked. Sasha pounded me on the back. "Wait," I gasped. "You couldn't have. What interview? Are you sure?"

"Of course I'm sure. It was you and Alex what's-his-cutey-face and the lady with red fingernails. On CNN. You looked dazzle."

"I don't get it," I said. "You're sure?"

Sasha just gave me a look.

"Oh my gladness. Well, how was it? How did I come across? Was it convincing? Do you think it'll make a difference?" I couldn't imagine what had happened. How did Alex get the video back? How did he get it all pulled together from Egypt?

"It was...um. You looked great." He stopped, obviously uncomfortable.

"What?!"

"It just...wasn't...exactly what I thought you were going to do."

I still didn't get it. "Can we just go home and watch the rerun?" I asked. "Please."

"Sure. Of course."

I had the most peculiar feeling as we drove, sort of giddy and weightless. It had run. I was on. National news. What was going to happen next? Somehow, unbeknownst to me, I had played my hand—read 'em and weep, Mr. President. But what cards was he holding?

Sasha came in with me, and we didn't have long to wait to find out. After about fifteen minutes of my nervous fidgeting, the New Flu theme music launched, and the logo spun across the screen. It was long past Focus with Fletch time, but yep, there was Alex on camera. No way to tell at that moment whether it was live or taped.

I listened. Cocoa slept on under the kitchen table, snoring and completely oblivious to my moment of truth. I nudged him with my foot. "Pay attention, you silly dope," I whispered. "Look what we started."

Alex spoke. "My guest Ms. Torrance Maddox brings some serious criticism of the protective isolation policy the CDC has imposed in thirty states to combat the New Flu strain of canine influenza."

That was familiar, from the interview.

Then there I was, on the news, on the screen, looking fairly dazzle, if I say so myself. And I said, "Quarantine just won't work. I have the answer. The easiest way for the government to stop the new epidemic in its tracks is to kill all the dogs. Eliminate the carrier."

What? That's not what I said, was it?

Then Narlee said, "Goodness, we'd hardly send out soldiers in the night to slay people's pets. This is America. Many people voluntarily brought their pets to the humane society or to vets' offices requesting that they be destroyed. This is precisely the type of panic we are trying to avoid with universal testing." She turned toward me. "I know you personally found it hard to accept when your dog turned out to have the New Flu."

Then the camera cut to me. Here's what came out of my mouth: "Okay, I did run away and I didn't catch it. Mr. Fletcher, I was horrified. Mr. Fletcher, did you know there were sixty million dogs in this country? I have the answer. Pretend to test the dogs, tell everyone their dog tested positive, take them away, and kill them in secret. That would guarantee an end to the spread of disease. Am I right?"

Jump to Narlee looking sad: "No dogs equals no flu. Of course. But as a protective measure it is inhumane and extreme and unnecessary. There is no reason for a single healthy dog to be destroyed as long as careful quarantine is observed. The government's releasing the stockpile of antiviral medications, tens of thousands of cases of N95 surgical filter masks. Homeland Security has spent a lot of effort preparing. We have the tools to respond."

There was a final cut to me. "Mr. Fletcher, I was horrified, and I had to speak out, no matter what. Don't underestimate the power of sixty million. Kill them in secret," I said.

"Tor?" Sasha's shock was obvious.

All the blood drained from my face to my toes. Darkness crept around the edges of my vision, and a whirring sound filled my ears. "That's not what happened," I whispered. "Not at all."

"Then what...?"

"They remixed the entire interview. They made me look like a monster! Like I'm the one who wants to kill all the dogs, and they're the good guys. It came out completely backward somehow."

"Why would CNN do that?" he asked.

"It wasn't them," I said. "CNN is the most trusted name in news. They wouldn't run something so...so wrong. Besides, Alex Fletcher isn't even in the country. He had nothing to do with this, I know."

"Then who?"

My shoulders slumped under the weight of my helpless fury. "It's the government. They're buying time while the killing goes on and doing a character assassination number on me to totally shut me down. Oh creeps. Look."

The feed cut to the President saying, "It's no wonder our young people are in such a panic, so worried in this time of crisis. My heart goes out to them, to all of them, and to the poor confused child you just heard from. But let me assure you, what you heard from our CDC physician is true. We have the tools to respond and our response is working and keeping you safe. We expect to announce a step-down right after my re-election. Some dogs are being released to their owners even at this time, cured and cuddly, thanks to the hard work of the great veterinarians across this great land of ours." He smiled benignly at the world.

"You freaping liar," I screamed at the T.V.

Sasha watched me crumple up and cry my heart out on the kitchen table.

CHAPTER NINETEEN

WALKING WOUNDED

Not only did I have an aching Rick-sized hole in my chest, now I was carrying a lead weight in my stomach. Cocoa patiently allowed me to cry hot tears into his neck fur day after day. Of course Sasha and Sioux and Rody believed me about what went down in Atlanta, but everyone else at school circled warily around me, wondering what kind of lunatic they harbored in their midst. Sophe and Valaree floated above it all, far more interested in debating whether TV made me look heavier. Mom and Dad gave me pitiful sympathetic glances that scraped like shards of glass across my soul.

Over the next few days I could hardly bear to watch the news. First of all, there were occasional reruns and clips of the CNN debacle, disaster, catastrophe starring Me. I had no way to figure out precisely who had done this to me—I only knew why it had been done. Second, since we were in the throes of the countdown to the November 8 election, the talking heads on the news made endless pronouncements and predictions, all pointing to a landslide victory for the smiling man. His election ads replaced all the slots usually taken up by drug commercials for incontinence and high blood pressure and insomnia and depression. It was enough to give you incontinent blood pressure due to depression-induced insomnia.

Worse yet, his re-election campaign ads were capitalizing on the stance the President had taken to crush my challenge. It made my stomach hurt to watch. They showed fake footage (it had to be fake) of people getting happy, healthy dogs back from the vet with a voice-over that talked about sensitive and responsive government. While the newspaper ran a back-page buried story about increasing numbers of people who were learning that their dogs had "died of the New Flu" while in isolation, the re-election noise machine ran ads emphasizing the lack of new human cases. That part was true, thank gladness. The potential disaster had been contained to a couple hundred people so far, less than the number killed any weekend on the highway.

At what cost? I still didn't know for sure. Alex Fletcher had been whisked out of town before he'd had a chance to locate that piece of the puzzle. All I knew was that the field was littered with casualties, and they had fallen without a whimper.

But still I watched, hoping something would change, hoping something would break, right up until the morning of the election. I forced down a piece of toast at breakfast. On the screen in front of me there was the guy with so much blood on his hands, grinning and mugging for the camera as he climbed down the rolling stairs from Air Force One to cast a vote in his home district. My eyes were drawn to those hands. He was holding a puppy. A puppy! A sweet, floppy-eared

Labrador puppy with a red bandana around his neck. He was adorable.

A reporter in the greeting line yelled out, "What's his name?"

"Chief," the President called back. "So when y'all play *Hail to the Chief*, he'll think it's for him." He scritched the dog behind the ears.

"I thought you didn't like dogs," another reporter said.

"Are you kidding? I've always loved them. This little fella was just born a few weeks ago back on my ranch. Now he's big enough to move into the Oval Office with me for four more years." He raised his hand in the four-fingered salute that was his signature campaign gesture. "He's the First Dog, don't ya know."

My blood began to boil. "You fraud! You phony!" I yelled at the TV. A few weeks back, he didn't even own a dog. More of a cat person, he had said. But who would remember that now? I waved my fist at the smiling man. "You jerk. You liar." The heck with four more years.

Rody thumped into the kitchen, dropping his loaded backpack on the floor. "Screaming at the TV again, Tor? That's getting to be a disturbing habit." He grabbed the box of Wheat Chex from the cupboard.

"Can you blame me?" I asked.

"Nope," he said. "It's a freaping shame after all our hard work."

I sighed. "It just kills me that people are out there now casting their votes, believing the country is in good hands. And all the proof is gone—my letters, my CDC friends, my interview, my video…"

"*My* video?" Rody echoed.

"Yeah, I'm sorry. They stole it out of Alex's safe."

"But what about the original?" he said.

My head snapped up. "The original. The original? What do you mean, the original?"

"On Sioux's camera."

"But she transferred it. Doesn't that erase it?" I asked.

"Of course not, you ignoramus," Rody said.

And I was so filled with desperate hope I didn't even want to hit him.

"Besides, you know her," he added. "She'd never erase anything without a backup."

I clasped my hands tightly together like a prayer. "Holy spit. A backup. A backup! Quick, call Sioux. Check." I hardly breathed as I listened to his side of the conversation. His grin told me all I needed to know.

"Yup, she's got it."

I threw my arms around him and squeezed. He patted me gingerly on the back, adding, "She just sent the file to your email."

"What? Noooo!" I yelled.

He jumped backward in surprise. "For creeps sake! I thought that's what you wanted."

"Remember, my account's been compromised. It's being spied on. And now they'll know Sioux's involved."

"How was I supposed to know that?" he argued. "I thought it was just your phone that was tapped."

"God, sometimes I think my whole life has been tapped." I sank into a chair and rested my forehead in my hands, trying to think straight. "Let's just check and see if it came through." I woke up the kitchen computer and called up my regular email account. "Oh yes." There it was, a freshly arrived message and attached video clip. "Faster than a speeding bad guy," I joked as I inserted a flash drive into the slot. In seconds I had it, safe in my hands, my last precious piece of evidence. Now what?

"Now what?" Rody asked.

Yeah. Now what? Excellent question. The polls had been open for over three hours already on the East Coast. The absentee ballots had been sent in long ago. If I'd only known, if I'd only realized, I could have done this a week ago when it might have made a huge difference. As it was, my proof of the President's role had changed only two votes so far, Mom and Dad's. Well, maybe Milly and Narlee's. And Alex's. Was I a day late and a flash drive short? Was it over already and I just refused to accept the obvious?

Heck, no. Never say die.

"Ahem, now what?" Rody repeated.

"Oh, sorry. I'm thinking. I have to get this into safe hands, as fast as possible." Alex Fletcher was marooned at the other end of the world. Totally unhelpful. Could I possibly wait till he was allowed back? Let the old-new President have his way with the country for weeks? How many dogs would be eliminated by then? I hated that option. Passionately.

The only other big player I knew how to contact was Steve Turner. Minion of...someone. How many times had Steve tried to tell me he was one of the good guys? How many times had Solly hinted that there was more to them than met the eye? They had followed my every move, always a step right behind me, it seemed. Sometimes a step ahead. But there was the other black car they ditched at the library, the search copter they promised they hadn't ordered, the MIB at the airport that Rick had sent off in the wrong direction.

Oh, Rick. I still couldn't rule out the possibility that he'd staged the CNN raid while I was distracted. But then I thought of the sorrow on his face when he realized he'd let Springer be taken, and I remembered the sincerity of his confession that he was rooting for me. Could I possibly trust these guys? I knew their duty had to come before their personal feelings. Part of the uniform.

What if I called Steve and handed over my last piece of evidence to the people sworn to stop me? I feared that option. Passionately.

I pondered aloud. "I suppose I could call Turner."

"Turner? Are you nuts?" Now it was Rody's turn to yell. "I thought you said they're the ones who stole everything in the first place."

"I don't know, Rody. I honestly don't know. I think it was another faction. I hope to God it was another faction, because I'm going to do it. Wish me luck and lend me your phone." I retrieved Turner's card from the fridge where Mom had stuck it while Rody fished in his pocket for his phone.

"You're sure?" he asked.

"Nope," I said as I punched in the number. I imagined this was exactly like jumping out of a plane, watching the earth zooming up to meet you and hoping the parachute would open. What the hell. Maybe I should try that, too. My lips curved into a smile at the image of myself hurtling toward a big white X on the ground.

"What's all the yelling?" Dad asked as he came into the kitchen. "Hey, a smile? What's that all about? I know this is an odd question, punkin, but why are you so happy? I haven't seen a smile on you for days."

I waved the flash drive in front of him. "I've got something to smile about. I'm back in the game. Just when I thought the deck was all used up."

"What's this?" He looked at the tiny object in my hands.

"More evidence," I said.

His face turned to stone. "No way. You're done."

"With what?" Mom asked as she joined the kitchen party.

"Political intrigue. Junior spy league. Everything," Dad replied firmly.

"But Dad," I protested. "I have to. This is vital!"

Mom put her hands on her hips in her authoritative way. "Is someone going to fill me in? Rody?"

"Sioux and I made a secret video at the vet center that basically showed what was going on. It's all Tor has left to prove that she was right—that she's not as lame as, sorry Tor, not as lame as that interview made her look."

Mom snapped the flash drive right out of my hand. "That's quite enough, Torrance. It's time for us to get back to normal. Your father's right." She held the stick away from me as I tried to grab it back. "I know exactly what to do," she said calmly. "We'll turn this over to that nice Agent Steven Turner, and he can take it from here. I have his card right here on the fridge."

I pressed SEND. "Mom, that's just what I was about to do." I held the phone up so she could hear it ringing.

My brilliant and dramatic moment was cut short by a loud rap on the door. I was closest. Huffing loudly in annoyance at the interruption, I flung the door open, saying, "Yes? What? Holy spit. Steve!"

Agents Turner and Solly lurked on my front doorstep. "You rang?" Steve said. He was holding his cell phone, which was ringing a duet with the one I was holding.

"How do you do that?" I asked. "How did you know?" He smiled mysteriously.

Cocoa pushed me out of the way and put his paws on Steve's knees. He panted with joy. Steve stroked his head, not even seeming to mind the sharp claws on his good suit. "Good to see you too, lad. Down, now."

"Please, do come in," Mom said. "The kids are just on their way to school, but there's something they wanted to give you. And I've just made a pot of coffee. Would you like a cup?"

Steve's eyebrows rose like a pair of question marks.

Mom trusted him. My dog loved him. He had to be one of the good guys. He just had to be, or I'd be doomed to lose faith in the entire world. I took the flash drive out of Mom's extended palm and handed it to Steve.

"It's video proof of the slayings at the vet hospitals," I said. "We still have time if we can get it on the news. The election isn't over yet."

"Excellent. Thank you." Steve pocketed the precious footage, and I desperately hoped I'd made the right choice. "Mr. and Mrs. Maddox, I'm afraid I need to borrow your daughter one more time."

Dad stepped in front of me. "No way. She's done with this."

"I certainly respect your feelings, sir, but she's needed for an important strategy meeting."

Dad pointed at the kitchen table. "Then you can have it right here, under my supervision."

Solly shrugged. It was nice to see him again. "Mr. Maddox, I'm afraid that it's a bit difficult to transport the other participants here. Tor will have to come with us. I promise we'll return her in one piece." He chuckled at his own joke.

"Then I'm coming with you," Dad said. "Every inch of the way."

Steve patted him on the shoulder. "I'm sorry, sir. You're not cleared for this."

"And she is?" Dad gave me a searching look then shook his head. "No. No way. She's been wounded enough in this battle, getting involved with your crazy schemes and power struggles and ruthless politicians. Remember, she's just a kid."

Turner coughed. "I realize how easy it is to forget that sometimes, but I know she's tough enough to handle this crowd. And right now, we need her voice. She's not only an important witness, but she's the instigator of this process."

"I'll go," I said. Instigator! Well, well.

"No, Tor," Dad insisted. "You can't. Enough is enough." He glanced over at Mom, who was nodding.

But I had to. I had to make them understand. "Look, Dad. This is my battle. I volunteered. Apparently, I even started it."

Dad opened his mouth to argue, but I cut him off. "I know you and Mom just want to spare me from getting hurt any more, but I'm in it for the long haul." I patted Cocoa's head. "These guys need someone to speak for them. Someone to protect them."

"But why you?" Dad asked.

"Because I have to. I fired the first shot, and I can't just walk away. Look, I've seen what the mighty can do. I'm not afraid of being hurt. Don't you get it? You were wounded a hundred times worse than I ever was, but I know you'd still go running into battle to protect us, to protect what you believe in. Of course you would."

His eyes flashed, and my hope rekindled. I was getting through. One last button to push. "You know, Dad, a friend of mine reminded me that in real life, there are no bloodless battles. I have to keep on fighting this thing, and if these guys have a way to win, then I have to be with them. We're...we're a unit."

Dad coughed. Mom gripped his hand, sensing him weakening.

"Please," I whispered.

Dad cleared his throat. "When do you all need to leave?"

Turner clapped Dad on the shoulder and gave him a tiny salute. "Well done. Thanks."

"Can I come, too?" Rody asked.

"Sorry, sport," Turner answered. "Just your sister. For now."

I glanced down at my distressed jeans and dirty sneakers. "Should I wear my power suit?"

"You bet," Turner said.

A mere half-hour later, we were on our way to the airport. Dad had given me a special talisman to carry, a medal for wounds received in action. Deep inside my pocket, my fingers slid along the ribbon of his Purple Heart.

I was flying as myself, with a signed note from my parents. A thought drifted into my head. How was Dad explaining this to the school office? I sat in the back of the quiet black car, this time not worried about the lack of handles on the inside. I was safe, unaccountably safe.

So far, Turner and Solly hadn't briefed me on what to expect. Maybe that's why I wasn't nervous, just excited.

"How are the kids?" I asked Solly, to make conversation and show there were no hard feelings, at least on my part.

"Hey, they're great. Not sleeping much, but great. Check 'em out." He handed back a picture of two tiny bundles, one pink and one blue.

"Oh my gosh, they're adorable. It looks like they have your hair." Like hardly any. "So Steve," I said casually. "How's Rick?"

The two men exchanged a look. Turner spoke first in an expressionless voice. "I pulled him off this case. Lost his objectivity, it seems. Situation called for a clean break."

"Break? Like vacation?"

Solly answered. "Like *not* vacation. Redeployed to analysis."

The meaning of his words gradually sank in. "But wait, that's not, he didn't, I mean…" I stammered uselessly. "I'm sorry," I said at last.

Without moving his eyes from the road, Turner said, "Ms. Maddox, you are a remarkable young woman, but you are temporarily trapped in the body of a sixteen-year-old. It would be best to remember that. Enough said."

I couldn't let it go. "But really, nothing—"

Solly cut me off sharply. "Did you know, Ms. Maddox, a fascinating feature of these cars? They all carry a recorder for the protection of the agents."

My life flashed before my eyes, at least one incredibly special moment of it. Recorded. Shared by others. I shriveled with guilt. I'm so sorry, Rick.

Turner coughed. Under his breath, he muttered, "Although sometimes they develop glitches, erase everything before it uploads. Sometimes. Damned unpredictable."

CHAPTER TWENTY

THE HALLS OF POWER

It was a long awkward plane ride after that. I was subdued, in a crushed sort of way. I squished myself against the window as tightly as possible and closed my eyes. Well, I had to, to keep the tears from leaking out. Idiot. I prayed that I hadn't screwed up everything between Rick and his dad, that getting "redeployed" out of his first field assignment wouldn't shove him off the path he was following to his dream.

Finally, on the last part of the flight, Steve decided I'd spent enough time beating myself up. He slipped me a handkerchief and patted my hand. "Let's consider it an avoidable accident," he whispered. "Not to be repeated. Not to be reported. That's enough now."

I nodded my remorseful agreement and blew my nose in his handkerchief.

A little louder he said, "Solly and I know what we know, but can you catch us up on what happened at CNN from your perspective."

So I pulled myself together and told them all about the taping session with Alex, about the disappearance of the cameras and Narlee and Milly. "And I have no idea what happened to them afterwards. When I tried calling the CDC, they said Narlee, Dr. Wave, was on leave and Milly had retired. You guys don't happen to have them, do you?"

"Not yet," Steve said grimly. "But we do know where they are, and they're perfectly safe.

I had to ask. "So it wasn't your guys who grabbed the cameras? They said it was men in black suits. With sunglasses."

Steve sighed and removed his glasses. My heart dropped two or three beats. His eyes were a piercing reminder. "Stupid uniform. No, it's not unique to us."

"Well anyway, the guys who did it obviously did the remix interview. Did you see it?"

"Oh yes. Crappy splice job, but I guess they were in a hurry."

A wave of relief washed over me. "Was it that obvious?"

"It was to us," Steve confirmed. "Then they conveniently got rid of Alex Fletcher, requested him to cover a high level meeting with the new Egyptian President."

"Is he coming to the strategy meeting?" I asked hopefully.

"No, but we've been in touch with him. He's not going to testify. But he will report. He wants to avoid an ethical conflict."

"Testify?"

"We'll get there eventually."

The plane touched down with a slight lurch at Reagan National. As we deplaned, Turner and Solly walked on either side of me, like my private body guards. I was wearing the same suit as I'd worn to

Atlanta, my only grown-up clothes. I caught a few furtive looks in our direction and some whispered questions as people pointed me out to their friends. I tucked my face toward Turner's lapels. "I think they recognize me," I murmured.

He slipped a hand into his pocket and pulled out an extra pair of regulation MIB sunglasses. "Here, put these on. You're part of the team now."

Warmer than sunshine was the glow deep in my chest. I was part of the team.

I straightened my shades, tossed my hair, threw back my shoulders. My high heels clicked sharply through the airport corridors. I was on my way to do battle.

Our driver dropped us off at an enormous building with imposing columns. Pennsylvania Avenue had flashed by on the corner street sign, illuminated by the orange glow of the street lights. It was after nine, and polls had closed across the entire Eastern time zone. Election Day would be over in a few hours. "Where are we?" I asked.

"Department of Justice," Solly said. "DOJ."

"Wow. That's a whole lot of justice." The building ran as far as the eye could see, taking up the entire block.

"Let's hope so," Turner said softly.

We entered between two huge metal doors, and Turner and Solly flashed their badges and retinas. I was scanned and patted and scanned again. I kept setting off the metal alarm. The guard gave me a curious look when we ultimately tracked the mystery to Dad's medal in my pocket. I didn't even try to explain.

My pulse raced as we made our way through the building. Excitement and anxiety fought for the upper hand. Part of me wanted to slow down, stop and gaze at the beautiful murals and sculptures along our path while my emotions sorted themselves out, but the men sped me along the gray marbled floors.

Finally we reached a reception desk where a kind-faced woman said, "Go right in. They're expecting you."

The door opened, and a silver-haired gentleman rose from a meeting table. He extended a hand to me. "Welcome, Ms. Maddox. I'm—"

"The Attorney General," I blurted out.

"Ah, you know me," he said.

I turned to Steve. "So he's your boss?" Steve gave a short nod.

"I see," I said. "Pleased to meet you, Mr. Attorney General, sir."

"Likewise, Ms. Maddox." His handshake was warm and reassuring. His pinky tickled my palm. He winked. "Permit me to introduce the rest of our little group." I was among friends.

My eyes flicked around the table. It was like Mount Rushmore in person. Holy spit. Scarcely able to breathe, I said, "Governor Benson, Washington, Democrat. Governor Reed, Idaho, Republican. Governor Stanley, Oregon, Democrat. Governor Mendoza, Arizona, Republican." Crisicles, so to speak.

Governor Elena Mendoza reached out to shake my hand first. "Well, I'm flattered that you know all of us on sight."

"Oh yes," I said. "I spent some time on all of your websites."

Governor Benson chuckled. "Oh yes, we know." He gestured to four pieces of paper in the middle of the table. I recognized them at a glance—the emails they had sent me. But how? Then I remembered who had ended up with the originals outside the library so long ago. Of course. The Turners.

Governor Reed patted the empty chair next to him. "Well, well, young lady. Have a sit. You've stirred up a mighty big pot of trouble here."

"I'm sorry," I replied.

The Attorney General patted me on the back. "No, no, Ms. Maddox. Don't be sorry. Don't be sorry. When the President played fast and loose with the truth and overstepped his executive power, it was indeed a sad day. But we're here to rectify that situation."

"So why didn't you do anything before the election?" I demanded. "It's too late now. If you knew, why didn't you warn everyone so he wouldn't get re-elected? Have you seen the exit poll results? It's a landslide."

"Timing, Ms. Maddox. Timing," the Attorney General responded. "If I'd let the President know I had a case to prosecute against him before the election, he would most likely have contrived to win it anyway in all the confusion, and tomorrow there'd be a new AG sitting in my chair, one of his cronies. And if he'd lost, well, he'd essentially be like a private citizen tomorrow. A lame duck, and not particularly worth shooting. The consequences don't compare to bringing a complaint of grounds for impeachment to the House."

Impeachment. Whoa. One more alternative popped into my head. "And if he'd lost, your party would be out and you wouldn't be here to follow through and nail him. I get it."

"Couldn't have put it better myself. Now this here bipartisan group of governors you so kindly rounded up for us has promised to testify in the House hearings. Ms. Maddox, there's a good chance you'll be called to testify in the House about the raid on CNN. That's a helluva charge in and of itself. A crime against our Constitution. Can you handle that?"

"Yessir," I promised. "I'll do my best."

Turner moved behind my chair and rested his hands on my shoulders. "She'll do brilliantly, sir. I'll vouch for her. She even managed to come up with another piece of evidence we didn't know about."

He placed Rody's flash drive on the table.

"That's my brother's work, to be fair," I said.

"Please thank him for us," the Attorney General said graciously.

The door opened and another familiar figure stepped into the room. Everyone stood up. "Everything good here?" he asked.

"Yes, Mr. Vice-President," Turner answered. "We're all set for tomorrow."

The AG shook his hand. "All set. Now get out of here before someone sees you. Go back to the victory parties. We'll see you in the House chamber first thing in the a.m."

"Okay then. Safe trip back, Ms. Maddox," the Vice-President said to me.

I became a statue.

Deer in the headlights.

I nearly fainted.

Steve nudged me from behind. "Say goodbye," he muttered in my ear.

"Goodbye," I echoed. "Thank you, Mr. President."

"Not yet," he replied with a wink.

As soon as the door shut, I fell into my chair. "That was so cool." Then my burst of spaciness wore off and I landed back in reality. I stood up, hands on the table and addressed the assembled pantheon. "What about the dogs, guys? While all this planning and scheming and *timing* has been going on, they've been rounding them up. *Killing them.* Does *anyone* know how many?"

The AG answered. "Best estimate we've come up with so far puts the toll at about twelve million." The silence after his words was profound.

"Damn," someone whispered at last.

He went on. "Tomorrow morning, right after the articles of accusation are read, the House will override the secret executive order and place responsibility for containment back on the States. Within a few hours we'll be back to quarantine, this time with materiel support—masks, vaccines, whatever you governors need. For crissakes, if this doesn't qualify as a crisis to dip into our stockpiles, I don't know what does."

I added, "Dr. Wave said her models showed this disease running its course in about three more months with good quarantine."

"Well that's the cheerfullest news I've heard today, young lady," Governor Reed said. His hearty voice helped lift the weight from our shoulders, the weight of twelve million lost.

CHAPTER TWENTY-ONE

CALLED TO ACCOUNT

It was November 22, two weeks after the election, a week after the House started formal impeachment hearings on the second term President. We were all glued to *Fletch in Focus*, waiting for his CNN Special Report. Mom and Dad had come home early from work specially. Sioux and Rody were holding hands on the couch. Sasha and Blade were sitting on the floor with Cocoa draped across their legs, enjoying all the attention. Almost all my best friends in the same room. I was the only one who felt the tangible absence of one more person. One more very special person.

The camera held Alex in tight focus as he spoke. "And now, a special report about an American who goes by the name Joe Citizen. Joe represents what we value in America—honesty with ourselves and each other, loyalty to our best friends, and the courage to take a stand."

Rody looked at me with an oddly proud look, and I blushed down to my toes.

"Joe Citizen, a sixteen-year-old girl, spoke truth to power and called a President to account." The camera panned back and there I was, sandwiched between

Milly and Narlee. Our guys had managed to subpoena the stolen news video before it could be erased, and Alex had been recalled to put it all together.

Mom and Dad exchanged that telepathic glance they do. My stomach had butterflies, monarch butterflies, with sharp pointy crowns.

It was amazing how Alex had crafted the story, interweaving veterinarian interviews with clips of the President speaking, shots of the long lines outside animal clinics, Rody's video of dead animals being tossed into trucks, the official CDC announcements, the governors' speaking out. He told the story of deception uncovered.

I watched my loved ones watching me. My life was about to take a sharp turn on a twisty highway, maybe head right on through the safety railing. I shuddered to think what my fifteen minutes of fame would bring this time around. Not just to me (I'd felt the long arm of the government before) but to the country. What had seemed like an automatic re-up for the President would be followed by his crash and very public fall from power. I hadn't been called yet to testify to Congress, but I knew that time was coming soon.

My shoulders twitched. My arms broke out in goosebumps. I wondered if right now the President I had once loved was ordering someone to nail me in an unexplained drive-by shooting.

My cell phone chirped with an incoming text message from a blocked number.

Well done, Spike. Don't worry. I've got your back. Keep the faith. RT

I will, I promised him.

Tor Maddox's adventures continue in

Tor Maddox: EMBEDDED

Life has been way too quiet for Tor Maddox since her fifteen minutes of CNN fame. Then agent-in-training Rick Turner reappears with what sounds like a simple assignment—to embed herself as his eyes and ears in her own high school. When she agrees to keep tabs on high school state swim champ Hamilton Parker for the Feds, she is plunged into the deep end of a sinister international plot. Knowing that freedom, justice, and lives are at stake again, Tor jumps in feet first, but has she gotten in over her head this time?

When observe and report becomes kiss and tell, Tor's first mission may blow up in her face.

Take a sneak peek.

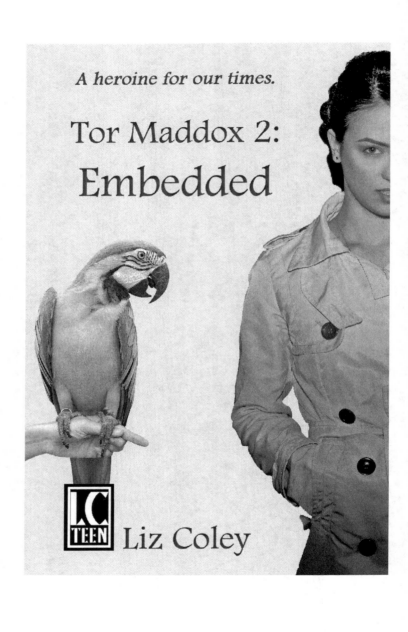

A heroine for our times.

Tor Maddox 2:
Embedded

Liz Coley

TOR MADDOX: EMBEDDED

by Liz Coley

CHAPTER ONE

LIFE MAKES A U-TURN

San Diego Union-Tribune. Squirrel implicated in three-car pile-up.

I swear it wasn't my fault. Not really.

You can't expect me to kill an innocent ground squirrel in cold blood. Anyone with even half a heart would have swerved—that's what I planned to tell the traffic magistrate. I just hoped he himself had at least fifty percent of a heart beating in his chest, because the lady officer who took the report and wrote out my citation certainly didn't. Appeals to her reason made not a single dent. Mentioning that I was personal friends with the President and the U.S. Attorney General earned me a hard, disbelieving stare. And for obvious reasons, my trembling lower lip and tearful brown eyes were wasted on a fellow female.

I had started the afternoon thrilled—you might even say *elated* or *euphoric* if you'd looked over my shoulder at my SAT vocab list for the week—to be holding my freshly printed driver's license. Four months past my sixteenth birthday, I'd finally logged enough supervised hours to qualify, and on the bright, sunny morning of March 4th, I tested and passed.

So what if it was the third try? Practice makes perfect, or, to be completely honest, eighty-five percent of perfect.

My fifteen-year-old brother Rody followed too close behind my size eight footsteps. Not only is he in my class at school (having squeaked by the age cutoff), but he was already brandishing his own provisional learner's permit and claimed to be a better driver than I was. He showed no brotherly enthusiasm when Mom and I returned with the happy news.

"Tor must have gotten a really easy examiner in a good mood," he said to Mom, throwing a bucket of cold water on my delight. "So...she didn't break any traffic laws *this time?*"

Brat. And to think I was just going to offer him the honor of first ride with me solo at the wheel.

Mom leapt to my defense. "Rodeo, sweetie, don't tease your sister. She did well enough to pass."

Rody mouthed the word "barely" at me and raised his eyebrows in mock-alarm.

Mom didn't hear him. "It'll be your turn soon enough."

"Not soon enough for me. Mom, you're still going to drive us to school, right?" he asked with that stupid, exaggerated, worried look on his face. "I don't want to become a statistic. I don't want to die young in a pool of blood and twisted metal."

"You faithless turncoat," I snapped back. "Just see if I'm available to drop you and Sioux at the movies next time you need a ride."

"You can't do that anyway, till you've been—"

"Never mind. I'm not offering anyway," I said a little too loudly. I glared him into silence. Can't do that until I've been licensed for a year. I know. That's the ridiculous rule. But everyone at school gives each other rides all the time, including Sioux driving Rody for their dates, and I'm quite sure he didn't want me bringing that up in front of Mom.

He correctly interpreted my meaningful glare and shut down.

"Guess I'll just take a victory lap by myself," I said. "That okay, Mom?"

Of course, driving alone with a new license is a complete anti-climax, as I realized three blocks down the road. I wanted to share the magic moment. No I wasn't *technically* allowed to drive anyone except a family member, but it was just a short spin, and I loved Sasha, my guy BFF and dance partner, *like* a brother. We'd grown up together—that counted as family in my book. So I texted him, and, unfortunately for him, as it turns out, he said, yes, he'd be happy to be my first victim.

Truer words were never spoken.

I swear I wasn't distracted, or I wouldn't even have noticed the squirrel until it was too late. Right?

Sasha and I were zipping along down a hill, and I had it all planned out to use the momentum to glide up the steep rise ahead, when the little gray fluffball dashed out of the pink-flowered oleander bushes and propelled itself in front of my wheels. With lightning reflexes, I jerked the steering wheel to the left and swerved onto the other side of the road, just as a dark gray car coming in the opposite direction topped the crest, headed straight toward us.

You could argue a more experienced driver would have veered back to the correct lane, right on top of the fear-frozen rodent, and apologized to God. But my instinct was to steer even farther left, trying to turn my swerving maneuver into a U-turn at 35 mph, which is, as I have now learned, apparently impossible by the laws of Newtonian physics.

They say these things happen in slow motion, but they're totally wrong. In horrendously awful, split second disasters, time speeds up. Something about relativity. Einstein should have figured that out. Before I knew what was happening, my front wheels bounced off the curb on the other side of the street. An ear-splitting explosion filled the car, the air filled with white dust, and my face filled with airbag. The car lurched sideways to a horrible symphony of tearing metal and breaking glass. Then, just as the unforgettable fortissimo of the impact faded, another vehicle came over the hill at top speed and rear-ended the one already embedded in the passenger side of my car.

An epic yelp pierced my right ear drum. *Sasha!*

I wiped airbag powder off my lips and rotated my head to look at him. My neck fought back. Sasha's gorgeous green eyes were filled with man-tears, and his chiseled face twisted in pain.

I gasped and coughed. "Sasha, are you okay?"

"Still alive, anyway," he said with the most desperate forced smile I've ever seen. "I think...I think it's just my leg. Except I can't actually feel it."

In spite of side air bags, the door of my tiny car was crushed against his right leg. "Oh spit, Sasha," I whispered. He planned on making a living off those legs. "I'm calling 9-1-1."

"Good idea," he said. And passed out.

I sent my shattered emotions off to their room to weep so I could call and coolly explain the situation to the 9-1-1 operator. Then I called Mom. Then I sat there and hung onto Sasha's hand for dear life as the wail of sirens grew closer. I breathed slowly through my nose while my heart attempted to pound its way through my chest wall. Tears drew tracks down the white powder coating my cheeks.

Cars slowed as they glided past and glared at the devastation I had wrought. The squirrel was nowhere in sight, long gone, free to live out the rest of his natural life.

Mom and Rody arrived at the same time as the ambulance and police cruiser. Oh why, oh why did she have to bring him? Mom ran to me, pulled me out of the car, and ran her eyes up and down my five foot ten frame, searching for damage. "Oh, sweetie," she said. "Oh, sweetie."

She wrapped me in a python hug. Over the top of her blond head, I fixed my eyes on the three-car medley. The accident scene leapt into vivid focus. The other drivers had untangled themselves from their own wreckage and moved to stand on the sidewalk along the road. I couldn't help noticing the contrast. The woman in the gray Lexus that had nosedived into my car was dressed for tennis at the club. She paced with a tight, angry stride on well-toned legs as she spoke in bursts to someone on her cell phone. The woman in the rusted, white Chevy who had rear-ended her was dressed for hard work, housekeeping by the looks of it. She stood rooted to the spot, dismay creasing her face. Both of them appeared unhurt, thank gladness.

A paramedic touched me on the sleeve. His ID tag said BOB in large, friendly letters. "Excuse me, miss. Were you driving? Are you injured?"

I tried to talk. Nothing came out. I nodded and shook my head and pointed to Sasha. BOB brushed past me to reach through my side of the car, checking Sasha's vital signs.

Rody ran his fingers along the buckled roof of the car, which was now three-quarters of its former width. "Holy crap," he said in a low voice. "I was only kidding." He put one hand on my back, about as much of a hug as I could expect. "You're shaking."

"No kidding."

"What happened?"

"There was a squirrel in the road."

"Um, I see." He frowned. "Tor, you know you're not supposed to—"

I cut him off with a glare. "I know."

The paramedic pulled his head out of the car. My whole world condensed to a Sasha-shaped bubble. Was he okay?

"He's okay," the paramedic reported. "Just passed out from pain. Looks like a broken leg, but his other vitals are fine. Your big brother?" he asked.

I wanted to collapse with relief, but I couldn't shake off the numbness around my brain. I tried my voice again. "Yes. No. Like one, though," I said. "Will you call his parents? I don't think I can...think I..." Hiccups, like the winds at the front of an emotional storm, stole my words. I swallowed hard and wrote Sasha's home number on the pad BOB handed me.

A policewoman was talking to the other drivers. Scratch that. She was talking to the housekeeper, a middle-aged Latina with black, curly hair and round cheeks. The housekeeper had her wallet out, explaining in accented but fluent English that she had her day-worker permit.

"Everything is in order," she was saying. "You see the dates. Not expired."

The policewoman shrugged and began placing flares around the accident scene.

We waited another endless four minutes for a tow truck to arrive to pull the cars apart so the paramedics could pry Sasha out of the mashed passenger compartment. I shook without blinking, without thinking, watching him for signs of life. He looked like a dark-haired, sleeping angel in a Joffrey Ballet Summer Intensive sweatshirt.

The scents of eucalyptus trees and flares and gasoline tickled my nose.

Gasoline? It must have been from the old car. Mine was all-electric.

I jumped away from Mom's embrace and hollered. "Someone's car is leaking gas. For creeps sake, move the flares!"

Concern flashed in the eyes of the woman whose crunched Lexus was being dragged from the clutches of my Chevy Spark, but it was the housekeeper who scrambled for whatever she'd left in her vehicle. An ominous dark puddle spread beneath it.

Too fogged into my own world of worry, I hadn't spoken to the other drivers yet. Now I staggered toward them, not knowing what to say besides sorry. "Is anyone else hurt?" I managed.

"No, thank God," the Lexus lady said. "Not yet. But my husband's going to kill me. We just got this car."

"Hey, what a coincidence. I just got my license," I said, with what I thought was a sad, ironic twist to the words.

The police officer pounced in on my words like a hawk pouncing on a mourning dove before it can even coo for help. "Just got it, you say? Within the last six months?"

"Within the last six hours, more like," I admitted with a tiny sigh. I hoped the *pathos*—the tragedy of my situation—would soften her heart toward me. "Here." I handed her my interim license, a flimsy piece of paper already marred with sweaty fingerprints.

"Well, goldang," she muttered. "It *is* less than six

hours. You didn't even let the sun set once before you joined the ranks."

"Ranks?"

"Of idiot sixteen-year-olds who lose their licenses. God save me from sixteen-year-olds. Save us all," she prayed with her eyes raised toward the eucalyptus tree canopy. "How's your big brother doing?"

"He's not…" I started and choked on a huge lump of sob.

"Not your brother? An unrelated passenger? Please tell me he's over twenty, or you've got another serious violation." Her red face grew larger and larger in my field of vision.

I tried to breathe, but the sudden rush of emotion back into my frozen brain clogged my windpipe. Someone adjusted the brightness setting on my eyes, making everything darker and smaller. The world spun. The sidewalk stood up and zoomed closer until it smacked me in the face. For just a second, it hurt like spit.

The next time I opened my eyes, a stranger in a dark blue jumpsuit was crouched over me, pressing a white cloth above my eyebrows. No, not a stranger, a BOB. The hard concrete beneath me pressed back. From the thobbing pain, I imagined my head resembled the watermelon the UCSD physics students drop off the top of Urey Hall at graduation every year—shattered rind and red pulp. In fact, a big splat of red stained the sidewalk next to me.

"Did she have a seizure?" Lexus lady was asking. "Is that why the car went out of control? Oh, the poor,

poor thing." She kneeled beside me and rubbed my hand.

I decided not to mention the squirrel at this juncture.

When all the details were reported, paperwork completed, and cars towed away, all that remained was fragments of shattered headlights, an evaporating puddle of gas, and the dried brown patch of my blood on the sidewalk. To the passers-by, it was like nothing had ever happened.

The officer gave the housekeeper a lift in her patrol car; Lexus lady's husband arrived on the scene, as advertised—beyond pissed; and three-quarters of the Maddox family (me, Mom, and Rody) followed Sasha's ambulance to the Palomar Hospital Emergency Room, where I knew Dad would already be pacing the intake area. From the car, I called Sasha's boyfriend Blade in case Sasha's parents forgot in all the panic.

Dad was supposed to be on weekend duty in the hospital pharmacy, but he abandoned his post to watch the suture tech stitch up my forehead, wincing with every stitch. Dad winced, that is—I couldn't feel a thing thanks to lidocaine. So everyone was present and accounted for by the time Sasha's lower leg was stuffed into a cast, and I was transformed into the Bride of Frankenstein with six stitches over my right eye.

They stuck us both in wheel chairs to take us out to our cars, Sasha with that huge, ungainly thing on his leg, woozy with pain killers, and me with a little bit of gauze taped to my brow.

Sasha smiled at me. "Getcha some scar cream or

you'll look like Harry Potter," he said in a slurred voice.

I pressed his arm. "I don't know what to say. I'm so incredibly sorry."

"S'okay," he said. "S'things happen. Sign my cast?"

There was only forgiveness, no anger, in his Percocet-blurred eyes. On the other hand, his parents, stiff professorish types, wished me a speedy recovery through clenched teeth. I sure wouldn't be calling them as character witnesses at my trial.

Oh yeah, did I mention? While the nice paramedic BOB had applied pressure to my bleeding head on the sidewalk next to the accident scene, the officer had handed me a green slip of paper. "Your driver's license is suspended for reckless endangerment. Your court appearance is Monday morning, ten o'clock."

Available June 1, 2015 in print and ebook formats.

ABOUT THE AUTHOR

Liz Coley is the author of the internationally best selling psychological thriller *Pretty Girl-13*, in 12 languages on 5 continents. Her last LCTeen novel, *Out of Xibalba*, was published in 2011. Her short fiction for adults has appeared in Cosmos Magazine, as well as numerous anthologies.

The new *Tor Maddox* series represents the lighter side of Liz.

Liz Coley makes her home in Cincinnati, Ohio, where she volunteers at her daughter's school, plays team tennis, sings in a choir, and enjoys the company of a supportive posse of Ohio YA authors.